"THE JESUS PROJECT"

By

JOHN DIGGENS

The characters and events portrayed in this book are fictitious. Any similarity to real persons, living or dead, is coincidental and not intended by the author.

Text copyright © 2014 John Diggens
All rights reserved.

No part of this book may be reproduced, or stored in a retrieval system, or transmitted in any form or by any means, electronic, mechanical, photocopying, or otherwise, without the express written permission of the publisher.

Published by Xflight Technologies LLC

ISBN-13: 978-1502905475
ISBN-10: 1502905477
BISAC: Fiction / Science Fiction / Time Travel

DEDICATION

To darling Anna - My whole life!

ACKNOWLEDGEMENTS

The first draft of this book was in 1987, the entire thing typed out the hard way by my wife. Naturally rejected by all the Publishers I sent it to.

Next left in the attic, gathering dust!

More recently, having acquired computer skills, and with the help of my step sons Mark and Stephen, the basic script was digitised and updated. They designed a snazzy cover for me, and thanks to the magic of the Internet here we are!

Contents

Preface
Prologue
Chapter 1 A Discussion on Time
Chapter 2 A Violent Interlude
Chapter 3 Preparations
Chapter 4 Off
Chapter 5 Joseph
Chapter 6 Jesus
Chapter 7 Grant has a Date with the Devil
Chapter 8 Judas
Chapter 9 The Crucifixion
Chapter 10 Joe's Story
Chapter 11 Future
Chapter 12 A Confrontation
Chapter 13 The Duel
Chapter 14 A Question of Honour
Chapter 15 A Little Coaching from "Big Q" and Friends
Chapter 16 Williams has a Fight, and wins a Lady's gratitude
Chapter 17 Grant shows his Mettle
Chapter 18 A Visitor from the Past
Chapter 19 Grant has Thoughts about Luck
Chapter 20 The Death of Close Relatives
Chapter 21 To Final Glory
Chapter 22 Finale
Chapter 23 A Little Spot of Trouble
Chapter 24 Home
Epilogue
End

PREFACE

This is a story of the past, and the future; of what has been, and what is to come. We live in a unique period of time; technologically we have developed further in the last one hundred years than the previous one million years. The average person in the industrialized countries has a quality of life in excess of anything that the serf of the middle ages or the subjects of Queen Victoria could ever have dreamed of.

Just think; every ten years our knowledge increases geometrically; computer and quantum technology will maintain this growth. What will we do with this accumulated knowledge?

Greed, the corruption of political power, big business, human nature, envy, extremism; all will combine to see that the meek and the poor will never inherit the earth. Three quarters of the world's population will still go hungry; the rich will get richer until the gold pours out of their orifices. On the other hand, hope and a belief in Universal Good may see that God's gifts of knowledge will achieve a fair and just order of things.

We have the science to: create a utopia; or a smoking nuclear ruin; to enter a golden age; or embark upon a downward spiral to hell.

Time is a great leveler, when the Grim Reaper appears it matters not whether you are a billionaire living a life of luxury, or a peasant trying to eke out a living in some dry God forsaken land.

Each small increment of time is unique for an individual, whether experienced personally, or collectively. Practically, at our present level of technology and science each instant of time Is irreversible, and therefore irrevocable; perhaps it will always be so!

Just think, one hundred years ago a mere handful of today's population existed, in one hundred years only a handful of us will be alive. What a thought! We live, we die, and we make our mark as best we can. We live on in memory, maybe for another thirty years or so for most of us, and a thousand years or more for those who were gifted, or special, or maybe just a pain in the butt; the Hitler's and the Stalin's achieve a place in the history books just as surely as the Newton's and the Einstein's.

What's it all about then? Is our life really to no purpose? Is it just a brief burst of energy, like sparks from a grinding wheel?

Far greater intellects than mine have given their lives to a study of life, the Universe, and the hereafter - the concept of Eternity!

William Blake in his poignant **Auguries of Innocents** best sums it up in the opening lines;

> **To see a world in a grain of sand,**
>
> **And heaven in a wild flower,**
>
> **Hold infinity in the palm of your hand,**
>
> **And eternity in an hour.**

My story explores some possibilities of our existence, both past and in the future. Speculation? Yes! But then who knows?

John Diggens, Guildford - October 2014

PROLOGUE

The twenty year old youth gazed across the bay. The water was calm and absolutely flat - completely protected from the raging seas beyond. It was a beautiful evening, with a glorious sunset. He would sit here for a while on the balcony of his parents' house, enjoying the air - tomorrow he would be dead. It just wasn't fair but what could he do. The "Grand Council" had decreed it. He had been given the customary twenty-four hours, after the declaration, to get his affairs in order, and here he was, now, enjoying his last few hours on earth in the place that he loved best. Tomorrow at 0600 hours the "Monitors" would come for him, and he would be taken away to the regional "purification" installation, and be exterminated in the "purification chambers". It would be quick and painless.

This fact did not prevent him suffering an uncontrollable fear - one of his shortcomings that had damned him in the first place. The "League for Intellectual Purity" had carried out the mandatory tests on him attaining his twentieth birthday. For some time now he had been aware that he might not measure up to the council's standards and, as a result, be, in the words of the council, "purified". He had thought of escaping before the fateful day, and joining the group which existed outside of civilisation known as the "Undesirables", but had decided against it. This would have meant disgrace, with the consequent lowering of status, for his family. The council could be very vindictive.

For hours he stared across the water, until his eyes ached and he dozed off. He came to with a start as he felt a hand on his shoulder. It was 0600 hours precisely. 'It is time,' stated a "senior monitor" of the "purification corps."

Vaguely, as in a dream, he got up and followed the monitor to the transporter. In thirty minutes he was being ushered into the purification chamber. He idly observed a "chief monitor" through the viewing panel, who was giving the computer its orders. In seconds the chamber would be bathed with purging rays, which would disintegrate his body into its component particles; eventually to be released into the vacuum of space. He could not be allowed to contaminate planet earth ever again - not even with his dead cells.

His whole body burned with excruciating pain - was this to be the painless death promised him? He mercifully lapsed into unconsciousness, and then awoke; it seemed instantaneously....

He stood in an open field wearing the same clothes as when he had entered the chamber. The important thing was that he was alive. Two figures in the distance were trying to attract his attention. 'Fore,' shouted one of them, he noticed that they were carrying sticks and some sort of long bag over their shoulders. He ducked as a small white missile shot past his head. The memories of his ordeal began to fade from his mind, and soon he was unable to even remember his name. He turned towards the two and decided to try and communicate with them. There was much that he didn't understand...

Chapter One

A Discussion on Time

'A thousand ages in Thy sight are like an evening gone'
From the Hymn 'Oh God Our Help in Ages Past'
Isaac Watts

'But surely Einstein's Theories have put practical barriers on time travel' said Williams, to his lifelong friend John Grant. The year was 2030 and two old friends were having an intriguing discussion.

Williams; a handsome man in his mid-thirties, with short brown cropped hair, stood over six feet tall and dwarfed Grant; a short stocky man with an unruly mop of jet black hair, a large prominent nose and sallow skin. Certainly nobody would have called Grant handsome and most would have said downright ugly. To his credit: he had dark laughing eyes, a fine set of teeth, and got on very well with both men and the ladies, due to his extremely pleasant personality, and his patience with people; when you spoke to Grant, he always listened; one of life's gentlemen; he was a leader of men, but had that priceless gift of humility. Grant was a man you would trust with your life.

'Yes Peter it would appear so, but even Einstein was not always correct; whilst Einsteinian physics upstaged Newtonian mechanics, without really supplanting it, so our present day theories on certain aspects of science have upstaged even Einsteinian theory without, again, replacing it. Consider the breakthrough in 2025 by Professor Sophia Massey and her team at Cambridge, in combining General Relativity and Quantum Theory.

Grant and Williams had been at Cambridge in 2016, when both had gained a first in Physics, and later Doctorates. They had gone their separate ways; although always keeping in touch. Williams had taken over his father's Electronics Company, and Grant had gone to America to work on various space projects including the manned shot to Mars. He had headed the Theoretical Physics Division, which had come up with the Fusion Reactor Drive; easing man's path into space, replacing the outdated rocket propulsion devices of the seventies and eighties. This had made possible the manned shot to Mars.

Grant excelled at everything he tried - a God given talent which he never presumed upon.

His areas of expertise included marksmanship with various weapons, fencing, athletics and unarmed combat. He had even found time to squeeze in a PhD; writing a thesis on "The Life of Christ and his effect on Mankind".

By far his most exciting venture had been into the world of the "Paranormal" Grant had a tremendous facility in this area. A wide range of tests had put him into a one in a million category. He could make very tiny particles, the size of pin heads move, and the standard tests with cards and shapes had achieved results way beyond anything randomly expected.

The current discussion between the two old friends took place in Sir Felix Mortimer's country house near Godalming, in Surrey. They were weekend house guests of Mortimer, who was chairman of the syndicate which was backing the massive research into time travel known as the "Jesus Project". It was even rumored that various churches had also put money into the enterprise.

After a magnificent dinner the two men, with their host, had retired to the library. Mortimer had left to make a routine check, by cell phone, on security at the research Centre nearby.

Grant and Williams pleasantly spent the time chatting, as friends often do. They were seated in two huge bronze-red leather armchairs, in front of a glowing coal fire, cradling glasses of some very old and expensive brandy in cupped hands. Around them were a superb collection of books arranged in shelves from floor to ceiling in glass units, which were controlled for temperature and humidity. Grant recognized several "First Editions" from the Dickens era, and marveled at the wide choice of literature. It was bitterly cold outside, and the sound of rain and driving sleet could be heard on the windows. Both men felt an inner feeling of wellbeing and contentment.

'Although Einstein was far from convinced that time travel could ever be practically achieved,' continued Grant 'he did prove that a sort of time travel was possible; as time slows for people travelling very fast, or hanging around in a high gravitational field near a black hole for a while. 'There is no doubt that travelling at speeds greater than light would logically result in time travel into the past. There was a famous limerick in the early sixties:

'There once was a lady called Bright, Who would travel faster than light, She went out one day, In a relative way, and came back the previous night.'

This departure from the serious discussion brought a smile to William's face, even though he had heard the piece on numerous occasions. 'This describes the phenomena exactly' Grant said 'Of course Einstein was right, under all known laws of physics during his life time practical time travel was not possible. However the theoretical Tachyon particle can only travel faster than light, and as a consequence seems to travel backwards in time, and over the last ten years new discoveries have been made; discoveries in theoretical and practical physics which would have made the old man's hair curl even more, and green with envy to boot.'

'Consider modern theory on "black holes" which may still be man's gateway to the stars - a star gate if you like; a means of beating the light barrier perhaps? Some curious results have been obtained in particle accelerators, which had many eminent physicists to conclude a faster than light phenomena.'

'OK! OK!' interjected Williams, 'we've discussed this stuff before, and got nowhere: or (thoughtfully) maybe you have got somewhere? Just what is this Jesus Project?'

'Well, Peter, I suggest we refill our glasses with this fine brandy, and I will tell you ; We have some time before Felix gets back; he always seems to natter for ages on the phone with Brownlow when he does those security checks of his. Always likes to keep people on their toes. Sometimes the old Bastard goes over to the center and raids it with a couple of his cronies - he knows the complete security system like the back of his hand, and knows the weak points. He has often caught security with their trousers down - leading to several dismissals and demotions. I believe he has finally got the system exactly how he wants it, despite nearly being maimed or killed several times in the process.'

'Anyway to get back to what we were talking about.' Grant held his glass out for more brandy, and Williams obliged. They settled back comfortably and Grant continued. 'Some years ago a Professor Bennett, of Yale, was experimenting in the field of anti-gravity. Initially he used high speed rotation to achieve a gyroscopic effect. Many of the earlier sightings of UFOs involved so called Flying Saucers. It was thought that their noiseless flight was in some way due to their rotation, producing anti-gravity; if in fact they actually existed. As part of his research he also messed around with high density magnetic fields, perhaps in a futile attempt to harness the earth's very weak flux - It is interesting to note that Hitler sanctioned such research during the Second World War - A further development was to combine the rotation with the magnetic field.' Grant paused before continuing.

'He had now got to the stage where he very badly needed a breakthrough; as funds were running low, and sponsors for the project were in short supply, due to its lack of any sort of success - however small! Failure followed failure, until one evening, whilst working late; he noticed that objects close to the device were acting in unusual ways, disappearing and re-appearing in different positions. Bennett found, after intensive study of the phenomena, that instead of inventing the first anti-gravity device, he had created a sort of time machine, capable of moving small objects back in time and space. He could not explain why he was achieving this stupendous effect - many great discoveries are accidental and, furthermore, the theoretical verification sometimes escapes suitable explanation for some considerable time.' Grant paused for effect.

'Steven Bennett, whilst wondering why Einstein's Laws were apparently being disregarded - certainly the Old Master would have had a more than passing interest in the device - redoubled his efforts in this completely new direction. Unfortunately he was never able to go beyond fifty-micro seconds back in time, and then only with small objects. Even this required huge magnetic densities, up to ten Tesla, coupled with a ten "g" force - created by rotation'

'Despondent, Bennett was almost on the point of giving up, when he happened to read a scientific article on E.S.P. research by Doctor Alan Donaldson of the "Institute of Noetic Sciences." Donaldson had centered his work on psychokinesis (P.K.) - the power to influence the movement of material objects by will - and psychical research - the scientific investigation of spiritualism. He found that some of his more talented helpers could "remote view" major historical events. His "guinea-pigs" told him that the mental images of the past were very poor, but that they had been able to get a fix on certain periods, due to the psychic energy being emitted.' Grant downed his brandy and poured himself another.

'Bennett got in touch with Donaldson, and both men came to the conclusion that perhaps, just maybe, the combination of the physical and the paranormal could solve all of their problems. That is how a project on time travel actually got started.'

Very early on, Williams, from showing a polite interest in Grant's discourse, began to pay real heed to the dialogue, leaning forward in his chair so as not to miss a word. The rain had stopped, but the wind had increased to almost gale force, and the clatter of several roof tiles from the four-hundred year old house could be heard; there would certainly be work for the builders tomorrow.

Grant went on with his story. 'It was decided to concentrate on the Jesus era, hence the name, as by far the best psychic emissions came from this period; and of course due to the tremendous controversy that surrounds the life of Jesus Christ. I was asked to join the team because of my knowledge of that age, as well as my other credentials.

'Raising the capital was a problem, initially; who in his right mind would pour millions of pounds into a project concerned with the Paranormal, and time travel? Eventually we asked Mortimer along to view some experiments. He was enthralled; and after that we had no money problems whatsoever.' Grant stood up - he was getting to the end of his extraordinary revelations.

'We have now made our breakthrough, and will be ready, soon, for the greatest adventure ever undertaken by man' Enthused Grant.

Williams had sat silent throughout Grant's amazing disclosures; towards the end his mouth fell wide open in sheer wonderment, wanting to query but unable to, but now the questions came.

'Have you tried to go into the future?'

'Yes we have, but with absolutely no success at all. There appears to be a barrier, whether physical or ethereal we don't know. I suppose we ought to pose the question; has the future actually happened? If we can go back in time then, for us, the future has happened. It becomes very complicated.'

'What about the Grandfather paradox of time travel, could you go back and meet yourself, or maybe kill your Grandfather?' Williams was really enjoying himself now.

'We really do not have the experience, yet, to even begin to answer those sorts of questions. This is the really big danger with time travel, the possibility of actually changing the future.'

Williams got up and stretched himself; he went over to the fire and, taking up the poker, stirred the glowing mass, watching the sparks fly. Next he carefully selected three large lumps of coal from the burnished brass coal scuttle, throwing them onto the blaze to feed the dancing flames.

'Isn't it bloody marvelous,' he reflected. 'Only the rich can afford this archaic, inefficient method of heating, the rest have to put up with central heating.'

A thought struck him, and he half turned. 'Have the Chinese or Russians got in on this particular act?'

'The ultra-atheists have been involved in research into the paranormal for years, without, of course, agreeing to anything spiritual. Our intelligence tells us that they haven't yet penetrated our security, and in any case their research is not moving in the same direction as the "Jesus Project."

'In the early days security got a bit paranoid and almost everyone was suspected because of the sensitive nature of what we were doing. There was an Australian by the name of Graham Davis who was a bit of a joker - his feet didn't touch the ground after an incident with a dummy bomb.'

'Actually our security is rather good, once Felix knocked off the rough edges - energy screens, electrified fences, armed guards, very tight security clearance, all that sort of thing. We really can't be too careful! If the wrong people got onto us...'

Just then they were interrupted, very suddenly, by their host bursting through the door. An imposing figure was Sir Felix Mortimer, Knight of the Garter, Minister for Engineering and Science in the United Kingdom, and one of the most influential men in the kingdom. He was a large man tending to run to fat, with iron grey hair, side burns and deep piercing black eyes, which seemed to penetrate into your very soul. At sixty he could look forward to many years of full vigorous life, thanks to the miracles of modern medicine that his great wealth could buy. The old biblical three score years and ten had been rendered obsolete for some.

The old man would be womanizing for a good deal longer yet - so said his friends and enemies behind his back. He didn't suffer fools gladly, and was ruthless when it was demanded. A good friend, but a very nasty adversary, it did not pay to upset Sir Felix.

The two young men gaped at Mortimer - he was a touch out of condition, very red in the face, and out of breath from his run down a long corridor and up a flight of stairs.

'A full security alert was called a few seconds ago, the Plant is under attack,' he managed to splutter out. Then still panting heavily, 'I really will have to get a phone installed in here.'

The library was the only room in the house where cell phone use was forbidden. The only room where you could remain relatively undisturbed. Sir Felix was now regretting his decision.

Grant and Williams leapt to their feet on receipt of the startling information, their drinks going flying as the small table between them went over.

The procedure, during a purple alert, was well established, and without a word Grant and Mortimer rushed out of the room, followed by Williams, who wondered what the whole thing was about, but thought it would be a good idea to find out anyway. The men were headed for the house armory to pick up weapons, and then over to the plant to see what was happening. Grant could not help thinking that perhaps it was another fool drill, called by Mortimer; but he had to admit that his host appeared in deadly earnest.

Who on earth would want to attack us, thought Grant, his mind rapidly turning over possible reasons for the alert. This was totally unexpected. They had prepared for any eventuality; but had never actually expected an attack. Was it the Chinese, the Russians, maybe the Islamic Extremists? If any of the world powers had got wind of the true nature of the research at the plant, then interest from them may have been a possibility; even to the extent of some subtle spying. But this!! An actual open attack on the plant; this could mean war, if it were true.

Grant had often considered the possibilities, that somebody might be foolhardy enough to attempt a break in, to steal the results of the research. You could blackmail whole nations, by going back into history, simply by what you might do to change the course of history for a country or, indeed, individuals.

Grant felt a tingling in his body, a sort of apprehension, was it a warning of events to come?

He often felt these sensations when some danger threatened. It was, he knew, part of his sixth sense - his awareness of something outside normal reality.

John Grant often wondered if he was, in some way, closer to a God than most of his fellows. He felt guilty about it in fact. Even as a child there had been a feeling of being different. He had never been deeply religious and had always felt the best way to please a God - should there be one - was to live your life treating people, as you would in turn want to be treated.

The three men ran through the house - Sir Felix taking up the rear with a great deal of puffing, punctuated with the occasional muffled oath. Through superbly paneled corridors they sprinted, making little noise on the rich carpeting which was everywhere.

The house had been in the Mortimer family since 1693, and had seen a lot of action - there was even a ghost, which Felix swore to have seen many times. Apparently a headless apparition, who had fallen foul of the axe man in a bygone age, when it was not prudent to upset the monarch of the period. Sir Henry Mortimer was the poor unfortunate third Earl of Godalming. Something of a black sheep it was said, although the present sixth Earl was quite proud of his history - ghost and all.

Down they went into the cellars to the armory. A portion of the house sub-levels had been fitted up as a weaponry range and recreation area. Grant had spent many happy hours here, sharpening up his skills with pistol, rifle and cross bow. In fact the place had become something of a second home; with the Earl as a sort of favorite uncle.

Now the situation was rather more serious, and this was reflected in Mortimer's face as he struggled with the super light body armor, designed to withstand light laser bursts. Grant helped him put the finishing touches to the buckling, and then helped himself to a Mark III "Westminster" laser, with two spare power packs. Williams followed suit, but Sir Felix settled for an LRAD weapon - The acoustic device had been developed to kill at maximum setting.

The quickest way out was the lift, which went direct to the garage. In seconds they were seated in the Rolls Royce Golden Cloud parked there. Exactly two minutes—forty seconds had elapsed since the extremely illuminating conversation in the library had been disturbed - it seemed much longer.

Chapter Two

A Violent interlude

'He who lives by the sword shall die by the sword'
Jesus Christ

Williams, for some unaccountable reason, found himself in the driving seat, and drove them to the plant along the special high speed road which connected house and plant, foot down to the floor all the way. The "Rolls" was the old man's pride and joy, and he grimaced at the savage treatment it was now receiving. The "Ferrari Super Sports" which normally did this trip was out of commission with transmission problems.

The Rolls held well on the wet icy road, cutting through the driving rain, which had just begun again. The cold cut into Mortimer's bones, and the thought flashed through his mind, that at his age it was no time to go off playing the hero, especially on such a miserably bleak January evening.

The five mile journey took just three minutes, and the powerful headlights took in some very pleasant countryside, pretty thatched cottages and nice neat hedgerows. The beauty was lost on the three travelers who stared ahead, their minds on other things; what for instance lay in wait for them at the end of the road.

They were met at the security gate by the Chief Surveillance Officer, Matt Brownlow; who had been in the service of Sir Felix for twenty years. A small man, with brown receding hair, Brownlow wore the tight fitting dark blue uniform signifying security service, with the Chiefs "pips" on his shoulders. An ex-marine sergeant major, he ran security with the same strict discipline as the services. He was a man that even the Earl had tremendous admiration for. Like many little men he had an evil temper when roused, and particularly when drunk - which was quite often - but always off duty. Grant had seen him beat two men senseless at the local "Hare and Hounds" simply because of remarks made about their local squire - the Earl.

The plant was a vast spread of buildings, laboratories, and workshops, with an outer perimeter fence eight feet high, and a smaller electrified fence inside. The entire complex was illuminated at this time of night. Each major building was protected by an energy screen.

The facility was protected from the air by an automatically triggered EM pulse defensive system, specifically directed to, and neutralizing any incoming threat to a height of twenty thousand feet and within a ten mile radius, this was backed up by an array of ground to air missile launchers. The defenses also included state of the art ABM systems; the whole project was off limits to everyone, excepting those actively involved. Ministry of Defense regulations and restrictions were in force at all times, and twenty-four hours per day warnings were broadcast on all frequencies, to keep clear of the area. The cover story was; that intensive research was going on into a defense against the Chinese latest secret weapons. Mortimer had "pull" in some very influential circles indeed - no less than His Majesty's Government.

The noise was deafening, and Brownlow had to shout to make himself heard above the alarm sirens and the sound of explosions.

'We have four men pinned down in the stores block,' yelled Brownlow.

'Did they penetrate the main laboratories?' Screamed Grant above an increasing noise level; as an afterthought 'Where are the security drones, we need them to monitor things and to add fire power.'

'No,' answered Brownlow. 'The energy screens held long enough for us to get there, with men to distract them, unfortunately the drone controls were the first thing they took out; inside knowledge perhaps? The main test facility was what they were after - they seemed to come from nowhere; out of empty space.' Grant noted this information, and filed it away for another occasion.

'How can we identify them?' asked Williams.

'They are clothed entirely in black. So far we have lost two of my best men' answered the security man, with regret in his voice, the sweat running freely down his lined battered face.

He looked as if he would have broken the attackers in half, if he could have got his hands on them - whatever else people said about Brownlow he was fanatically loyal to his men.

Grant took command of the situation. 'Get your men to cover the exits,' he ordered, 'And for Christ sake somebody turn the blasted alarms off before I go deaf.'

'Peter, Sir Felix, come with me, and keep your heads down!' He concentrated for a second, fixing his mind on the four men. Focusing his attention on their leader, he was assailed by thoughts of such incarnate evil that he momentarily reeled. Never before had he experienced such depraved vileness; such utter corruptness. He forced himself on despite feelings of nausea. The three men went through a store security door, and spread out, taking cover behind the numerous large crates lying around. There was hardly any lighting, as most of the lighting tubes had been destroyed by their adversaries in order to conceal their intentions?

'Get some auxiliary lighting over here' yelled Grant over his shoulder to Brownlow who covered the trio from the door. Two minutes later two searchlights appeared and were immediately eliminated by well-directed bursts of fire; this accompanied by indistinct curses from the Security Chief.

'Leave it, 'ordered Grant.

In the dimness he saw something moving behind some machinery, and blazed off five seconds worth of pulsed laser fire, without success, except to draw a similar burst in return. Then, thinking quickly, he set fire to a pile of cotton waste lying in a corner. Momentarily there were no problems with illumination, and Williams took out one of the four, taking off the top of his skull when it appeared just above some cover.

What happened next was pure chaos as the sprinkler system triggered, and the complex was plunged into near darkness again. It was at this point that Sir Felix took a wound in the arm, and was forced to retire from the scene, being dragged out by Brownlow. Luckily his amour took most of the blast.

'If you surrender' shouted Grant to the enemy left, 'you will be well treated, let's have no more bloodshed.' He was nearly slaughtered for his pains, as concentrated power from three sources completely obliterated the wooden box he crouched behind. He threw himself to one side a split-second before losing its protection. Everything was now soaking wet, but at least somebody had the sense to turn off the sprinklers.

'What a cock up,' exclaimed Grant. He was prevented from further self-assessment by a shadowy figure, making a break for one of the side doors. He was hit full in the back, not by Grant or Williams, but by his own men. 'Nice people!' commented Williams.

The next hour saw the remaining protagonists sitting it out, with further attempts to settle the thing quietly; without success. Grant had given firm instructions to Brownlow not to send in any reinforcements, to avoid more unnecessary deaths. They all set shivering in the darkness; Williams, more than once, worried about catching pneumonia from the ordeal.

'Surely you can see that the position is hopeless,' said Grant trying just one more time. 'We cannot get to you, not yet anyway, but you certainly cannot escape us, please give yourselves up.' Silence was the answer to that one.

At last Grant decided to be bold, he crawled over to Williams, and they had a brief whispered discussion on tactics, which involved moving their positions, feinting an attack on the flanks, before making a concentrated frontal bid. This was achieved by throwing bits of old iron and wood to the flank before Grant, covered by his friend, launched himself forward, leaping over the crates which hid one of the remaining men in black.

The only problem was that he lost his footing and his weapon in the fall, and found himself looking down a very large laser pistol. This was the first time that Grant had got a good look at the opposition, and in the split second of life left to him, as a finger closed on the trigger, he saw his foe, dressed from head to toe in a body stocking of black. It was the exposed face which really caught the attention, chalky white, cold pale eyes, without expression...

Grant, covered by his friend, launched himself forward, leaping over the crates which hid one of the remaining men in black. The only problem was that he lost his footing and his weapon in the fall, and found himself looking down a very large laser pistol. This was the first time that John Grant had got a good look at the opposition, and in the split second of life left to him, as a finger closed on the trigger he saw his foe dressed from head to toe in a body stocking of black. It was the exposed face which really caught the attention, chalky white, cold pale eyes, without expression...

Grant had a vague impression that something out of the ordinary was happening!!
Next a wonderful piece of luck - a click of the trigger without result and suddenly Grant realized that the man had run out of charge. With a quick Karate blow his jaw bone was smashed and his neck broken.

'Are you Okay?' Inquired Williams anxiously.

'Yes I am!' gasped his friend 'Let's keep the last one alive if we can, he is the leader, and I need answers to a lot of questions.'

Their last adversary, seeing he was now hopelessly cornered, began a suicide run at Williams, his high-energy laser firing rapid bursts from the hip. Peter hit him in the shoulder with a needle beam of fire; but still he came on. He would have put paid to Williams if Grant had not put a wide angled beam into his right thigh from his pistol, now retrieved, which left him with a bloody stump; his severed arteries spurting torrents of blood at each heartbeat. Grant tore off his shirt and attempted to stem the flow.

'For God's sake get a medical team here pronto,' hollered Grant at the top of his considerable voice...

***

The head of the Medical Centre, Surgeon in Chief Helen Wood looked up from ministering to the very sick man in the bed. 'Ah! Dr. Grant, we have hooked him up to the E.S.P. booster as you suggested! His brain pulses, particularly in the alpha range are very weak, but you may get something out of him. When you have finished there is something I must tell you.' Her face was flushed, and she could hardly contain her excitement as she handed Grant the electronic E.S.P. booster attachment. She obviously had something very important to reveal. But in the meantime there were other fish to fry; information had to be obtained from the dying man.

Grant attached the device to his forehead, and for the second time that night, reeled, this time nearly fainting. The man on the bed died within minutes of the electronic interrogation, but during this short interval Grant experienced mental images such as he had never dreamt of; even in his most vile nightmares. There were black magic rituals, and human sacrifices. People were burnt alive, and subjected to the most horrible tortures.

Grant got distorted views of a hooved creature, it was grotesque, a hideous apparition, which could have only been the devil himself. Naked young girls were subjected to the most hideous sexual attacks by the creature. All the time there was a mental attack against Grant; trying to force him into submission; attempting to kill him. It was fortunate that he had such a strong will power. The problem, at the end of it all, was that they were no further forward - they had obtained no information of any real substance.

***

Grant looked in on his Chief. A pretty nurse was just putting the finishing touches to the dressing on Sir Felix's wounded arm; he had had a very lucky escape, and would be up and about in a few hours. Sir Felix was already beginning to feel more his old self, and had already asked his nurse out for dinner, and had been given her phone number to call her. He had a nice line, which never seemed to fail. Grant thought that he would ask him about it someday - he was always willing to learn from an undoubted master.

'How are you, Sir?'

'Not bad at all,' with a knowing wink.

'Did you get anything from our black friend?'

'Not a lot chief, he pegged out soon after I tried the mind probe; although it's obvious that he is into black magic,' answered Grant. 'Helen came up with something however. Our intruders have some rather strange characteristics; their blood is, microscopically, subtly different from normal; on the other hand it still has a nice red color, as I found out a short time ago. The bone structure is also marginally different from conventional Homo sapiens.

'The most outward and visible difference are the six digits on hands and feet.' Grant kept to himself the even more significant fact that the men had similar birth marks on various parts of their bodies, which resembled three sixes.

"And that no man might buy or sell, save he that had the mark, or the name of the beast, or the number of his name. Here is wisdom. Let him that hath understanding count the number of the beast; for it is the number of a man; and his number is Six-hundred threescore and six."
Revelations Chapter 13 Verses 17 and 18.

'Well! Well! Well!' mused Sir Felix, 'What does it all mean? I think, John, we should discuss the possibility of bringing our "J" date forward. I wonder if we are ready. I am still against sending you on this mission: you are the single most important member of the team; you have coordinated the whole thing, as well as taking an active part. On the other hand! Your qualifications are impeccable in every single respect, and under the circumstances we may only get one chance, and for that we must send in our best man. I would like young Williams involved as well - please ask him to attend the meeting tomorrow.'

Sir Felix's mood changed, suddenly, and he started to ramble.

'God how I envy you, to think you will see "Our Lord" in the flesh.'

There were tears in the old man's eyes. Grant had never seen him show weakness in anything before; it embarrassed him. He had never thought of Felix as a deeply religious man, and this behavior was completely alien to his normal rock hard character. Perhaps it was his age; perhaps the shots he had been given; or a more deeply rooted personality emerging - rather like people showing their true side after having a few drinks. Anyway it was disconcerting. Grant said his goodbyes, turned quickly and left.

Mortimer had arranged a meeting for the following morning at 1000, which was in precisely six hours and forty minutes time, and he felt very tired and longed for a bath and some sleep. He went off in search of Williams as he was in need of a lift back to Guildford where he had decided to spend the night.

Travelling back in Peters vintage 1958 Ferrari 250 Testa Rossa, Grant told his friend that Sir Felix had asked him to attend the meeting; to become involved with the project.

'John, that's the best news that I have had in a long time. Frankly I am bored stiff with my life these days. The company is running like clockwork and I tend to be nothing more than a figure-head, only attending the odd board meeting. My life lacks a challenge. About the only challenge I get nowadays is competing on the ladder at the squash club.

Williams dropped Grant off near his flat.

'Goodnight John, see you tomorrow.'

'Thanks Peter, I look forward to it.'

***

Grant walked the short distance to his modest flat. He breathed in the cold night air, it was crisp and clean, the streets of Guildford were deserted at this time of the morning. His mind went back to the history of the late Twentieth and early Twenty First Century when it wasn't safe to walk the streets in many of the larger Inner Cities in Britain; there was overpopulation and a lack of basic housing for so many.

Through the New Millennium; when Muslim extremism held sway; corruption of the Financial and Banking systems by greedy Bankers and Business Chiefs; MP's fraud; an incompetent and inefficient Police force; an avaricious Legal and Accounting system - all contributed to the decline of a once great nation!

Membership of Europe didn't help; with their Court of Human rights, which allowed religious extremists, thieves, murderers, rapists, extortionists, gangsters, and fraudsters to elude justice.

Successive Governments did absolutely nothing, always going for the soft option to placate the minorities.

Eventually "Sweet Reason!!!!" - An accelerating crime rate,

combined with a seriously declining economy, resulted in a tremendous backlash from a disgruntled populace. A strong Coalition Government was formed, steps were taken to prevent the criminal excesses of the past being repeated. Britain got out of Europe and ran its own affairs

In the past habitual criminals got off, aided by a weak legal system. The "Mr. Bigs" of crime got off Scott free due to so many anomalies in the legal system. A minority of Trade Union officials, who were the catalysts of mob violence, was never charged with their numerous crimes against society; for years they had held the country to ransom for their selfish ends. Social misfits and sports hooligans - both players and spectators, had for years been treated charitably - more sinned against than sinning. Being deprived; being a different race; following a particular religion, any excuse was acceptable for not toeing the line.

With this background, legislation was framed to change the whole system of crime and punishment: violent crime including sexual offenses such as rape and child abuse was dealt with severely, with capital punishment sentences being handed out by the courts in extreme cases. Society demanded vengeance on the basis of the Old Testament "An eye for an eye and a tooth for a tooth" rather than rehabilitation as a soft option - the victims forgotten, their lives ruined.

Any connection with hard drugs and extortion brought the death penalty. Major organizers of crime also suffered the supreme penalty; much of this was possible due to the abolition of the jury system; being replaced by a court council of five people, qualified in law and with an experience of life at all levels.

The anachronism that was the "House of Lords" was abolished, The Royal Family was severely curtailed in its scope, and being relegated to merely a showpiece - The farce of police protection for anything up to the fiftieth in line for the Throne was ended.

Having departed Europe, Great Britain was now "Fortress Britain" And Britain took total control of its affairs. Illegal immigrants and foreign criminals, responsible for much of the crime, were forcibly deported instead of being kept at huge expense in prison and holding centers.

Benefit systems were radically overhauled, if you didn't take on work which was allocated you lost your benefit, simple as that! The other aspect was that the old system paid out benefits to the disabled, who were becoming more prevalent due to medical science. In the 40's and 50's disabled people were virtually unknown. Now one in five! In order to largely alleviate this state of affairs all pregnant mothers were subject to gene therapy, any fetus found to have long term medical issues were aborted!

Hundreds of billions of pounds were immediately released to the economy; by the simple idea of formalizing euthanasia - three doctors being convened to judge whether a person's quality of life had sunk to such a low level as to warrant a quiet dignified death.

Virtually overnight many of the thousands of care homes, charging anything up to £1000 per week, catering for the senile-people with no hope or quality of life - were closed. The NHS was the major beneficiary, with the pressure taken off due to the demise of so many of the older population.

Many of the thousands of people on life support - with a vanishingly small chance of recovery - eating up the NHS budget uselessly had their plugs pulled - again with safeguards in place

The upshot of this was that funds were now available to give the young and the deserving a decent start in life, instead of pouring money away on totally lost causes.

Corporate greed was, quickly, curbed by the simple process of ensuring that no employee could earn less than one fiftieth of the top earner in an establishment employing more than 10,000 people, with a pro rata arrangement, in law, for lesser organizations. This meant that the old minimum wage immediately became redundant. Similar rules were in place for all working environments; including Parliament, the Civil Service and the Judiciary. Pension plans operated similarly - fairness for all at last!

Non-violent crimes, such as theft and fraud, tax evasion and the like, were punished by the confiscation of twenty times the value of the crime, plus a stiff prison sentence, with hard labor. With a system of zero tolerance in Schools and Colleges they quickly got back to centers of learning, instead of centers of juvenile delinquency.

Most crime was stamped out in a year. Not that this action by the state signaled a move to either the extreme right, or left politically. Both rich and poor were treated alike. Each exemplary sentence received wide publicity. Even vehicle license and insurance evasion was harshly punished by the simple process of confiscating the vehicle. Cheating the state was not a worthwhile occupation.

In three years Great Britain, from being second rate, once again took its place with the top flight industrial countries. From being one of the leading debtor nations, it now had a healthy balance of payments; with the wealth so generated being used to improve the lives of all.

Great Britain now set the pace and example, for others to follow. A major breakthrough in the field of technology came in 2020. Japan, America and Great Britain had for some time been involved in a joint project, to develop a fusion cell based on hydrogen. With oil rapidly running out the spectra of energy starvation was removed, once and for all.

There were still clouds on the horizon; vicious strains of disease were a planet wide problem. For a short time their progress had been halted but due to molecular development the viruses always kept one step ahead of a permanent cure. The reckless prescribing of drugs by some Doctors did nothing to help matters. Then the development of nano techniques which was seen as the savior of mankind; bringing medicine out of the dark ages in the bid to fight disease. Grant came back from his ruminations with a start; he looked up. A young policeman stood there, 'I wonder, Sir, if I could see your identification please?' He was obviously concerned at this little man walking the streets at four in the morning.

'Of course,' answered Grant, 'With pleasure.' The policeman quickly checked the information, together with fingerprints, DNA and retina using a small hand held device which relayed the information to the National Computer Controlled Center. With national finger printing, DNA and retina scans, and identity cards, crime detection was very much simpler.

'Sorry Dr. Grant,' the young constable was obviously impressed by his title. 'Just a routine check; hope you don't mind, it's just that it is rather early in the morning, and you might have been a cat burglar after all!'

Grant smiled - were the police really looking younger nowadays?

'That's okay; I would rather you checked than miss something important.'

'Goodnight Sir'

'Goodnight constable'

Grant let himself into his small self-contained flat. He sat down and poured himself a stiff whisky. He lived alone, and the flat bore witness to this fact. The rooms, whilst clean and tidy, were austere, lacking a woman's touch. His parents had both died, when he was still a child, in an air crash, and he had no living relatives. He was however very close to the Williams family, who had fostered him immediately after that fatal accident.

Grant finished his whisky, and looked round at his modest surroundings. He was glad that he had no romantic ties; he had had his moments with the opposite sex, had relished them, but had never fallen in love. His great love had always been his work.

He bathed, and slept. Before he dropped off he wondered what lay in the future or in the past for him.

***

Was that a knock at his door? Grant swung his legs over the edge of his single bed and stood up, swaying a little. He glanced at his digital clock; it showed one thirty. John scratched his head; surely it was four-twenty when he had climbed into bed. Perhaps the clock had stopped. Better check his wrist watch. No, that confirmed the time - what the hell was going on. Again that knock on the door - louder this time. Grant swore under his breath and went over and opened it - nobody there! He turned and stubbed his toe on a chair...

...Again that knock on the door - louder this time. Grant swore under his breath and went over and opened it - nobody there! He turned and stubbed his toe on a chair...

Grant shook his head and rubbed his eyes; what was up with him? The air around him started to shimmer with a strange green light, he stumbled and fell over, and trying to get up was like balancing on a trampoline. What was happening to him? - For God's sake, what was happening?

The room whirled round him, a feeling of being pulled to another place.

He woke, the sweat pouring down his face, the bed linen soaked. A glance at the clock; six o'clock - had he dreamt it all? His big toe throbbed with pain. He turned over; striving for sleep, but it was a long time coming.

***

'You fools' said Project Leader Klein to the cringing technicians before him, 'You have again failed to pick up the man Grant. I now have to explain your failure to our Masters. Then to the armed guards, 'Take them out and give them twenty lashes each.'

Klein would have probably settled for a punishment of twenty lashes from his superiors, but could expect much harsher treatment unless he could offer a satisfactory explanation.

Failure at his level usually meant a death sentence. Equipment malfunction was to blame for the two abortive attempts to capture Grant. He really must be a very important man. Klein drummed his six digits on the table, what excuses would he give.

The speaker on the desk buzzed, 'Come into us now Klein, we are ready for your report...'

Chapter Three

Preparations

'Be prepared' — *Scouts motto*

Grant shambled into Sir Felix's office at the plant next morning looking decidedly the worse for wear. He hadn't even had time to shave, and the dark circles under his eyes did not enhance his appearance. Mortimer lounged in his swivel chair, looked up, and laughed at the sorry sight.

'Rough night John?'

'A little,' was the curt reply; then remembering his manners 'How's the arm?'

'Not bad; not bad at all - a bit sore, but Wood said a couple of days and I'll be as good as new.'

Just then Williams came in looking very sharp in the latest style in suits, a clean shirt with matching tie and, if you stood within a ten meter radius, a nice line in aftershave. Staring at his friend he was about to open his mouth when Grant put up both hands exclaiming 'Yes I know! No sarcastic remarks please, I've already had Felix on to me,' and holding his nose, 'There's a funny smell in here, is it the cats?'

They were soon joined by Bennett and Donaldson, and the meeting, under the chairmanship of the good Earl, was brought to order. Grant yawned expressively, quickly stifling it after a stern glare from the chair.

'Would you like to update me on the position with regard to the "Jesus Project" please gentlemen. Perhaps you could start us off, John - you could stay seated if you wish,' the Chairman ended with a grin.

'Thank you Sir' - now a little more brightly - 'Professor Bennett says the hardware is ready, but there are problems with the computer simulations the coordinate calculations are causing some difficulties.' Bennett nodded in agreement and he broke in 'Yes that's right, I have got my boys running the stuff through the computers; even working overtime it may take up to six weeks.'

'Thanks Steven, I think that's about right,' commented Grant. 'Perhaps we could hear something from you Alan - how is the E.S.P. side going?'

'Pretty well,' observed Donaldson, 'you, we are happy with, but we are still experimenting with some electronic gear, which we hope will make the transition back in time more comfortable for you.'

Sir Felix sat back in his chair, his fingertips together, forming an arch; he pursed his lips together, a sure sign that he was about to make a suggestion. 'I think that Peter should be part of John's pay load, he could prove most useful to the project. I know that this changes things somewhat, and that some modifications may have to be made. But if we kick off in say two months, that should give everyone ample time. Besides, at that time we will have to make less adjustments to our calculations, due to the relative positions of Earth and the other planets in the solar system being closer to their corresponding positions, during that crucial period in Judea.'

'Will that create any sort of problems?' asked Mortimer.

'No problem!' affirmed Bennett. 'All we need are Peter's accurate weight and measurements.'

'Well Peter what do you think?'

'I thought you would never ask,' joked Williams. 'This is the best offer I have had for years; yes you can count me in.'

'Good,' said Sir Felix glancing around the group.

'Any other comments?'

There being none he adjourned the meeting.

From numerous research experiments, on a small scale, the scientific team had found that the negative energy required for the trip back in time could be extracted from the universal "Dark Energy" The ESP man acted as a mental relay, releasing quantities of energy, which could not be tapped for any other purpose but time travel, it appeared that those who had been on record as stating that there was no such thing as a "free lunch" had been proved wrong; at least for the time being. This energy was channeled, using suitably designed equipment: Nano science, micro-electronics, software, and of course the human linkman.

The discovery of this phenomenal source of energy was a real bonus to the project, as a considerable amount of power would otherwise have had to be generated for the jump back in time. The top brains in the fields of ESP and Physics were still trying to fathom the theoretical complexities; but the point was, it worked!

One theory that had been put forward was that the combination of the magnetic and "g" forces had put the "payload" onto some sort of time lines rather like train rails. Once on these rails the E.S.P. linkman was able to, mentally, push the load in one direction - backwards in time. Nobody had yet explained why it was impossible to move forward along those same lines.

What was not clear was why such large amounts of energy were required. It did not seem to matter how far back the time jumps were, the same considerable quantities of energy were soaked up, according to the instruments which registered the power consumption.

The energy required was dependent upon the mass of load only, rather than the length of time jump. This almost certainly meant that once on the time lines, only a small amount of mental energy was necessary to create movement through time - rather like the small effort required to overcome the resistance of a linear air bearing. This further meant that the vast majority of the energy was used in getting onto the lines in the first place.

With the free energy thus available many men and supplies could be transported. However, the sudden appearance of tons of equipment, and a regiment of men, might have tended to scare the natives a little. There was also a fear that the course of time would have been altered, although nobody was really sure. It was thus decided, very early on, that a small inconspicuous expedition of one or two men, with minimal equipment, would be best.

The next few weeks were very busy. Grant briefed Williams on takeoff details, the era they were visiting, and other information that he would need.

Both men took a course of vitamins, keeping off their normal diet, to give them a lean and hungry look. The indigenous populations of Judea in 33 AD had nowhere near the same quality of life as the middle classes in England during the twenty-first century.

Williams took a crash course in Aramaic, using the brain tutoring device; he ended up with a passable knowledge of the language, but would rely very heavily upon Grant who spoke the tongue fluently.

During their free periods, Grant and Williams exercised vigorously. They battled against each other, using the short stabbing broad swords popular with the Romans at the height of their Empire; with staves, a weapon used by the Jews; with knives; in fact anything that might prove useful in Judea at around the birth and death of Christ.

It must be said that the men were rekindling their youth together during this time; they fought hand to hand, fenced, and swam; loving every minute of it. Grant had only been five years old when he became an orphan; and had been taken in by Peter's family. The two boys had been brought up as brothers. John and Peter complemented one another wonderfully, and the bond between them was very strong. Both men were extrovert and decisive; Williams on the one hand was a bit of a joker, and loved acting the clown, Grant on the other hand was more serious. They loved music of every type, and variation. Their measured IQ was somewhat in excess of 195, but in addition they had the gift of commonsense - something sadly missing in many of the super intelligent.

One evening, after what passed as dinner - vitamin pills washed down with water - the men were at a loose end. They had taken up residence in Mortimer's house at his behest. 'I want to keep an eye on you two, just in case you get into trouble,' was his muttered comment.

'Fancy a game of snooker' asked Grant.

'Yes, why not, I think I'm up about seven to six in our series, don't see why I shouldn't improve on that.'

'Fat chance!' was the rather belligerent reply.

Williams had just racked up the balls, when Grant started to sweat, and feel groggy. The room seemed to sway around him, he glanced at Peter - he was concentrating on his shot. Again that insidious tug that he had felt before...

...Williams had just racked up the balls, when Grant started to sweat, and feel groggy. The room seemed to sway around him; he glanced at Peter - he was concentrating on his shot. Again that insidious tug that he had felt before.

Suddenly the room, Williams, the snooker table, all vanished.

The hapless Grant found himself in a large half lit covered arena; he was surrounded by what at first appeared to be several statues. The center piece of the area was a large marble floor, which was in the form of a chess board. Grant was standing on one of the middle black squares, with the figures scattered around him on the other squares in various poses. Closer inspection showed that they were in fact giant chess pieces, in reality dressed up human beings.

Abruptly a fierce looking black knight moved the regulation number of squares by walking stiffly - like a controlled robot. On getting into position a short sword was produced, and plunged into the white Bishop who was previously the sole occupant of the square. What looked like blood poured from a gaping wound in the Bishops chest, and he collapsed in a heap emitting a cry of anguish in the process. Grant realized, with a terrible shock, that the chess game was for real, with the flesh and blood pieces paying the ultimate price for being taken.

There were a lot of the human chess pieces dead or dying. The macabre game seemed to be coming to an end, the Black pieces greatly outnumbering the White. Where the hell was the white King? Thought Grant. He felt a compulsion to walk to an adjacent square. A black pawn - a simply clad foot soldier - armed with a knife moved to the right hand square next to him. He tried to fight the compulsion to move in and kill the pawn. He managed to compromise by chopping the soldier on the neck, rendering him merely unconscious. Grant noticed that the man offered no resistance. Grant detected a movement to his left. The black Queen moved into a position three squares from him, with nothing in between.

'Checkmate, I think friend Grant,' said a voice from the far corner of the board.

'We have been trying for some time to get you to join our little game - thank you for coming 'Well played,' said another, deeper, voice. 'An excellently fought match.'

Out of the corner of his eye Grant saw two dark robed figures sitting on a raised dais, viewing the proceedings. Before he could take in more detail the remaining black chess pieces were on him, and he had to defend himself. He picked up a fallen sword and hacked around him, all thoughts of any finesse gone. Grant felled three of the pawns and the rest of the black pieces surrounded him. There was the Queen, a Bishop, a Knight and two Pawns. The Queen pulled out some sort of strange mechanism and pointed it directly at his chest.

He was suddenly overcome by a paralysis which was almost total - he could just about blink his eyelids. One of the pawns caught him before he could fall. The Bishop took two paces forward and took out a knife; raised his arm, the weapon glinted in the half-light before plunging downwards in the direction of Grant's heart. He had time to notice that there were six digits grasping the knife handle.....

***

'Alright, John, your turn, I haven't left you much'

Then sharply 'John, where the hell are you?'

Williams searched round the games room, looked in the toilets, absolutely no sign at all of Grant. He knew that his friend was not one to joke around in this fashion and rang Sir Felix on the house phone. Mortimer came down; he was wearing a lovely red dressing gown and had obviously been preparing to retire for the night.

'What in blue blazes do you mean by it? Is this another of your cock and bull stories?' grumbled the Earl.

Williams explained again what had happened, and Sir Felix calmed down somewhat.

'How can a man vanish into thin air?' He exclaimed. Then thinking 'Of course! If he was travelling through time or space he would suddenly vanish, just like on our own tests. But how could he without all the equipment and backup systems?

'John may be in terrible danger, how can we possibly help him?' Williams was becoming distraught.

Without a word Felix took out his cell phone, he dialed a number and was soon in contact with the living quarters at the plant.

'Alan, come over quickly, we have a very urgent problem to deal with. I suggest you bring over the ESP amplifying unit, with a three way access facility.'

Fifteen minutes later, in the games room, three men sat intensely discussing the problem. Donaldson had the floor.

'Our only chance is, I believe, a three way mental hook up on the amplifier, which I think was your idea, Sir, (nodding to Mortimer), when you suggested I should bring over the apparatus.'

'That's right, let's get on with it. When we get wired up if we all mentally think of Grant back in this room, that might, with God's help, do the trick.'

Minutes later each man was concentrating very hard, until their heads were pounding.

'It's no good,' uttered Peter. 'It's just doing no good at all.'

'Shut up and keep with it,' ordered Mortimer savagely.

***

The knife arced down and Grant thought grimly of that game of snooker that he had so recently left. The sharp point of the knife was one millimeter away, when he was suddenly yanked hence and dumped unceremoniously on the snooker table, in front of a startled trio, who had almost given up all hope.

There were a few seconds of absolute silence from the three men, whilst Grant ruefully and painfully disentangled himself from snooker balls. Then everyone started to speak at once...

Finally John Grant was allowed to tell his story. Although still suffering from the effects of his traumatic experience, and still half paralyzed, he was able to blurt out the main details, before passing out on the floor.

Three days under medical care, in the plant's hospital, saw Grant better, but still a little groggy and bemused by all that had happened. The big fear was that the unknown enemy would try to lift him again. He was obviously extremely important to them, simply because he was the mainstay of the "Jesus Project". Speculation was rife on the connection between the six fingered men in black and the project, but nobody had yet come up with a rational theory. Indeed the facts of the matter had been programmed into the project computer, which kept showing on its screens **"INSUFFICIENT DATA"**.

It was decided to maintain the original schedules. Grant himself was now mentally prepared for any further eventualities and it was unlikely that another attempt to capture him would succeed. Preparations for the critical **"OFF"** date went on a pace. The entire project team was working full out, grabbing sleep and meals where they worked. Everyone was tired and edgy.

In the last few years Grant had, during experiments, been back in time frequently, but normally for only a few minutes at a time. He had felt sick and disorientated, and had quickly returned before any harm could come to him. It was soon concluded that nature abhorred imbalance, and that movement of a body through time created such imbalance. In other words Grant was being pulled, like a homing pigeon, to his starting point datum, with the consequent discomfort.

The scientific team had eventually come up with a solution, an energy nullifying device simply implanted in Grant's head. Once in the past Grant mentally activated the device, which comfortably kept him there; rather like throwing another mass onto the pan of a scale, to maintain balance. The complex and tiny relay control system was only possible due to the development of the latest nano-technology.

Many years ago, if someone wanted to indicate the impossible, it was to write the Ten Commandments on a pin's head, now the electronic equivalent of millions of bibles could be so stored.

The technical stuff was now reaching a satisfactory conclusion, what remained outstanding was, in a way, more difficult to organize and control. There had been numerous discussions and arguments as to how the time travelers would conduct themselves in Judea.

Finally it was decided that Grant and Williams would act the part of Jewish Merchants.

Even now skilled tailors were working on the outfits they would be wearing; perfection was the aim, so as not to arouse any suspicions. To lend further authenticity to the act, coinage of the period was duplicated.

Their belongings would also contain; nutria-foods; the latest nano activated antibiotics; emergency medical gear;

laser hand guns; miniature grenades; cameras and digital recording equipment.

Grant intended to take along a few home comforts, including Scotch whisky, and some soap. This supposed that Sir Felix did not become suspicious, and carry out a pre-trip check on their gear.

As well as numerous physical tests on Grant and Williams, during the various preparations, they were also psychologized at regular intervals. This had become something of a standing joke between the two men, as they tried to score points off the very pretty, but apparently humorless psychologist, who ran the tests.

Ms. Curtis complained bitterly to Mortimer after each session, and even his charm was beginning to wear a little thin, until eventually she quit in disgust; she was never replaced. Mortimer thought that the boys were about as psychologically stable as it was possible to be.

***

The night before the expedition, saw Grant and Williams taking a night cap with Sir Felix whilst he gave them a final briefing.

'On no account must you interfere with the events of the period that you will be entering' he lectured. 'Otherwise you may not have a home to come back to. Consider the world today without Christianity. Our sociologists have done several quantum computer scenarios. There is no doubt that due to man's darker instincts he has used religion, particularly Christianity and Islam, to inflict a great deal of misery on his fellow beings; the treatment of women as a lower class being; denying them education and free will; the Inquisition; the burning of so called witches; the Dark Ages, where scientific development was held up for hundreds of years; the cruelty inflicted on Muslims during the Crusades by Christian Knights; all in the name of religion.

'In one scenario we had reached our present technological development in 700 AD,' Sir Felix continued. 'However in another, due to the lack of spiritual comfort and moral guidance over the centuries, evil and devil worship became the normally acceptable doctrine and technological development was completely crushed.'

'I hate to strike a discordant note in all this,' interrupted Williams. 'What if we get there and there is nothing out of the ordinary happening; that the scriptures are a load of bunk.'

'No chance,' answered Grant. 'There is absolutely no doubt that the period is unique; the tremendous psychic activity, particularly on the day of Christ's death, completely refutes that scenario. As to the meaning of it all who knows?'

'Anyway, please record as much as possible,' interjected Mortimer. 'Without,' he added, 'arousing any suspicion.'

'What about the Aliens?' asked Williams?

'We can only think that they are out to stop us at all costs,' answered Sir Felix. 'Where they come from, God or the Devil only knows. We must investigate when we have less pressing matters to consider; it must be obvious that, from your written report, John, they are anti-Christ. I cannot, for the life of me see why they are interfering with our project. Do they want the secret of time travel? Surely they could have used more secretive methods to this end. Are they even of this world?'

Just then the security alarm, triggered from the plant and installed in the house after the last fracas, went off. Communication with the complex revealed that it was under very heavy attack by up to one hundred men in black costume that had seemingly come from nowhere. They had heavy laser projectors, and had almost reached the takeoff laboratory; which was their goal. Felix silently thanked the Almighty that he had seen fit to quadruple the security just recently - he hoped it would be enough.

'Come with me quickly, we have little time to spare,' ordered Sir Felix as he led the way down to the wine cellar, and into a small room with a simple lever control on the wall. This crisis situation had been foreseen and prepared for in advance. He quickly slammed the lever down. The very air seemed to vibrate momentarily, and then all was still again. Sir Felix operated the door, and they stepped out into the takeoff facility in the maximum security lab. Williams and Grant looked at each other, and then at Sir Felix, quizzically.

'Either, Sir, you are a magician, or you know very much more than you have told us,' exclaimed Grant.

'We will discuss that another time,' insisted Mortimer. 'You are taking off now!' The sounds of fierce fighting could be heard beyond the thick walls, and the energy screens of the building. 'In the circumstances you will wear full body amour under your robes, no! Do not ask why, you may find out soon enough.'

With practiced skill John and Peter got themselves ready. Mentally they had not yet acclimatized themselves to this sudden moving forward of the whole operation. Physically it was a race between them getting off, and the attackers breaching the laboratory defenses.

As they struggled with their preparations various thoughts ran through Grant's mind: would the jump in time be successful? Would they return intact? What if Williams's doubts about the period were true and they found nothing out of the ordinary? Maybe he would end up on a sacrificial slab, a victim of the devils excesses...

***

Twenty miles beneath the earth's surface, in a dimly lit chamber sat the servants of the "Dark One". The six black clad members of the high council of the "Dark Brotherhood" were in major session. The head of council, the ordained Leader, is speaking.

'Please report Samus'

'I have sent one hundred men, handpicked, to the "Jesus Project" complex. We have had no reports since they left. This time with our superiority in numbers, and the heavy laser projectors I have sent with the force, we are guaranteed success.

Leader's cruel white face turned to Samus, and gazed at him. His pale blue eyes seemed to bore into the unfortunate man.

'I hope you are correct, we must not, cannot have another failure, or your life will be forfeit.'

Samus was silent; he knew that he dare not protest for fear of bringing Leader's wrath down on his head. Great Satan! He would make those pigs of his suffer if they failed him. He would deal with them, before the council dealt with him. The security leader was used to this sort of pressure since he had taken over four years ago. He sometimes wondered if the place on the council was worth it all. Five of his predecessors had been executed, and he wondered if he might not be the sixth.

'Professor Deimos' rapped out the Leader.

'Yes Great Leader,' answered a fat, bloated man, with a triple chin; his eyes buried in a mass of flesh like tiny buttons. 'Report on the development of your project, please Deimos.'

Deimos rubbed his hands together, a rather irritating habit that he had. Leader noted this, and marked it up as yet another weakness of these spineless fools. How could he serve the dark God when he was so poorly served by his own council?

'The weapon will soon be operational, just another three weeks, we still have to test it thoroughly, and will do so against the island of Japeen, it is about time we set an example; and they have been asking for it for a long while.'

'That is true Deimos, you have done well.' Leader's voice was now soft and dripping with honey. Deimos inwardly preened himself - it did not do to show too much pleasure in front of Leader.

'Thank you, Sir - my Leader,' he stuttered.

'Let us get on with it,' said Leader impatiently. 'Foss, you next; please report on the slave regions. Has the production quota increased as I ordered last month?'

Foss, a short man, bald with wide set eyes was sweating, and he could feel the perspiration dripping down his chin. He had been fearing this moment. The odious little man was supervisor of the African continent. He was responsible for the output of the very important mining operations, as well as all other production including food and livestock. The operations were totally dependent upon slave labour.

'Ah! I..., Ah! I ... am sorry Great Leader.' Foss managed to get out.

'Come come Foss, please explain yourself,' Leader almost whispered, the menace in his voice hardly disguised.

'What you are trying to say,' he continued, 'is that instead of increasing production, it has fallen.' Leader motioned to his personal guard.

'Take this cretin away, and eliminate him,' he said. A ripple of apprehension went round the table. Foss was hustled away, begging forgiveness and mercy - it fell on deaf ears.

Foss' second in command, who had been waiting outside, came in and took his place.

'Ah! Vint, glad you could make it. Please tell us what measures you intend to take to improve your production quotas.'

Vint started his maiden speech on the council with some confidence. 'Great Leader, I appreciate your confidence in me. I have already taken steps to see that your wishes are carried out. Every ten thousandth person, drawn by lot, in the African continent has been burnt alive, in public. More are promised if quotas in every area are not improved...'

'Excellent! Excellent!' Enthused Leader. 'You have done exceptionally well.' Vint had, in fact, been specially selected as a possible future Leader. He was known for his abject cruelty, and had ingratiated himself with the present Leader because of it. Just then a deep resonant booming sound came from far off, being repeated at regular five second intervals.

'Well gentlemen,' said Leader, 'We are being called by the "Dark One" to black mass, let us go quickly, lest he becomes angry.'

The whole Council arose and filed out, with Leader at their head. Further on down the passage there was a huge oak door. It took two guards to open it. The stench coming from the large cavern of a room was overpowering, although these men were used to the stink of death.

Leader lit some giant candles in the great room beyond the door, which closed shut behind the group when the last had passed through. At one end of the room was a blood stained slab, on which a rotting body lay. The members of the Council knelt facing the alter.

A grotesque figure suddenly appeared, squatting on the slab like some great toad, green slime dribbling from its gash of a mouth; crab-like hands resting upon its pot belly (This was one of the manifestations of the Devil). The next hour was spent in dedicated worship of the beast, Leader being in constant mental contact with the fiend from hell.

At the end of the hour the door was opened, and a very young, naked, girl was brought in; she was drugged, as she made no attempt to escape, though that would have been pointless. The girl, hardly fifteen years old, was then strapped down onto the slab, her legs apart. Then the beast "took her" brutally, the huge serrated organ tearing into her virginity, causing the blood to flow down the poor unfortunate girl's legs.

After this exhibition, watched with delight by the assembled councilmen, the girl was carried out. She would carry the devil's spawn, until its birth nine months hence.

Two small babies were next brought into the room, their throats were cut and their bodies offered up to the creature. He gorged himself on them, the blood mingling with the slime now pouring down onto the slab, coloring it afresh.

The figure on the slab grew indistinct, and then disappeared from view. They waited for a few minutes in reverence, before returning to the council chamber.

***

We will draw a curtain over the excesses of the Devil, and his brood, and return to Grant and Williams, fighting against time in order to manipulate time.

Chapter Four

Off

'The Most Incomprehensible Thing about the Universe is that it is Comprehensible at all'
Albert Einstein

Grant and Williams were bustled into the time chamber; they were changed and ready, all contemporary articles such as watches and rings were removed or hidden. Their makeup, considering the short period of time available to implement it, was as perfect as modern technology and artistry could make it. Even their inoculation marks were disguised.

Grant was attached to the electronics which controlled the whole system: the huge magnetic coils wound around the chamber, the chamber itself, and the circuitry which amplified his E.S.P. capability, and would be instrumental in catapulting them back in time.

The chamber rotated horizontally at extremely high speeds, it was the high "g" forces, combined with dense magnetic fields, up to twenty tesla, which formed the physical part of the system. Grant was the link between the physical, and the psychic energy which finalised the transfer back in time.

The co-ordinates for the transfer were a combination of the gravitational value, and the flux strength of the earth's weak magnetic field, to six places of decimals. Both parameters alter with time, due to geological changes, but techniques recently developed enabled these changes over the centuries to be calculated, and allowed for. Slight adjustments were made for the ten hours or so early start now forced upon them.

Near Jerusalem, where the transfer was to be made, the coordinates were 9.809182 m/s/s and 60.121274 micro Tesla. The year, month, week, day, and hour of transfer was dictated by the E.S.P. linkman and the associated systems.

Another factor also had to be considered, the relative positions of the planets in the solar system at the time of transfer, and at the other end. Any slight error and the two adventurers might find themselves breathing vacuum.

The practice of transfer in time worked fine, the theoretical niceties were still being studied. Grant would, at the critical moment activate the necessary circuitry, using the chamber controls and the nano-relay control locked in his brain. The relay, and associated computer links would do the rest. Everything, except the chamber and associated equipment, within three meters, would be transferred with the pilot. On return, Grant would activate the control mentally, reversing the whole process back to the laboratory chamber. Williams' departure and return, together with his physical stability in Judea would depend upon the nano-electronics embedded in his friend's skull.

The main grid transformer had been destroyed by the attacking force, but the auxiliaries had immediately cut in - two large, and very powerful, hydrogen cell powered steam turbines. Both would be needed at maximum power to deliver the ten mega-watts required to activate the "JESUS" chamber.

Grant and Williams were belted into cushioned seats, rather like potential astronauts, this to relieve the six "g" force that, momentarily, they would be subjected to. Grant concentrated deeply, he pressed buttons and the chamber started to rotate, building up speed quickly. Another button activated the relay which operated the huge contact breakers spilling current, one-hundred thousand amperes, into the coils. The massive superconducting coils were cooled within an ace of absolute zero, at which electrical resistance is zero - hence no heating effect from the huge currents involved.

With "g" and magnetic forces at a maximum, Grant pinpointed the exact psychic time coordinates. Everything went blank...

Neither Grant nor Williams experienced anything during the transfer. Grant, during his previous momentary visits to the past, got the feeling, just prior to the jumps, that he was about to hurl himself into empty space without a parachute. If truth be told both men were scared, although they wouldn't have admitted it to a soul.

John and Peter were the stuff that heroes were made of. In another age they would have led the "Charge of the Light Brigade" or fought the "Battle of Britain"; they would have been an Alexander the Great, a Pompey, or a William the Conqueror, a Richard the Lion heart, or a Wellington. Grant and Williams were the very best examples of Twenty-First Century Alpha Males.

***

Grant found himself lying on a hillside, overlooking Jerusalem, with Williams next to him. They had only a few seconds to take in the general surroundings. It was a fine evening - the time was six o'clock and the sun well past its prime. Grant was about to comment on the marvelous sight of the "Holy City" some miles from them, when the two men became aware of a group of Roman soldiers of contubernium or platoon strength - eight men; The Decanus, a surly brute of a man, said 'Where in Jupiter did you come from?'

Grant, in perfect Aramaic, his arms raised in a submissive pose, answered, 'I am sorry Sirs we didn't mean to startle you, and we are strangers here; just passing through.'

'Right lads,' said the surly one, 'Let's have a bit of fun with these Jewish pigs.' He spoke in his native Latin, but his meaning was all too clear as he drew his sword. His men quickly followed suit - there might be rich pickings here. The two men looked well fed and prosperous. The soldiers licked their lips in anticipation of a good share out from two bulging purses.

The Romans sent their riffraff to Palestine, and after a turn of duty in that forbidding land the motley crew could have done with some fun; a chance to relieve the boredom, of what up to now had been an eventless patrol.

Unfortunately for the soldiers they had picked on the wrong pair to have fun with. Grant's physical qualifications have already been described. Williams, if anything, was even better qualified in the field of martial arts; being a Cambridge blue in boxing, and an Olympic standard exponent of Judo.

The Romans were all a full head shorter than Williams, and about Grant's size. They were no match for the two ex-varsity men. In twenty seconds flat the grass covered hill was scattered with some very bemused Roman soldiers, in various states of fracture, with several of them unconscious.

'Frightfully glad to have you along,' said Grant to his friend. 'Glad to have been of service,' replied Williams touching his forelock in mock salute. The two of them had enjoyed their brief workout.

'Let's get out of here quickly, and set up headquarters somewhere, said Grant; getting back to the reality of the situation, after the exhilaration of the fight. At a fast trot they left the scene of battle, before their adversaries could gather their wits together, enough to call for reinforcements.

***

The two made headquarters in a small cave in the hillside, it was dry and warm and they made themselves comfortable. They had arrived seven days before the crucifixion, and had decided to try and see some of the events described in the scriptures which preceded the major event; to report back to the many interested parties in their own time.

Grant sat on the cave floor, cross legged. 'Can't you feel the fantastic psychic energies Peter?' he asked. 'It's as if we were at the center of the whole Universe at this time in history. I really cannot figure it out. What is the purpose of it all? I know we are here to find the truth of the whole religious bit; but why should a man, the so called son of God, die painfully, just to wash the sins of this world away? A Priest would explain it all I suppose, in their convoluted fashion. What I would like is a practical down to earth answer to it all. I suppose that I have always believed in some sort of divine entity; some sort of omnipotent scientist I suppose.

'There was a fellow in the seventies' replied Williams, 'now what was his name?... Ah! Yes, I remember, Erich Von

Daniken: he wrote many books on his research; trying to link happenings in history, the bible, the supernatural; with science, space travelers, and the like. To him the ancient Gods were in fact spacemen. Perhaps we shall now find out at first hand. As for the psychic energy, I obviously have no E.S.P. facility whatsoever, as I cannot feel a thing.

'John,' went on Williams, 'I have just had a thought, and I hope that none of those soldiers we have just worked over are fore-fathers of ours or of someone like Galileo, Michelangelo or Newton. I am sure that a couple of them cashed in their chips, and I gave one of them such a heavy kick in the marriage arrangement that I should think that further potential in the fatherhood department would be zero. You know what Sir Felix said on the matter of physical intervention,' he added darkly.

'Unlikely,' answered Grant, 'Our sociologists did a statistical computerized prediction of such events occurring. People like these soldiers have only a ten to one chance that their line will get past the 700 AD mark. On the other hand the aristocracy of the period, who are much better cared for, may present a problem; so I suggest that you don't do any damage to them, as there is a better than evens chance that their blood line will not die out. In killing them you may well affect the future. Perhaps only marginally but...

'Another thing,' interrupted Williams. 'The Romans had gained and kept most of the civilized world by this stage in history, how on earth did they do it with the rabble we have just encountered?'

'Don't be taken in by their performance against us,' answered Grant. 'The basic Roman fighting machine was, sorry, is, superb for this period in history. The Roman Empire was all powerful for around nine hundred years; at its height it extended across a territory 3000 miles east to west, and 2000 miles north to south,' informed Grant.

'The Romans brought their form of civilization to all the people that they conquered. Although totally ruthless, and sometimes cruel, they forced nations into a totally new era. Their secret was their discipline, and ease of mobility in adapting battle formation - this gave them military superiority over the known world. Their swords and spear tips were of shear steel, produced in Spain; consider steel against bronze weapons!'

'Their tactics were usually to kill as many of the enemy with javelin spears, whilst defending themselves with their shields. Once at close quarters their short stabbing swords were brought into play very effectively. Each maneuver was carried out with complete discipline. As they took over each area of conquest, the Romans pressed the cream of the men still left alive into their service and most joined willingly, keen to enjoy the fruits of that service. Better by far to be on the winning side. Sociologically the Romans were excellent administrators, encouraging the populace into their ways and style of living; bringing such luxuries as baths and plumbing to their lives.'

'I see!' exclaimed Williams. 'It sounds very fascinating; I wish I hadn't neglected my history quite so much now.'

'You always were a bit thick in that area' countered Grant. 'We really ought to get ourselves sorted out, lets inspect everything to see if there are any problems - our lives may depend on it later' he added thoughtfully. 'Then we must get our heads down, we need to be really sharp for tomorrow.'

The next hour saw them checking all the equipment thoroughly; including Grant's implant with a special micro testing system which you could fit in a matchbox. Everything seemed perfect, and the journey through time and space had not affected either them or the supplies.

They had thought of discarding the body armour, as it was inclined to be uncomfortable if worn for long periods, but had decided against it; remembering Mortimer's very serious warning. Instead they planned to keep it on at all times for the seven days or so that they would be around in this foreign land - just in case, although neither of them really thought that there would be any modern weapons in this era except their own-how wrong they were!!

'Let's turn in now, Peter'

It had been a long hard day, and Williams readily agreed. They stripped down to their body armour, and got into the sleeping bags - very cozy and snug against the evening air which was getting rather chilly.

Grant was just about to fall asleep when Williams queried sleepily 'What about that matter transmitter in Sir Felix's home then? And what the hell do those men in black have to do with it all?'

'Oh! Shut up and go to sleep,' was the curt reply.

***

Sir Felix watched the large time chamber as it rotated up to maximum speed. He was, indeed, too old for all this excitement. He had supervised the takeoff right up to the last minute. The spinning of the drum had a hypnotic effect on him; he thought about getting to the security doors to assist in the defense of the laboratory, should the energy screens fail. The boys must have somewhere to come back to. He decided against it; he would not make that much difference and he wanted to make sure that they got off alright. The sounds of battle intensified; and a fear gripped him such as he had never felt before; his head and chest started to ache.

The light pulsated off the rotating system, and his mind went back to when Mary had been alive; dear sweet Mary! What times they had had. He had asked her to marry him when he had been twenty-five; a young engineer with Rolls Royce. Perhaps if things went well with the time machine he would get John to take him back to that terrible day in 1995 when Mary had been taken from him. Independently wealthy, he had become an extremely successful mechanical engineer, and had eventually become president of the Institute of Mechanical Engineers. He had received his K.G. for services to the engineering industry of the United Kingdom, a few years before.

On that fateful day in April a runaway car had mounted the pavement and struck his wife down; she had died instantly. If only he could get back and somehow prevent the whole episode; the whole tragic event.

Mortimer could still see his Mary's face, she had been lovely; a real English rose. They had never been able to have children, something they both bitterly regretted; something to do with his sperm count - apparently nothing could be done, despite numerous consultations with the best medical minds in the country. The tears welled up, and his eyes glistened, all the old feelings of grief were coming back.

Over the years he had tried to get it out of his system by taking on a succession of women, but none of them came close to making him forget. He knew what they called him behind his back: a lecher, a pervert. What did they know! He thought furiously. He would have given anything for just one more moment with Mary; just one more kiss.

Felix soldiered on for years; his work keeping him going. Then, the chance of a lifetime, the "Jesus Project". After seeing the demonstrations he was filled with wonder, and a longing to help. Later he had met Grant, and immediately took to him; here was the son he had never had from his loins; second best would have to do.

He wondered; should he have told the two, Williams and Grant, what he knew about those devils in black, the attacks, that matter transmitting chamber? Would it have done any good?

But what was this, the chamber was slowing down, and he could still see Grant. Had something gone wrong? Sir Felix was immediately alert again and very very worried...

Chapter Five

Joseph

*'Time is like a river made up of events,
and its current is strong;
no sooner does anything appear then
it is swept away,
and another comes in its place,
and will be swept away too'*
Marcus Aurelius

    The two men went to sleep, having set up a small security device at the mouth of the cave. They were awakened in the middle of the night by a tiny buzzing sound - the electronic device had been triggered. Before they could do anything the cave was bathed in bright light from flash torches and a voice in curious broken English, from behind the wall of light ordered 'Put your hands outside your sleeping bags where we can see them, we do not wish to harm you, but have orders to kill you if we have to - do as you are told and you may live.'
    Blinking back the sleep, and trying to adjust to the suddenly improved illumination, Williams and Grant eventually saw that they were being covered, with what

appeared to be high-energy lasers, by two men in black robes.

'Careful now,' they were warned, as they slowly attempted to ease the sleeping bags free of their shoulders, so that they might comply with the order.

Grant was furiously trying to get his mind in gear. Their security had been very slack; they should have paid more attention to Mortimer's warnings. They hadn't even taken the precaution of keeping a handgun in the sleeping bags ready for instant use. They really would have to sharpen up, Grant decided - that is if they got another chance.

Their hands were now in clear view: 'Now roll onto your stomachs,' was the next order. Williams was a little slow in this maneuver and received a kick in the ribs to help him on his way.

Their captors were part of the same brood that Grant had had so much trouble with lately. He was now well experienced with the general characteristics of these evil men; pale blue eyes set in a cold white face, with cruel thin bloodless lips. Something out of your worst nightmares.

Just then a seemingly amazing thing happened, both of the black robed men suddenly toppled forward without a sound.

'Please do not be alarmed,' said a deep voice from the cave's entrance, 'I do not think that they will give you any more problems!'

Picking up one of the fallen torches, Williams scrambled to his feet and pointed it at the voice's source. A large man, wearing grey robes, was illuminated; he held a small but lethal hand weapon. Casually the man walked into the cave and over to the bodies kicking them face upwards before checking for life signs.

'A pity they are both dead, we may have got some information out of them' he commented. Then as an afterthought, 'I had to make sure, a disabling shot may have put you in danger.'

The man was tall - about the same height as Williams - with huge shoulders. He looked like a weight lifter, and Grant could only imagine the power residing in the muscular frame beneath the robes. His face was smooth, and very handsome; with pleasant brown eyes, and a nice tan. Obviously of Latin origin - probably Italian.

'Permit me to introduce myself, I am Joseph,' he gazed at Grant and Williams, and at their pile of belongings, with some suspicion.

'May I ask who the hell are you?' He continued. Before the two could reply:

'I assume that as these dogs wished to do you harm, that you must be friends of mine.'

He grinned at them, and they noticed his teeth; very small, even, and very white. (Funny the things you notice - thought Williams - even in times of adversity)

Grant was first to reply, 'Let me introduce Peter Williams, a good friend of mine. My name is John Grant. I believe, Joe, that we owe you our lives. He offered his hand in time honored fashion, closely followed by Williams. Joe accepted with a handshake which left them both wincing.

'In answer to your next question: we are from the future as indeed you most obviously are; our year of origin is 2030 A.D.' Joe looked somewhat taken aback by this revelation. 'That's funny I am from the year 6034'
'AD?' queried Grant.

'I don't understand,' exclaimed a very puzzled Joe. Grant decided to enquire further, doing some quick mental calculations. 'If you are from the future, would it be exactly 1997 years?' The big man's face was a picture as he too did his sums.

'Yes that's precisely right, why?'

Grant glanced at Williams to see if the penny had dropped. Suddenly the dawn of realization on his friend's face.

'Well, I'll be damned.'

'When you two have finished your nice little double act, perhaps you would explain it all to me,' Joe growled.

'Yes, sorry Joe, what I am about to tell you will, to put it mildly, seem rather implausible,' said an apologetic Grant.

'I assume you do not have a religion called Christianity in your world, furthermore I am willing to bet that the Old Testament is part of your literature, and that your calendar starts at Genesis - let's see now - 4004, this is 33 AD, add 1997 onto that, and we get 6034 in your world or 2030 AD in ours.' Joe looked at Grant as if he was mad. 'What are you talking about? He exclaimed incredulously. 'I mean that we are talking about a parallel world, which you are from, where a religion called Christianity never got going.' 'That's the only possible explanation,' interjected an excited Williams, who had been hopping up and down, waiting his turn to get into the conversation. 'Exactly where are you from, Joe?

'From the land mass of UROPA, specifically a small island called BRITANNIA, but I still don't see'...Ignoring the man's lack of understanding Grant probed further. 'What is the state of your world and why are you here at this time in history? You seem to know about our dead black friends over there.' Pointing to their recently deceased antagonists. Joe's mood changed to one of melancholy.

'My world is on the point of being taken over by an evil sect dedicated to the worship of Satan,' he exclaimed bitterly. 'There are two distinct areas of my planet, UROPA where there is a thriving God fearing civilization. The rest of the planet is ruled by what can only be described as disciples of the Devil, led by a Dark Brotherhood, a couple of examples are over there' Joe continued with some distaste. 'They have, as you can see, six digits on hands and feet.'

Some people say that they have been spawned by the Devil himself. The Dark Brotherhood controls a highly developed scientific culture, and has recently manufactured what they call the "Ultimate Weapon". Our spies inform us that it will destroy us; there is no defense. Our last hope is, myself, I have come into the past to see if there is any way that our future may be altered'

It appeared that the world of Joe was markedly different from that of Grant and Williams. Jesus Christ had never been heard of, and they concluded that there was a good chance that the period of history they were now in, was the era where the amazing division had taken place.

In Joe's world, as well as the normal advances in science - much the same as the alternate world - there were some fantastic developments in the psychic and Para-normal. The world had divided into good and evil, or white and black geographical areas. The Dark Brotherhood ruled by fear and cruelty - human sacrifices were normally accepted practice. They seemed to derive their strength from the suffering of others. In Uropa life carried on in a rather more democratic way.

Joe continued 'Our people will risk anything, even if it means that I radically alter the future by some drastic act. The Dark Brotherhood also has an excellent spy system; as well as having just developed time travel. They have pursued me back; to keep an eye on me. They are able to do this with their highly sophisticated personnel detecting devices - that is how they managed to find you. I think that they must have mistaken you for me. I followed them; the rest you know.'

'Am I correct in the assumption that you came to this period due to the psychic energies being emitted?' asked

Grant.

'Yes' answered Joe. 'Our time travelling device homes in on anything that looks remotely interesting; I have already been to various periods of history without success. I thought that I was onto something in 5,504 in Spane - but it was only a bunch of perverts getting their kicks torturing peasants for their own gratification. There was nothing mystical about it at all. Certainly nothing to do with the Dark Brotherhood, even though it had their hallmark, I managed to kill a few of the bastards anyway,' he added with relish.

Grant reflected that Joe was not the sort of man to get on the wrong side of; he could only imagine the carnage that the man had created in that backward culture with modern weapons. They had probably thought that "Old Nick" himself had something to do with it - not a man from the future.

'The Dark Brotherhood also appears to have the facility to jump into the alternate world - our world!' Exclaimed Williams.

'That's bad,' said Joe, 'If they have that ability, it means they know the exact reason for the alternate future for this planet. If that is so then your future is in jeopardy as well as mine.'

'They certainly did their best to stop us coming,' commented Williams.

'Mmmm... Did they know,' Joe was deeply concerned at the information he was receiving.

'What's it all mean? Mused Grant 'When did the future divide into two, and for what reason, that's what we need to know.

'I suggest we join forces, and see what we can come up with,' suggested Joe.

'OK!' agreed Grant, 'Any objections, Peter?'

'None,' affirmed Williams. 'We really have no choice as I see it.'

The three men spent the next few hours questioning each other about their respective worlds and comparing equipment...

Later the three men tried to grab a few hours' sleep. Grant could not get the idea out of his head that mankind's future happiness might possibly depend on them. Much of what had happened was now explained: the men in black, the last thoughts of the man he had mind probed, that desperate attack just before they had lifted off, his experience on the devils chess board, with human pieces being sacrificed.

Tomorrow, according to the Gospel, was Palm Sunday, and the three men were to try and witness the event. But tomorrow is another day thought Grant wearily.

***

Joe, or more formally Joseph Vincent, took some time to get to sleep. What had he got himself into? These people from a parallel world seemed decent enough, but did they realize the stakes that he was playing for; a whole world and its future. How he hated the Dark Brotherhood. He smiled to himself as he thought about the two recently departed members of that order, now outside the cave, buried under piles of rock. He savored the thought; how easy it had been, a quick burst with a needle beam through the back of the neck at close range. That would go some way to paying the lot of them back, for all the suffering they had caused.

'What am I turning into' He thought. If I go on like this I will be as bad as they are. It was very hard to be rational when faced with such a foe as this.

Joe's mind went to his homeland, Britannia. He came from the northern area of Yorkland, where he lived with his wife and three young children: Delia, Ali and Adam

He was well known as a bit of a hard man and had joined the Uropa security forces on leaving college, at twenty; now thirty one he was a colonel, having risen very quickly through the ranks, he was very smart, very ruthless, and extremely resourceful! Regular testing had shown that he possessed exceptional mental potential, although largely latent, and untapped. For three years he had been receiving special training in order to unlock his special "gifts".

His training had been long and arduous, for months on end he would be away from home; but Ann and the kids had been very understanding about the whole thing. His guarded, 'of tremendous international importance' sounded pompous; but nevertheless had to do. It was the children in particular who kept on at him; they wanted something to boast about at school. He had to keep putting them off, until eventually he lost his temper, and there were tears; Joe wished that during this particular period he was single again, without the worries of a family. Then he looked across at Ann and smiled; he apologized to his children. The details of his present tour of duty weren't mentioned again.

The murmurings of a "terrible weapon" grew weekly and Joe's superiors were becoming decidedly edgy. At last the day of his mission had come. Intelligence reports had indicated that the "other side" was very close to their goal.

His final briefing had been by Uropa's "Chief of Security" no less; the venue was somewhere in central Lunden.

The "Chief", Boris Von Cram, resplendent in his War Marshal's uniform, was a tall, slim man, about six two. A German of middle age, he spoke good English, and expressed himself most forcibly.

'You, Colonel, have been selected from over 500 eminently qualified candidates for this mission; your training has been more than thorough. You are as ready as our considerable resources can make you. I cannot tell you how to play it, only you can decide. Depending upon what you can achieve, you may come back to a world free of that abomination - the "Dark Brotherhood", or to God knows what!'

'The lives of us all depend upon you,' he continued, with even greater intensity, punching out the message with his raised fist, his face registering the hope and fears expressed by all the free world.

'All I can say to you is good luck, the prayers and best wishes of Uropa go with you.' He shook Joe's hand firmly and saluted him. Joe returned the salute, about faced, and marched out of the Marshal's office.

***

Joe dozed off, and then came to with a start; he thought he heard a noise from outside the cave. He glanced over at Williams and Grant; both sleeping like babies. Should he wake them up? He was getting a bit jumpy. No he must not disturb their beauty sleep; the small one could certainly do with it, he chuckled to himself. Probably only a small animal anyway.

Another thought struck Joe Vincent: could he really depend on the two of them in a crisis, they might even in some way, be in league with the "Dark Brotherhood". No - putting the thought from him - he must take the risk. The odds were very much in favor of them being friendly.

In any case the two of them were expendable if the going got rough; they would have to prove themselves to him first before he fully trusted them. Joe slept fitfully for some hours before finally settling into a deep sleep around four o'clock in the morning.

***

'The time is 1941 precisely, and this is your science correspondent, Charles Frampton reporting. You will have noticed that between 1902 and 1933 we have been off the air. This was due to massive magnetic disturbances over the South of England, which affected all telecommunications, as well as most modes of transport.'

'London and the Home Counties have been particularly hit, and there have been a number of tragic deaths due to the phenomena.'

Viewers noticed a bead of sweat on Frampton's upper lip, and he did not look his usual cool, calm, analytical self- quite the reverse! His owl like countenance, enhanced by thick horn rimmed spectacles, peered out of millions of screens. He seemed decidedly agitated.

'The center of the disturbance,' he went on, 'appears to have come from a top secret establishment somewhere in Surrey.' Frampton managed to inject a darkly significant tone into this statement. 'Investigations are underway, but the Ministry of Defense have put a complete blanket on the details. Immediately after this bulletin there will be a discussion, chaired by Sir William Franklin, ex-Chief Scientific Officer of the M.O.D. with representatives from various industrial and research establishments, on the possible cause and implications of the disturbance. This reporter has never in his experience come across...

Frampton got no further as the screens were again blanked out - this time due to official government intervention. Millions of people were left to wonder; and various official establishments were soon swamped with calls. The screens soon lit up again, and the public settled down to its diet of inconsequential entertainment. How were they to know that efforts were being made, on their behalf, to ensure mankind's continued wellbeing.

Chapter Six

Jesus

'Tell the daughter of Sion here is your king coming to you, he is gentle and mounted on an ass, and on a colt, the foal of a beast of burden'
St. Matthew Chap.21 Verse 5

Early the next morning the men, only partially refreshed from their few hours' sleep, packed a few essentials - everything else was hidden in the cave for their return - and breakfasted on some green colored tasteless pills. Then they set off, optimistically to witness and record an event chronicled in the New Testament; Christ's triumphant ride into Jerusalem.

The date **SUNDAY, MARCH 29th 33 A.D.** Both Williams and Joe Vincent had to stoop in order to disguise their large six-feet plus frames. Men of their statue and bulk were uncommon in this area and period in time. None of the three were in a talkative mood, and kept themselves to themselves, each with their own private thoughts on the situation they had been thrust into.

After the initial adventures of the previous day, and the sudden exodus from the scene of the battle with the Roman platoon, neither of the friends had had much time to survey the Ancient terrain of Judea. Grant was very interested to see the contrast between his own time period, and this one. He had visited the area on numerous occasions during his extensive research; but the modern state of Israel was likely to be very much different from the one he now found himself in.

They were approaching Jerusalem from the Mount of Olives, which was on the East side of the city. The view was absolutely magnificent, spread out as it was before them; an archeologist's dream. The area was very rocky and hilly. Grant, however, noticed that there was more grass on the hillsides than in modern Palestine, probably due to the herds of sheep and goats that had nibbled away over the centuries.

It was the city itself that really took the eye. The history of Jerusalem, since it had been established in the Early Bronze Age, around 4,000 B.C., was bathed in blood. It had been raped, razed, sacked and pillaged many times. In the twenty first century there was almost nothing left of what the three men now saw.

The first recorded history of Jerusalem began around 1000 B.C. when David captured it. He foundered the joint Kingdoms of Israel and Judea and the city became the Jewish capital. David's successor King Solomon extended the city.

Grant wanted, eventually, to explore the various avenues of time of the city in detail; after the successful completion of this sortie. He often wondered why there had been such a history of carnage connected with such a "Holy City" - maybe a meeting place of good and evil throughout the centuries.

Although there had been periods of peace for the city, its history, up until Grant's real time, had read something like a who's who of disaster; he remembered from its recorded history:

922 B.C. - the Egyptian pharaoh Sheshonki sacks the city;
850 B.C. - the Philistines plunder the city;
604 B.C. - Egyptians despoil the city, and its king is deported to Babylon;
600 B.C. - city and temple are totally destroyed, and its inhabitants taken as slaves by Egypt;
333 B.C. - and Alexander the Great - the Greeks take over;
167 B.C. - Seleucid Antiochus IV desecrates the temple, followed by a revolt - the Selecucids are expelled and a Jewish state is formed;
63 B.C. - Pompey captures the city for Rome;
40 B.C. - Herod appointed king by the Roman Senate. He largely rebuilds Jerusalem;
66 A.D. - Jewish Rebellion;
70 A.D. - the city is besieged, and almost totally destroyed by the Roman forces;
130 A.D. - city partially repopulated;
132 A.D. - unsuccessful revolt by the Jews;
135 A.D. - Hadrian builds a "Roman" city on the site;
324 to 614 AD - building of Church of Holy Sepulchre - a golden age for the city;
614 A.D. - Persian invasion. Inhabitants of the city are massacred and the churches are destroyed;
1010 A.D. - Egyptian caliph al-Hakum orders the destruction of Christian shrines.
1071 A.D. - Seijup Turks displace Egyptians as masters of the Holy Land;
1187 - Saladin and the Crusades;
1244 - sacked by the Khuarezm Turks;

1247 - the Holy City falls to Egypt;
1517 - Sultan Selim I inaugurates a Turkish regime to last 400 years;
1917 - British troops enter Jerusalem;
1948 - city is divided between Arabs and Zionists;
1967 - east city annexed by Israel during the six day war;
2020 -another Holy war between Israel and its Arab Neighbours. The United Nations intervenes, and the city is taken over by them; and is administered by them. Peace at last, even if supervised!

Over the years the city had housed many religions and Jews had lived with Muslims and various Christian factions including: Orthodox, Monophysite, Latin, and Protestant. It was not called the Holy City for nothing!

The chronicles of the area went through Grant's mind as he surveyed the 33 A.D. version. It was of course much smaller, and completely different from its modern counterpart, which had swallowed up many of the biblical landmarks such as Calvary; where the Crucifixion was supposed to have taken place.

Grant studied the scene intently taking pictures all the time with a concealed camera. The city, over the centuries, had been the focal point for many of the major religions of the world; but its striking feature was its size, it only measured around one thousand meters square and was totally enclosed by thick high walls. Antonia, previously Herod's palace, but now the Roman fortress and prison, dominated the city to the north. Just below Antonia was the temple; the center of religious life for the Jews. On the summit of the western hill, above the city, was another even larger palace; the present residence of Herod. The three towers called Hipparchus,

Phasel, and Mariamme were plainly visible, as no man of Grant's time would ever see them.

The air was clean and fresh on the hillside, due to the altitude of the area - 800 meters above sea level. There was something of a hot spell at this time, and the temperature was 28°C., such spells were common here at this time of the year; they were called "sharavs".

As the three men approached the "Golden Gate" to the City there was a mood of excitement and expectancy as the crowds gathered, they could not help but get involved in the event that was unfolding before their eyes.

Grant recalled the words from Matthew Chapt. 21 Verses 1 to 4:

'When they came near to Jerusalem, and had reached Bethphage at the Hill of Olives, than Jesus dispatched two disciples, saying to them 'Go to the village in front of you, and you will at once find an ass tethered, with a colt alongside of her; untether them and bring them to me. If anyone says anything to you, you will say that the Lord needs them; then he will at once let them go.'

The trios mingled with the crowd, and immediately were assailed by the stench from the unwashed sweating bodies around them; but were impressed by the happy smiling faces that they encountered. The crowd were already cutting palm branches and strewing them on the dirty road, together with articles of clothing. They were shouting:

'Hosanna to the Son of David! Blessed be he who comes in the Lord's name! Hosanna in high heaven!'

There was occurring a sort of mass hysteria amongst the throng, everyone vying for a better position. Despite themselves the three adventurers found themselves caught up in it all. Grant was pushed and jostled, and nearly became separated from his companions. He could only think that perhaps there were elements of truth in the New Testament after all.

Grant's head was ringing, then a tremendous sense of tranquility came over him. He was receiving psychic emanations of purity and goodness; he felt the tears rolling down his face. Glancing at Williams he saw that even his friend was visibly affected. Joe gasped in amazement as he too succumbed.

In the distance they saw... Him.., riding on an ass. An aura surrounded the man; it could only be Jesus Christ. The act was played out with deep emotion by all concerned. Jesus actually came so close that Grant could have touched him; it was all he could do to resist. It was all over very quickly, with Jesus and his disciples disappearing into the city, closely followed by the rabble.

'Quickly' said Grant. 'If the Gospels are correct he is going to turn the Money Changers' tables over.' They pushed through the throng, but it was now so dense that they didn't make it, and by the time they reached the temple, Jesus had gone, probably to Bethany - a small village outside Jerusalem. The three were in something of a mental daze. Later, when Grant had time to think about it, he realized that their modern minds were, relatively, highly developed, and thus probably more susceptible to the supernatural, in this case the "Holy Ghost" Later they realized that in the excitement they had forgotten to record anything...

***

Too late the men became aware that the Jewish crowd had dispersed, and that they were surrounded by at least one-hundred Roman soldiers who had suddenly converged on the area. What was worse they seemed to be of a rather higher caliber than those that Williams and Grant had so easily disposed of just a short time ago.

'Let's be taken quietly said Grant' under his breath. 'We cannot afford to be hurt in attempting an escape.'

The centurion obviously expected trouble. Why he should have thought that three Jewish merchants would offer resistance to such well-armed representatives of the Roman Empire, Grant could only speculate... He was soon to find out.

'We want no trouble,' said Grant. 'We only wish to go about our business in peace.'

Quickly, and with a disciplined precision that surprised Grant and his comrades, they were taken and their arms bound, before being frog marched ignominiously through narrow streets to the Roman fort at Antonia. Here they were flung into a cell several levels down, lit only by a flickering torch which was on its last legs. Their belongings had been taken from them. Luckily they had left most of the modern equipment back at the cave, excepting the recording stuff.

The cell door was thrust open and a young tribune - equivalent to the rank of a 21st century Colonel - strode in, flanked by two black robed men, who held some very sophisticated weaponry. The Dark Brotherhood had certainly established themselves with some powerful allies since coming to this time period.

'I want to know who you are, and where you come from' said the Roman with menace in his Voice.

'We are just poor merchants trying to earn an honest living' answered Grant. 'We can pay if you to let us go' - he knew that this would probably do them no good at all, but thought that it was the established custom; when the Romans held rich looking merchants, for the merchants to offer bribes. Just then the tallest of the Dark Brotherhood interjected, 'the plain fact is that we know who you are, and why you' Pointing to Joe, 'are here. 'What we don't know' he continued, 'Is why you other two are here, other than to observe? We have been loath to kill you, as this may affect the critical balance of energy that was necessary to bring you here; to this age.' Grant later thought of the analogy - a balanced beam with masses on either end; suddenly the masses on one end are removed, the beam goes down with a bang. The result, as far as time was concerned, could be disastrous; perhaps the rending of the fabric of time itself, creating inconsistencies in history, throwing the future into chaos.

Williams caught Grant's eye, and the horrible realization sunk in - Joe had, of course, killed two people from the future just a short time ago. The black robed leader, his name was Cato, saw their obvious discomfort. 'Yes,' he remarked, 'we know you have killed two of us, but our superior technology has taken care of any problem in that direction. Marcus here' - indicating the tribune - 'will be taking care of you for the next few days, then once we have settled matters here we shall take you back to our homeland to be eliminated'

The Roman officer nodded agreement. 'I believe that a squad of our men ran into you yesterday, with some rather nasty results. You will behave yourselves, otherwise you will be sorry, and we can do many unpleasant things to you; without actually taking your life' he added nastily.

The heavy door slammed shut and the three prisoners were left contemplating their fate. To make matters worse the torch had finally given up the ghost, the only light coming from torches outside, dimly illuminating the interior of the cell through a narrow slit in the door. There was also a very nasty smell in the cell from an un-emptied slops bucket.

Williams voiced the thoughts of them all when he commented 'Who would choose to live in this inhospitable land. Since coming here we have been almost killed three times; apart from nearly choking to death on the filthy smells which seems to pervade every fiber of my being. Thank heaven we had a full set of "jabs" before coming here. I hope that there isn't some sort of super bug which is impervious to our modern drugs,' he added with some fear in his voice.

Williams outburst was met with silence, further comment was completely unnecessary; what was uppermost in their minds was how they were going to get out of this mess. They soon loosened their bonds, and Joe with Peter started to feverishly examine their prison; looking for any weaknesses.

***

John Grant, on the other hand, closed his eyes, and relaxed. He found it desirable, when time permitted, at times of impending danger, to mentally distance him from the center of crisis, and to lose himself in his own thoughts; a habit that those nearest to him found most disconcerting.

Grant was back in the Williams' house in Camberley. Mrs. Williams, a large motherly woman, was wiping his nose; he and Peter had been fighting and John had ended up with a bloody nose.

'I don't know what I am going to do with you both,' said June Williams, dabbing at the small ten year olds nose with cotton wool. She hugged John to her; he smelt her perfume, and the freshness of her pinafore. Grant wished that Williams and he were ten again, and back in that kitchen in Camberley.

Mrs. Williams was still alive, God bless her. She and Mr. Williams were now in happy retirement; the two boys regularly visiting them. Fred Williams didn't get about much now, due to a touch of gout, but otherwise they seemed in good health.

The scene changed again, Grant and Williams were seventeen and coming home from school across the fields, when suddenly they had been set upon by a group of local "toughs". The two of them had fought back to back with their fists and feet until the louts, some more than five years their senior, had fled.

How Grant had loved those days in Surrey. Each season had something special about it: winter, cold and usually raining, when the family would crowd around a log fire; spring, blustery with more rain, and green sprouting prolifically from the trees and plants; summer, sometimes very hot, sometimes mild, a time for swimming, fishing, riding, and walking; autumn and the color, unmatched anywhere in the world, with the reds, rusts, gold's, and infinite shades of brown.

Next, the tears from Fred and June Williams as John and Peter went to take their places as "freshmen", at Cambridge. The two were then twenty, and almost full grown.

Then Grant's first love. He had met her whilst on holiday in Cornwall, during their first summer break from university. The Williams' always rented a cottage, for ten weeks, at that time of the year. She had been seventeen, skinny, but very pretty with an elfin face, long black hair, and a bubbling personality. John had loved her with an intensity which only the young, in their first serious relationship, could possibly feel. He lost her after eight weeks to a young man from Surbiton, who spoke as if he had a plum in his mouth. John Grant had been heart broken, mentally vowing never to involve himself with girls again.

> *The fountains mingle with the river*
> *And the rivers with the ocean,*
> *The winds of heaven mix for ever*
> *With a sweet emotion;*
> *Nothing in the world is single;*
> *All things by a law divine*
> *In one spirit meet and mingle.*
> *Why not I with thine?*
>
> *See the mountains kiss high heaven*
> *And the waves clasp one another;*
> *No sister-flower would be forgiven*
> *If it disdained its brother;*
> *And the sunlight clasps the earth*
> *And the moon beams kiss the sea;*
> *What is all this sweet work worth?*
> *If thou kiss not me?*

Love's Philosophy - Percy Bysshe Shelley

The memories welled up in Grant's mind. There was that terrible day when he and Williams had decided to walk across Dartmoor. The mists had come down, and they had become disorientated and lost. Peter had broken a leg when he fell into a pothole.

John Grant made his friend as comfortable as possible, and waited for the mist to lift. He had then carried him two miles, on his back, to the nearest habitation, and eventual hospitalization. Infection had set into the injured leg, and at one time it appeared that Peter might lose it - he still bore the vicious scars to this day. Grant had spent hours by his bedside praying for the miracle that would save the leg.

***

Suddenly Grant was back again to the present, and its reality... Joe had been watching him for the past ten minutes and had begun to worry about his seemingly comatose state. He had just decided to give him a bit of a shake when Grant suddenly came to, shook his head, rubbed his eyes and glanced around him as if just emerging from a deep slumber.

'You look as if you have been away from us for a while,' joked Peter, knowing Grant's little ways.

'I wish it was that easy to escape.'

'It is' answered Grant,

'But I didn't want to risk the mission by making the transition to our real time. Only if it becomes absolutely necessary, but in fairness to you both, I need your agreement on this.' He got it without discussion.

Chapter Seven

Grant has a date with the Devil

'The Devil as a roaring lion, walked about, seeking whom he may devour' Peter Chapter 5 Verse 8

'What do we do now?' questioned Joe, after some time had elapsed; their guards well out of the way. 'The walls and door are solid - the door is barred from outside, and no amount of force from this side will do any good.'

'We must put our thinking cap on, that's what we must do,' answered Grant. 'Let us wait an hour until things have settled down a bit. It is midday now, the officers, and probably Cato and his men will be having a meal shortly; then, with any luck will be sleeping it off. We should have only the ordinary rank and file to deal with. Whilst we are resting perhaps, between us, we can come up with a workable plan to get us out of here; to put a stop to any nasty plans that the "Dark Brotherhood" may have for our future.'

After an hour or so of further investigation and discussion they came up with a plan of sorts.

'Guile rather than brawn I think,' mused Grant. 'First bang on the door and see if we can attract somebody stupid, it's worth a try, if we get lucky and they open the door then bingo, our second phase can go into operation.'

After a minute's shouting and thumping there were voices outside. A gruff voice enquired, between cursing them, and casting doubts on their respective parentage, what the matter was. Their guards had obviously been otherwise engaged, probably gambling, or maybe dozing.

'One of us is dying,' said Grant. 'Your master would not want that.' There was a brief conference, followed by the sound of the external bar being taken off. The door opened to reveal the prisoners, still apparently bound; Joe feigning illness. Four men stood in the doorway, two held nasty looking clubs, and their companions short but powerful bows ready cocked. Grant had not bargained for this, but still decided to go through with his escape plan. Joe moaned with his "stomach pain", rolling around the cell floor - he would have done very well in an acting career. The two Roman soldiers, with clubs, came into the cell, being covered from the doorway. They bent over him, and momentarily shielded him and his companions...

Williams had been waiting for a chance such as this - his heart was thumping, pumping the blood around his large frame, the adrenalin flowing into his system. Like a large cat he sprang into action, shoving the two soldiers inside the cell against their comrades before they could fire their weapons. The four tumbled into a heap and were quickly overcome after a short sharp fight; and before an alarm could be raised.

The Romans were bound and gagged, and would not cause any problems for some time; being locked in their own prison cell. No doubt they would be in a lot of trouble with their officers and Cato at a later time; discipline in the Roman army was very harsh.

The three men waited to see if anyone had heard the commotion. All seemed quiet in the labyrinth under the fortress. They had been put into cells at the lowest level. Grant wondered where the officers and Dark Brotherhood members were, hoping against hope that they didn't turn up.

'Let's get out of here,' said Joe, picking up a club.

Grant led the way, armed with one of the discarded bows. The trio overcame the two occupants of the guard room and was able to pick up their belongings. Later they found the recording devices and camera was missing. They went up many stairs and through filthy passageways and out into the courtyard, without meeting opposition. They were half way across the yard before they were noticed by the guard on the gate.

The wall guard was alerted, and was taking aim with his bow, when Grant took him out with an arrow through the chest. Williams felled the two gate guards with a couple of terrible blows, and out of the fort the three ran. They lost the pursuing group of soldiers easily in the maze of alleyways around the fort. Quickly the men made for the north city gate of Benjamin; before the hunt widened. Grant was thankful for the lack of modern communication facilities in this age.

Nobody attempted to stop them as they ran. The Jews were no different from anyone else in not wanting trouble for themselves; from any quarter. They reached the open countryside, and were making their way to their hideout when they found a group of about twenty Jews barring their way. The group were thieves and cut throats, out for rich pickings from the merchants that used this road. The bandits were armed with staves and knives, and obviously relied upon weight of numbers to make their mark. If a Roman patrol happened along, they would melt into the back ground in seconds.

Their normal plan of attack was to beat their victims to death, then to strip them absolutely clean of everything. Every society had its murderers, its thieves, and parasites; those who lived on the backs of others. This period was no different than any other. The group now facing them had not heard about the meek inheriting the earth, or about brotherly love. Silently the mob surrounded the three; then they closed in staves at the ready to deal out death. Grant ducked under a raised stave and hit the man in the throat with a karate chop; killing him instantly. At the same time Williams seized a man in each arm, and crunched their heads together. Joe, a very mean fighter indeed, killed a fourth with the club he had kept from their fracas at the fort. In no time at all they had cut a swathe five meters in diameter around them. Another attack; this time more intense.

Now Grant and Williams were armed with staves, and silently thanked their lucky stars for all the practice they had put in, Joe weighed in with his trusty club. Six more Jews went down, their heads fractured. Things were really hotting up. The rest fled, they really were not used to this sort of opposition, and they would certainly be very careful who they tried to rob in future.

In the distance the sound of many horses could be heard.

'Quickly, off the road,' ordered Grant. 'The Romans have, I think, got themselves together; and that appears to be the posse.'

Round a bend in the road appeared a company of Romans, on horseback, with Marcus and Cato in the lead. The group stopped at the sight of the bodies of the Jewish thieves in the road.

'The dogs have been here recently,' snarled the tribune to

Cato. Cato looked around; concentrating. Grant, from his concealed position knew what he was trying to do, and desperately attempted to shield his mind from the Dark Brotherhood leaders probing.

'They are very close,' said Cato finally. 'Get your men to search both sides of this road for a stretch.'

Marcus barked out his orders, and then turned to Cato 'I am sorry for the shortcomings of my men, those fools will be sorry, I will have the skin off their backs for this!'

'Don't be too upset,' reassured Cato. 'These men are very clever, and more than a match for your soldiers; as they have already proved. We must hope that they can be found quickly. In any case I do not think that they will interfere with our plans, as they know so little of our intentions here.'

The fugitives had, by this time, split up, agreeing to meet back at their headquarters later on; providing they managed to elude capture. This they did despite a few close calls.

Getting back to the cave they organized themselves, dressed the few minor wounds that they had, and moved into another cave; just in case they received a visit. There were scores of such caves around, and they had taken steps to screen their energy sources, the power packs, from prying energy detectors.

Later they introduced Joe to Scotch whisky - he seemed to like it.

'What religions are there in your world Joe?' asked Grant.

'We worship Mohamad. There are various other minor religions around of course, and in fact they are encouraged in the free world; but over the centuries the Dark Brotherhood has stamped out most of the religious factions on the other continents.'

'You do realize, of course, that we may change the course of history for your world this week, and that you may no longer exist or have ever existed,' said Grant.

'That is a chance I take,' replied Joe. 'You know the alternative for us; my world.'

'I tell you what' interjected Williams, 'I really could murder a good steak with all the trimmings.' So saying he crammed his daily ration of vitamin pills into his mouth and washed them down with some evil looking water, which even the purifiers had failed to put any sparkle into. The other two grinned at each other, any observation completely unnecessary.

'Tomorrow we must look around some more to see if we can track down Jesus and his followers. I want to see some of the miracles at first hand,' said Grant. 'However, we must, of course, be very careful, and keep a look out for the opposition.

'The way things are going that could include the whole population of Judea,' commented Joe, with pique.

Over the last few hours Joe had been very impressed by his two companions; they had after all saved his skin. He warmed to them, and knew that he did not stand alone anymore in this alien land; he had decided that he could and would trust them with his life.

'I say, Peter, is there any more of that rather nice drink?' asked Joe.

'Here you are, son,' exclaimed Williams, passing the bottle over. 'I thought you would have invented some decent booze from where you come from.' 'Naturally we have wine and beer,' answered Joe, 'but nothing as good as this.' He smacked his lips as he drank from the small container - obviously alcohol was allowed in Joe's, alternate, Muslim world.

Williams tipped the last of his Whisky down a cavernous throat, yawned, and said, 'Well lads it's been a pretty heavy day; I really could do with some sleep. Goodnight all.' The others mumbled their goodnights, and soon the cave was silent, punctuated only by the sound of intermittent snoring from Williams.

***

The communicating device by Samus bleeped, he picked it up and spoke softly into it, then turned to his superior.

'Great Leader, my men are just on the point of breaking into the main laboratory, only a matter of seconds now; we can listen if you wish.' Leader waved his hand in assent. Samus switched the device over to the main speaker within the meeting chamber.

Samus brightened considerably; perhaps he might get out of the situation with a whole skin; even now...

***

In the quiet of the cave John Grant was just settling down in his sleeping bag when he started to get some rather curious sensations in head and body, similar to those experienced when the Dark Brotherhood had whisked him away to that insidious game of chess.

(Oh no! Not again! Please dear God, not again!) He thought in anguish.

He was about to voice his condition to Joe and Peter, when he was physically taken, and transported through time by an entity considerably more powerful than he had previously encountered. Mental opposition by Grant was useless; on the other occasions he had at least been able to hinder his eventual abduction.

Grant found himself standing alone in the open air. It was night time, but a full moon with a clear sky illuminated the surrounding terrain, which was vaguely familiar. Yes that was it! The area over which his comrades and himself had been chased by Cato's company just recently. But where on earth was Jerusalem? It should have been just over to his left three or four miles away. Where the city ought to have been was just bare rock.

Looking upward the time traveler scanned the night sky in which thousands of stars were visible, like diamonds set in black velvet. He failed to recognize any of the constellations - the eighty-eight groups of stars in named patterns, some of which had been acknowledged since the time of the ancient Greeks. This led him on to another thought; was he in the past or future - either was possible - but if so it might have meant maybe millions of years either way; because of the absence of Jerusalem and the familiar heavenly configurations. The most important consideration why had he been dragged through time at all?

It was only now that he noticed the extreme cold - well below freezing - although there were no visible signs of sub-zero temperatures such as frost. He shivered and discovered that he was only clad in light underclothes and his body armour, in preparation for sleep in his warm sleeping bag.

Grant suddenly felt a presence. 'Greetings John Grant' said a soft sweet voice. I have been waiting for you.'

Turning slowly, and with some caution, Grant found himself looking at a small figure, completely covered from head to toe in black; a hood covering the face.

'Hello, I find myself at something of a disadvantage,' he stuttered.

The hood was pushed back to reveal a woman's features. She had wild black curly hair, full red lips, lovely smooth pale skin, without a blemish, and coal black eyes. He could only guess at the marvels which were hidden under the black cloth. The woman extended a dainty well-manicured hand, and Grant automatically reciprocated, lightly gripping the exquisite palm.

Too late!!! He realized, with dread, that the hand had six digits. He tried to snatch his hand away, and found that he could not extricate himself. It was like touching a block of super cooled ice, the skin on his fingers was stuck to the tiny palm, which was sucking up his bodily heat at a great rate - his arm started to go numb ; at this rate of heat loss in a few minutes he would be dead. He tried to wrench himself away again, this time with an effort born of fear; like a wild animal whose paw has been caught in a trap. With a blinding awful pain the flesh ripped from his fingers, and he tore free.

The woman's face contorted into a hideous death head, with blood oozing out of the eye sockets. She, or It, advanced upon Grant, who had almost fainted from the pain and had fallen to his knees. He looked up, saw his impending doom, and put up his arms in a pitiful attempt to defend himself, crying out to his maker in his hour of need; as many of us do in times of extreme crisis. The deaths head changed to a man's features, with a full beard and black piercing eyes. The body supporting it, under the robes, increased in size, until the figure towered over the trembling Grant.

'You fool' uttered a booming thundering voice. 'Do you really think that your God will help you now; you have caused my servants great inconvenience. You must die, and be cast into hell for your audacity to the "Prince of Darkness"'

Grant was utterly powerless during this tirade, the man's black eyes hypnotizing him, boring into him like twin lasers, turning his mind to jelly.

'I have brought you here, fifty-million years into your future to destroy your body, and (he added significantly) soul.' The beast, for such it was, stretched out massive hands to cup Grant's head, to tear it from his shoulders, and, to hurl it into oblivion.

Suddenly, Grant was bathed in a warm soft light and he was lifted clear of the groping hands; with the putrid flesh dropping from the bones. His adversary jerked back from the warmth with a bellow of pain and rage, the quarry lost.

Grant spent, it seemed, many hours in his cocoon of healing energy, resting physically and mentally after his ordeal. In fact he was no longer in real time, but in a sort of limbo or hyper-space, a timeless condition outside of real time. Eventually the power, or entity, that had rescued him saw fit to deposit him back to continue his adventures.

***

Grant awoke to find himself in the cave, snugly wrapped in his sleeping bag. He had a blurred feeling that something horrendous had happened to him, but could not be sure. Joe and Peter were still asleep. He looked at his watch - 0245. He had only been asleep for a couple of hours. Ah well!! He thought, better sleep while I can. Without thinking he looked at the fingers of his right hand. He had a suspicion that something was a little different. The tips of his fingers were smooth and pink, as if recently healed from injury, not like the other hand, hardened from rough usage. He just could not pin it down in his own mind

Chapter Eight

Judus

'And forthwith, he (Judas) came to Jesus and said
Hail Master and kissed him'
St. Matthew Chapter 26 Verse 49

For several days the three travelled around, trying to get on the track of the Messiah. They had vacated their cave headquarters permanently, taking with them their entire arsenal of weaponry and their supplies. Their travels took them to many places in and around Jerusalem. It seemed that they always just missed Jesus, although there was always spiritual and physical evidence of his having been there, the bright happy countenances of people that he had spoken to, and those that had been cured of all manner of terrible ailments.

They saw at first hand the magnificent temple just below Antonia, which covered one sixth of the area of the walled city. It was larger than York Minster of Grant's England;

having a facade of gold. Some of the stones measured ten meters in length. Unhappily some thirty-eight years later it was to be completely destroyed, after the Jewish rebellion, by the Romans. What a terrible waste, thought Grant. Man builds and man destroys!

They walked to Bethlehem, the birthplace of Jesus, a few miles south of Jerusalem; just a small insignificant village, with nothing to see of any consequence. Without arousing suspicion Grant carefully questioned some of the community about Christ, gaining more information to add to their already impressive intelligence on this era.

There was no doubt that the Jews were a down trodden race. Evidence of this was everywhere - the way people would not look at you directly when talking to you. Their general physical condition. Only their religion seemed to keep them going. The fanatical belief in a God that would see them through all adversity.

On more than one occasion Joe and Peter commented on how little God had cared for his chosen people. John Grant could give them no valid argument on that. The word was out on the trio, and a large reward had been offered for their capture. They had to slip several Roman patrols during their walkabout. Their cover held up pretty well, and nobody attempted to turn them in for the reward, but Grant suspected that this was in part due to the general hatred felt for the oppressive regime.

They tramped for miles. Although super fit they all found the footwear of the period tough on the feet, and they suffered in their various ways from blisters, but had the benefit of some rather good medication. Williams never seemed to stop complaining and Joe, more than once, threatened him with physical violence if he didn't shut up.

***

Thursday, late afternoon; they went to a secluded garden called Gethsemane. The garden was just below the Mount of Olives, and was full of ancient olive trees; centuries old. There was a large mob with swords and cudgels led by a man in black robes. There was a smaller group close by, whose leader they immediately recognized as Jesus. The man in black went up to him and embraced and kissed him.

'Good Lord,' exclaimed Grant. 'Judas is one of the Dark Brotherhood.' His brain whirled with apprehension and wondered how this fitted in with the scheme of things. The Dark Brotherhood appeared to be helping with the capture and eventual crucifixion of Christ. Whist witnessing the scene before him, his mind tried to assimilate the intelligence it was receiving. He remembered Felix's warnings about meddling with events - he felt powerless - to do nothing spelt disaster, to act could prove equally calamitous.

One of the men with Christ, a big man, by local standards, lunged with a sword at the man next to Judas, cutting off his ear. Grant was close enough to see everything. Jesus picked up the severed ear and placed it back into position. It was as if nothing had happened; as if the sword had never been used, as if the blood had never poured from the wound. It was ... a miracle! There were no spacemen around with healing machines; no trickery, Grant would have staked his life on that. The scene was to live with him for the rest of his life. If any proof of Christ's power was necessary this was it.

Jesus was quickly hustled away; to his trial. The big man, Peter, went away to his own personal humiliation. Judas was shouting and gesticulating. It was obvious that he wanted Jesus murdered there and then, another twist to the plot, yet another surprise; but the servants of the Chief Sanhedrin priests, who had been sent with Judas, had their orders; to bring Jesus to them and ultimately to be handed over to the Romans.. The alien black Dark Brotherhood's first plan had gone badly wrong. Grant wondered why that member of the black order now went away and hanged himself. It might have been due to the failure of the plan, or the New Testament may have been incorrect in this case - he would never know.

Joe, Williams and Grant started to walk away when a voice called to them from a clump of trees. A small man waved to them from his cover. 'Be very careful,' warned Grant; but it was too obvious to be a trap. They sauntered over, keeping a wary eye open. They found the man waiting for them; he was of the Imperial Army, in full uniform, and of some rank.

'I am Gaius Marius, a Centurion in the Roman army. I serve under Marcus Gracchus, tribune of the First Cohort. I am a Christian; following the man called Jesus. He cured me of flesh rot (probably gangrene) from a sword wound in the arm. The arm would have been lost but for him - or maybe I would have died from the surgery. The Dark Brotherhood is out to kill Jesus. Marcus Gracchus is completely in their power. They have given him much gold to do their bidding.' Without pausing for breath the man went on quickly, as if he didn't have much time.

'Tomorrow morning, early, I am to take some picked men to a narrow section of the road which leads from Antonia to the crucifixion site at Golgotha. Apparently Jesus is to be on this road at that time, under armed escort. Some of the men amongst the guards have also been bribed to make abduction simpler; we are to take Jesus away and kill him quietly. Every man on this special, private, detail is to receive one thousand denari, which is over four years pay for an ordinary soldier. I am to get three thousand denari for my part in it'

Gaius went on with further details of the plot. It transpired that rather than conspire to kill Jesus; he had decided to try and rescue him with the help of the time travelers whom he had recognized from their imprisonment at the fort and new how important they were to the "Dark Brotherhood".

The Roman suddenly stopped in mid-sentence, with a gurgle, as a spear struck him in the back. He had been followed. Williams ran to the deep shadows from where the missile had come. Too late! The assassin had vanished to report the success of his mission; another centurion would lead Gaius' group tomorrow. Gaius was very dead, the three were horrified, but had to make the best of it. 'Let's find somewhere to hole up until tomorrow,' suggested Grant.

They found some old ruined stables close by, and settled down to discuss what had happened, to consider the latest information, and what they were going to do about it.

Joe was all for the three of them going to Antonia, with grenades and other weaponry of an equally destructive nature, to take the Governor hostage, and to free Jesus. He argued that surely such drastic action must change the course of history, and create a more suitable climate for his world - hopefully one without the Dark Brotherhood. Grant listened carefully, and could see that Joe was desperate for positive action. He was allowing his heart to rule his head, in an attempt to expedite matters. Grant knew that the Situation was very delicate and going into it like the proverbial "bull in a china shop" would not help matters.

'Any attempt to free Jesus must be prevented at all costs,' said Grant in a tone that he prayed sounded conciliatory. The next few minutes could prove difficult; if he couldn't make the two of them see sense...

'But why for heaven's sake!' Exclaimed an agitated Williams. 'If Christ lives longer, think how much more good he can do.'

'I agree,' chimed in Joe.

'I believe you miss the whole point,' answered Grant. 'Christ must suffer on the cross for mankind's sake, and he must be seen to suffer, and to die; indeed he must also rise again. If this does not happen he will only be known as a small time magician, whose memory will die in a few short years. Don't you see that the crucifixion is the culmination of Planning at a much higher level than mere man? The reason why Joe's world, the alternative world to ours, Peter, is in the grip of evil is that Christianity never took off.'

'There is evil rife on this planet, today, that will do anything to see that the crucifixion doesn't take place - to see that man's oppression continues for ever, to see that man has no hope for the rest of eternity. Whoever, whatever has set this whole thing up knows that an equivalent sociological period may not occur again for a very long time? We are, gentlemen, mankind's only hope for the foreseeable future, we must ensure the crucifixion takes place so that all the rest may happen, including the salvation of Joe's world.'

Neither Joe, nor Williams, could immediately think of anything to say after Grant's little speech...

'Can't you see the sense of it,' cajoled Grant, desperate for some sort of agreement. Looking first at Joe then at Peter. He wanted to shake both of them for being so slow in seeing what he could now see with crystal clarity. Peter nodded slowly, 'Yes, on reflection I think that you are probably correct John. There is really only one explanation for what has taken place. We are certainly going to be involved in events over the next few hours, but can we predict what is to take place, so that we may take appropriate action?'

'We have the information given to us by Gaius, as well as this' - Grant tapped a copy of the "New Testament" 'We must trust to luck, and the Almighty, to see us through to the finish.'

'That's all very well,' argued Joe 'but that is taking a chance, considering the stakes we are playing for. I am still not completely sure of your theories.'

'The Gospels have been pretty accurate so far,' commented Williams. 'I go along with you John.'

'Seems I am outvoted two to one,' growled Joe. 'So be it! We must trust to your testament of events - but I can't say that I like it much.'

Grant silently gave thanks, a crisis had been averted. There had been, for a time, a real danger of Joe acting on his own initiative; going berserk with modern weapons in this age would not have been a good idea. John Grant could see that to maintain the status quo for this world, would probably give the necessary change that Joe was seeking. This required some very subtle tinkering with events that were now unfolding...

***

A few miles away another conversation was taking place in the living quarters of the colonel of the First Cohort.

'Have your men still not managed to arrest our enemies?' asked Cato impatiently.

'I am afraid not,' answered Marcus Gracchus. 'But at least Marius, my Centurion has been silenced. This Jesus seems to have a curious ability to sway people to do his bidding. Even members of the Imperial Roman Army are not immune. The sooner the upstart is killed, the better. I still do not know why you want him assassinated privately. I assume you know your business - you are paying me enough, anyway - but remember the price for failure is high. It could mean my life and disgrace for my family.'

'The price for failure is very much higher than you think, my friend,' commented Cato, stroking his long chin reflectively.

'Yes, there is much that you have not told me' complained Gracchus.

'The less you know the better. Just remember tomorrow you will be a rich man. You will be able to resign your commission and return to Rome, where you can bid for a place in the Senate. Your wealth will be such that none will oppose you. But to get back to our problem, please redouble your efforts to capture Grant and his men. I will feel a lot happier if they are under lock and key by tomorrow. If needs be we must bring some of your fellow officers into our confidence.

'That would not be a good idea, my fellow Tribunes are already suspicious, and would report me to the governor if even a hint of our arrangement became known. They have been plotting my downfall for some time now, and would be only too pleased of the chance of something specific against me. All of them are very rich, with powerful friends in Rome so couldn't be bribed in any case.'

'I see! It seems as if I picked the right man for the job. Refusal of course, would have meant death, Gracchus went white as he looked into Cato's face, and knew that he meant every word. At that moment he wished that he had never met the tall man in black, but his personal ambition had outweighed any conscience he may have had at the start of their relationship.

'Pour me some more wine and then, please, leave me,' ordered Cato. Gracchus obliged with some haste, eager to leave the presence of his paymaster. He considered eavesdropping on Cato - he had often heard him talking to himself - but decided against it.

He cheered up, somewhat, when he remembered the treasure he was to receive tomorrow. He strode off in the direction of the interrogation room. A young Jewess had been brought in for questioning an hour ago, and he felt like conducting the session personally and without help...

***

There were many observers of the solar system that night, and the following day. A fantastic florescence emanated from this "backwater" of the Galaxy, this light permeated hyper-space, reaching the watchers instantaneously.

Some astronomers in the galaxy thought that it was merely a super-nova - a star bursting forth before it died.

The center of this amazing spectacle was earth, upon which an event was occurring unequalled in the history of that planet. Scientists witnessed the happening as millions of instruments recorded the phenomena, and the disturbance created a ripple through space which lasted just one earth day; the day of the crucifixion.

Scientists argued for years afterwards as to the phenomena's origin, and principle.

The majority of earth's people were blissfully unaware of the "happening" Only a handful even had an inkling of it, and its subsequent importance.

Chapter Nine

The Crucifixion

'This is the king of the Jews' St. Luke Chapter 23 verse 38

Friday, April 3rd 33 AD dawned - the most important day in the calendar of Christianity, and probably the whole world. Grant and Williams, with Joe, checked their weapons and other equipment, and then moved out into the dawn. It was 0600 hours; and very cold. At 1500 hours a man was due to die; to expunge the sins of the world, and to give man hope for the future.

The three of them had to make certain that it actually took place. Climbing tackle had been included in their original equipment list and would prove very useful on this particular sortie, as the city gates were closed during the small hours, and it would be necessary to scale the walls. The information they had received from Gaius, before he was killed, made them backtrack to Antonia, which also housed the Governor's residence, where Pontius Pilate was now holding his court; soon to wash his hands in symbolic rejection of his own guilt in the matter of Jesus.

The rescue and eventual assassination of Christ was to be attempted by picked men from Marcus' cohort; without help from the Dark Brotherhood - they thought that any assistance from them could well affect the situation adversely for their future.

The plan was to dress the men in Jewish garb, to overcome the official Roman guards at a convenient point along the road, to take Jesus away and kill him out of sight of his followers, and dispose of the body. In this way he would never become a focal point for the masses; and Christianity would soon die.

Despite the cold Grant felt the sweat dripping down his face and off the end of his nose and chin. This was due to some extent to the hard pace that they set themselves, but also his own forebodings. He glanced at his companions; nobody had spoken a word since leaving the stables. Even the normally exuberant Williams was silent. Joe was ashen - even showing through his tan.

Well, thought Grant "A man's got to do what a man's got to do." Even this rather humorous quote, taken from hundreds of Westerns; seen in his childhood, failed to bring him any joy. The awful thing was that they didn't really know what they had to do. It was just one big gamble, with humanity as the prize.

The trio was armed with modern weapons, which they sincerely hoped they wouldn't have to use - but if needs must! They also carried swords, staves, and knives. They hoped that with their considerable physical skills, that the latter would be sufficient. God willing they might still be victorious in their holy crusade. In their wildest dreams they had never thought that they would be involved in this most important of events.

Having scaled the city wall they reached the Governor's residence, where they had so recently been imprisoned and then proceeded to trace the road from the fort to Golgotha - the place of the skull - where Jesus was to be crucified. Up ahead was a narrow section in the road. 'That's the place' said Williams. 'Let's circle around this block of dwellings and take a look at the opposition. We may be able to climb on to those flat roofs, and get a good view from there.' In fact they did manage to clamber onto the roofs and look down. On either side of the road, were hidden eight disguised Roman soldiers, relaxing before the intended abduction.

'What's the game plan?' whispered Joe. 'We have an hour or so before the pre-crucifixion procession' responded Grant. 'It is quiet now, and I have a feeling that this may be as good a time as any to strike, everyone is asleep, and if we are quick and quiet nobody will be any the wiser.' He then made a decision that he hoped he would not live to regret.

'Yes' continued Grant, in a low voice, 'Let us wipe them out now; with our laser weapons. We must be sure of killing them all; I definitely feel this may be our best bet. Any other way may result in the premature murder of Jesus; and injury or worse to us. Besides we do not want to cause too much commotion with hand to hand fighting, otherwise we may attract some patrols.'

Joe and Williams accepted Grant's decision without question. They adjusted their weapons to wide angle kill. They knew that the risks of using modern weapons were great, but the thought of failure in this enterprise was too horrible to contemplate.

At a pre-arranged signal the three men sprayed the area where the Romans crouched. The whole group was wiped out in seconds, without really knowing what hit them. 'May God forgive us' agonized Grant, 'I felt that... this slaughter was the only way.' The decision to mete out death in this manner had really upset him.

On the other hand luck had been with them and nobody seemed to have heard the terrible carnage as the lasers dealt out silent death. The men dragged the bodies away from the main road, hiding them down a blind alley. Those finding them later would wonder at the terrible burns on the bodies, but such wonderment would soon be superseded by the events to come this day.

By the time the procession passed by it was as if the proposed ambush had never existed. Grant and his two comrades mingled with the crowd, the scriptures were surprisingly precise in what followed: the man called Simon carried Christ's cross, a crown of thorns had been placed on Christ's head, and removed prior to the procession, blood oozing from the wounds and running down his face. The procession included the two thieves, who were to be crucified with Christ; staggering under the weight of their posts, groaning and blaspheming.

Just then Joe shook Grant's arm with some urgency 'Look over there John, three of the Dark Brotherhood.' Luckily they hadn't been spotted by the members of the black order, and ducked down behind the large crowd, which was forming in the wake of the procession, pulling Williams with them.

'The whole situation is very delicately balanced,' observed Grant. 'Let's keep out of sight of them, and see what happens. They may decide to interfere somehow; their other plans have failed. They cannot afford to do anything stupid, on the other hand...'

He left the sentence unfinished, raising his hands in despair as it all seemed suddenly to be beyond his control.

The three members of the Dark Brotherhood appeared to be arguing amongst themselves. More than once the smallest of them made as if to draw a weapon from beneath his robe, and was restrained by Cato. The leader wanted to play it cool, which suited Grant just fine.

Grant had wondered if the Dark Brotherhood's representatives might try to persuade Marcus to order Christ's execution cancelled. The problem was that the Governor had already signed the order, and any action of this kind would have been taken as treason against Rome and the Emperor Tiberius. Even the tribune's position would not have saved him from death.

None of the three had been able to watch as the nails were driven home into hands and feet - the method of execution was undoubtedly barbaric; but as far as the Romans were concerned it helped to keep their provinces in order.

The crosses, with the men nailed on them, were raised into the vertical position, the thieves screaming with the pain. Roman guards laughed and joked amongst themselves as the sign indicating Christ's status as "King of the Jews" was placed above his head. Then the final humiliation; they gambled for his clothes in a small dip behind the execution site.

There were many followers of Christ there that day, watching; many openly weeping. Aged men and women with wrinkled skin like old parchment; young people, who as yet were unmarked by the ravages of life in this cruel pitiless period of history. Others in the crowd were simply there for the entertainment, their mouths open, and the saliva running down their chins; enjoying the spectacle. Grant had seen such people at the scene of major accidents and disasters, they would have been present at public hangings and floggings during the dark ages, and would have witnessed the massive executions after the French Revolution, using Madame Guillotine. Some people didn't change no matter what the period was, ancient or modern, thought Grant.

The air was heavy and oppressive; It began to get dark, the eclipse of the sun was actually happening. Grant remembered the controversy over this particular point. The generally accepted view was that the darkness was due to a dust laden sirocco wind, strong enough to split the curtain of the Temple.

In 1984 a Dr. Waddington and Dr. Humphreys of Oxford University stated, from their private research, that an eclipse had created the darkness for three hours. The amateur researchers had been proven correct, thought Grant with a wry smile; despite the fact that such an eclipse was physically impossible at this time. Miracles were a reality where the "Son of God" was concerned. There were certainly awesome powers present to apparently create such movement of the heavenly bodies, producing the eclipse.

At the back of his mind Grant wondered whether they were all being affected by hypnotic suggestion on a grand scale. Grant bitterly regretted the loss of all their recording equipment. But then he thought he still had the best recording system ever made; the human brain!

All eyes were on the crosses; at three o'clock in the afternoon the eclipse ended, and Christ was dead.

At Precisely that time the three black robed members of the "Brotherhood" winked out of existence. Grant just caught the phenomenon.

'Did you see that?' He whispered to the other two. Williams had been looking hypnotically at the crosses, and hadn't. 'Yes, I did' said Joe breathlessly. They had to explain it to a bewildered Williams.

Joe touched Grant on the shoulder. 'I have to go now; there is something that I must do.' Without another word, he left. It was Williams who caught on first.

'My God, I remember now, Joseph of Arimathea he exclaimed! He was the guy who asked to bury the body of Jesus, wasn't he?'

'I believe that you are absolutely right' confirmed his friend. Later on, when it was all over with, in a light hearted moment, Grant kidded Peter that his days at Sunday school hadn't all been wasted. The clue had been when Joe had mentioned earlier that he had actually materialized in Arimathae, a small village about 20 miles north-west of Jerusalem.

They were to meet Joe again, but not for some considerable time. 'I wonder if he will get back alright?' asked Williams.

'That, Peter, we shall never know. What we do know is that the elimination of our black friends must have meant that they and the Dark Brotherhood will not exist either now or in the future, ours or Joe's. The paradox is that we know they have existed.' 'Joe must be OK and have a future. The elimination of the Dark Brotherhood's men didn't seem to affect him at all,' answered Williams.

Grant was thoughtful. 'Our worlds were divided at this point in history; in one the crucifixion took place with all the attendant publicity, in the other something happened to Jesus before the crucifixion. We have prevented that. I am just wondering what effect that would have on Joe's world; surely the whole population would not be eliminated like the Dark Brotherhood. There must be factors here completely beyond our understanding. Joe is living proof that, in all probability the alternate world does still exist. Ah! Well! Perhaps we shall get to the bottom of it someday' he concluded.

'I think, Peter, it's about time we thought of going home.'

The two friends turned and departed from the scene. They did not look back. They could have stayed and seen the ending; or was it the beginning? The Resurrection and the Ascension. There was no need. Peter and John knew, in their hearts, that it was all true, the whole damn lot!

Grant and Williams picked their way through the crowd, some kneeling and praying, others lying prostrate upon the ground, the eclipse were lifting; the sun came out. After the terrible events of the day, the two men's spirits lifted, everything was going to be airtight; two worlds had been saved, theirs and Joe's. Best of all they were going home.

***

In another time, and another place:

'Great Leader what is happening to you?' Samus looked across, firstly at the figure at the head of the huge oak table, then at the other members of the council. He could see through them; they were like ghosts. The sounds of battle started to splutter and then die from the speakers. Leader's mouth was working vigorously, but no sound came from the thin bloodless lips. A rushing sound impinged on Samus' ears - it was the air which his body displaced, but was now filling the space which used to be him. - He screamed without making any noise at all...

***

'Some fool is manipulating time' exclaimed Volta, a 'Watcher" of the planet Overon in the Orion Nebula.

'Patience my young friend,' said the "Chief Scientist" of that planet.

'As soon as reports came in, that area was monitored, via hyperspace tube. We have pin-pointed the disturbance. It appears that it emanates from a level four solar system, and specifically a grade five planet called earth. There is also another phenomena occurring which we are at present analyzing.' The grey bearded scientist paused for breath before going on.

'Immediately we pin-pointed the planet I sanctioned "Special Investigator" Vins departure to that area. He has just got back, and will report to the "High Assembly" in fifteen time periods.

'But surely we must act against that system,' argued Volta. 'Time manipulation from a backward planet such as this could cause problems for all of us. Major time periods ago the "Assembly" ruled that time travel was only allowed under the strictest control, and then only if sanctioned by ninety percent of the Assembly. You know the problems inherent in the manipulation of time,' finished Volta.

'Calm down my son,' said the older man. 'You really must control yourself.'

'No' exclaimed the younger man 'The distortion created by time excursion; due to the vast quantities of energy required; which affects the universal entropy balance, is the problem, as you, Sir, well know. The practice of time travel has been outlawed by us excepting under very exceptional and controlled circumstances.'

'All true commented his mentor' kindly. 'Come, let us attend the meeting, and hear the report first hand.'

Assembly Chief Cron nodded to Vins to begin. Jon Vins was a little nervous, he had never addressed the full assembly before, but he was an articulate man, and soon got into his stride. He quickly completed the preliminaries, telling them how he had landed on earth, and monitored the events leading up to Grant's movement through time, and what had happened subsequently.

'Opinion, please, Vins,' asked Cron.

'It is obvious that they have no idea of the danger. But this is not the only reason I am recommending you take no action against them.' answered Vins.

'Yes!' exclaimed Deputy Kes.

'Grant and his friend have saved their own world, and its alternative, from a terrible disaster; this is why I strongly urge a more gentle approach.'

There was a long and acrimonious discussion, during which both the young Watcher and Chief Scientist were called to give testimony. One of the major points made was that other powers were at work; the curious luminous effect through hyper-space was, as yet, unexplained. Many of the assembly expressed fears of what might happen if an intervention was made. Perhaps this unknown element might unleash tremendous forces against them. But to their credit they also took into account Vins recommendations.

And so it went on, like politicians are wont to do. Eventually a vote was taken and the decision to take no action was almost unanimous.

***

Grant concentrated deeply, just as he had done six short days ago. He and Williams sat, on a hillside, taking a last look at the city, their belonging around them. Again the two men experienced blankness as Grant activated the nano-circuitry lodged in his brain.

Grant came to and looked around, he didn't believe what he saw, he momentarily panicked...

Chapter Ten

Joe's Story

'And after this Joseph of Arimathaea, being a disciple of Jesus, but secretly for fear of the Jews, besought Pilate that he might take away the body of Jesus: and Pilate gave him leave. He came, therefore, and took the body of Jesus'
Saint John Chapter 20 Verse 38

Evening had come, and Joe found himself at the Governor's residence. He asked to see Pilate. As if pre-arranged the big man was escorted into a large richly furnished room. Joe was greeted by an aide who took him aside.
'What is your business?'
'I wish to see the Lord Pilate on an urgent matter.'
'He is busy.' Pointing to two men at the end of the room in deep conversation.
'But I must see him now.' Loudly!

One of the men turned at the sudden raising of Joe's voice.
'Bring that man to me.'

Joe strode over. He recognized the other man as the centurion, in charge of the crucifixion - making his report to Pilate.

Pilate was of medium build, totally bald with a tired, worn, lived-in face, which showed the stresses imposed on him during his tour of duty in Judea. It was his eyes which showed the full cost of his service to Rome. They were cheerless, sad eyes. Here indeed, was the man who had passed the sentence on the "Son of God".

'Please wait whilst I finish with the centurion.'

Joe waited patiently whilst the report was made.

'Is the man called Jesus dead?' asked Pilate.

'Yes Sir, I ordered one of my men to thrust a spear into his side, towards the end, just to make sure. There was absolutely no sign of life when we took him down. I don't think that we will be bothered with him or his followers again. Nothing like a good crucifixion to serve as an example eh?'

'Thank you centurion. What of the other reports which have been coming in: the temple's curtains have been torn - probably some vandals stirring up trouble, Romans disguised as Jews, found mutilated - this may mean reprisals against whoever is responsible. Kindly set up an enquiry into each event.'

'Yes Sir, I will organize it immediately. I really do not know what to make of it at all. Perhaps Jesus really is the son of God.' The soldier laughed nervously. Pilate did not share his attempt at a joke, and turned to Joe.

'You wish to speak with me?'

'Yes Sir, Lord Pilate, I have been asked to obtain the body of Jesus, for proper burial, if that is alright with the authorities' pleaded Joe. 'Of course, we do not want to appear ungracious. Centurion please see to this man's request.'

Joe was given the body, and with the help of several of the disciples wrapped it up in clean linen clothe, with various spices to preserve it. Then they carried it out of the city to a new cave, recently hewn out of the rocks. They gently deposited it near the back of the sepulcher. The entrance was then sealed with a great stone. It took all of Joe's considerable strength, with the help of two others, to finally ease it into place. The body would now be safe from wild animals.

Joe said his farewells, and started on his journey to Arimathaea, from where he would depart to his own future - unlike Williams and Grant his system necessitated him finding the exact spot on which he had arrived, in order to facilitate a successful return. He was nearly at his jump off point when he finally came out of his dreamlike trance. Shaking his head, to try and clear his befuddled brain, he mentally backtracked over the time when he had left Grant and Williams.

'I didn't even say goodbye,' he moaned out loud to himself. Somehow Joe had been subjected to mild hypnosis, and in this state certain suggestions had been imprinted on his brain cells. This had led him to carry out the various tasks, as described in the scriptures.

'Oh! Well, I had better get on with getting back home, I suppose.' Joe went through the ritual, using a small hand held device, which did the same job as the one surgically locked into Grant's brain. The device was activated, and the rocky ragged landscape gave way to nothingness...

***

Joe found himself in the takeoff laboratory, spinning vigorously in the time chamber. It quickly came to rest; he unstrapped himself, clicked open the door, and stepped out into the large airy room. Joe examined his surroundings. Were they exactly the same as when he had left? He had had a nasty thought that perhaps he would have no home to go back to, but here he was, apparently safe and sound. He ambled towards the far corner of the area, where the small control/ viewing room was. There was something odd about the lab, but what was it? Ah, yes! That was it; the decor was a pastel blue instead of green. Now, how could that be? He knew of no plan to re-decorate the facility.

Approaching the observation windows of the control room he spotted four figures inside. They were talking to one another excitedly. Joe was looking forward to seeing the four men: Ted Palmer the Project Director, Isaac Stern the Chief Engineer, John Fenner Chief Scientist and Dick Harper the Medical Advisor. He had come to know them well during the months of preparation for his trip.

The door of the viewing room slid open, and he was greeted by a very puzzled looking Palmer. Was Joe going color blind? When last he had seen the Professor he was surely wearing a red bow tie, now it was blue - perhaps he had changed. Another thing, Ted was wearing glasses. As far as Joe knew the man had 20/20 vision - perhaps they were safety glasses. Palmer peered ahead, scrutinizing Joe.

'Is that you Joe? Where the devil is your special environmental gear? What the hell is going on?' The other three emerged and Joe noticed subtle differences from when he had last seen them. Dick Harper asked, 'Are you Okay Joe? This trip seems to have altered you somewhat. I had better give you a complete check over before we go any further with this'.

Joe and Fenner's objections were waved aside. Harper had complete jurisdiction as far as medical matters were concerned. Joe was quickly escorted away to Harper's surgery. His clothes were whipped away as soon as he had stripped, for analysis he guessed. Joe decided to go along with it all, he knew, eventually, that he would get the answers to his questions; he would just have to wait.

He was made to shower, and to excrete, the water and the results of his efforts being spirited away for, he assumed, more scientific studies. His checkup was very thorough, including both physical and mental tests. Harper was an extremely competent man.

'Well,' said Harper, 'You seem to have suffered no ill effects from wherever you have been, other than a slight touch of malnutrition. I suggest you go and have a good meal, I will put in my report to Palmer, who will then, presumably, convene the debrief.

'Thanks Doc, see you later.' After eating he went off to try and have a word with the security monitor, Major Roberts, he wanted to get in touch with Ann as soon as possible, to let her know that everything was alright.

He walked into the monitor's office, and found a full Colonel behind the desk - a Colonel Franklin - to whom Joe took an instant dislike. Franklin seemed to know Joe very well. His request to ring Ann was turned down flat.

'Sorry Vincent, but that is not possible until after the debrief, I didn't even know that you were married.' Joe frowned, things did not feel right. He asked after Major Roberts, and was greeted with a blank stare from Franklin. Joe walked to his quarters in something of a terrible daze. It was to get worse; his room and belongings were, to all intents and purposes, the same as when he had left, but there were some slight differences. The most outstanding variation was the photo of a lovely young girl signed "To Joe from Julie with all my love"

This replaced the family portrait of Ann and the children. Was somebody having a joke? Surely nobody would dare. Joe was well known for his quick temper, and he did not suffer fools gladly. A polite knock on the door. 'Yes, come in'

A corporal entered, 'Beg your pardon Sir, but you are required in number one room immediately. I was told to tell you that it was urgent. Thanks Corporal, be there right away, by the way you haven't been messing around in my room have you?'

'No Sir, it has been locked up whilst you have been away.'

When Joe got to the debrief he found a lot of people waiting, far more than usual for this sort of thing. He was able to identify Palmer, Franklin, Stern, Fenner and Harper; there was also the departmental psychologist - Joe felt a little uneasy at his inclusion; a brigadier with an aide; and a couple of others that Joe could not place. Palmer started the proceedings.

'We would like to make this meeting as informal as possible. Please sit down Joe whilst you give your report. Although Doctor Harper has given you a medical okay, it appears that you are suffering from fatigue and mental strain. Please let me know if, during this hearing, you feel unable to carry on at any stage, and we will adjourn until you are up to it.'

'Thanks Professor, I think that I should be able to see it through.' (Providing I don't get a lot of damn fool questions, Joe thought darkly).

'Before we begin I would very much like to ask a question.' (Might as well get it over with, thought Joe).

'Fire away.'

'What has happened with regard to the Dark Brotherhood, and their ultimate weapon, since I have been away?'

The ensuing silence could have been cut with a knife. Joe seemed to have captured everyone's attention, especially the brigadier and his aide, who prior to Joe's question seemed to be having their own private meeting. Suddenly everyone seemed to be talking at once, and Joe noticed that the psychologist, on Palmer's right hand, was whispering excitedly into the chairman's ear.

'Jesus Christ, Colonel,' Joe noticed the sudden formality in Palmer's tone, what sort of a question is that? We send you off on a routine experimental mission, and you come back in different attire asking moronic questions.'

'He was acting very strangely as soon as he got back,' interjected Franklin. 'I can only suggest that we adjourn this debriefing and isolate him in order to psychoanalyze him. There is of course another explanation, our Russian comrades may well have got to Vincent in some way.

Joe looked around the group, hoping that he was just having a bad nightmare from which he would soon awake. Then he realized that Palmer had begun his tirade with a rather peculiar expletive "Jesus Christ". It appeared as if his excursion back to Judea, and the subsequent events, had altered the history for his world. When was somebody going to realize that there was a lot more to this than a psychotic colonel?

'Gentlemen, gentlemen, perhaps I might be allowed to put forward a rational explanation, which does not involve the imagined sabotage of our project.' Thank God, thought Joe, for somebody with sweet reason.' It was Fenner, the Chief Scientist, who had spoken and, at least for the time being, held the floor.

'This is obviously a marginally different Joe from the one who left us. In our various computer simulations and scenarios of the McDonald space and time effect, it was postulated that we could get some curious results, involving parallel worlds and the like. I will not bore you with the details, but this debrief will be a waste of time until Joe has been thoroughly interrogated, using drug induced hypnosis. We may then establish just what has happened.'

'What sort of scientific mumbo-jumbo is this,' exploded the brigadier. 'What we have is a security breach, plain and simple. Colonel Vincent, if it is he, has been bought by the enemy to sabotage this project. He must be put under arrest immediately.'

Joe did not like this unfortunate turn of events. The brigadier was an arsehole, just like Franklin. The problem was that they were arseholes with rank.

'If I could elucidate. There is a perfectly good explanation for all this.' Joe said with all the conviction he could muster. 'Please extend me the courtesy of listening to what I have to say, you may then verify what I have said under hypnosis, as Doctor Fenner has suggested.'

'Good idea,' said Stern, 'I move that we hear Joe out, and then validate what he has to say. Afterwards we can then take whatever action is necessary. I have to say that, as a humble engineer, I am looking forward to his report.' Joe was glad that there was general approval for his suggestion - the military delegation being the exception.

***

Hours later, the interrogation over, Joe's amazing story was validated, using irrefutable scientific evidence. Later Fenner took him aside for a chat. Joe again requested that he phone Ann and his family, just to tell them he was alright.

Fenner took him by the shoulders, and looked at him directly. 'Unfortunately, Joe, the Ann that you knew does not exist, at least not in this world. Your three children are not here either.' Joe visibly slumped. He had been half expecting something of the sort from Franklin's comments to his original request. Was this to be his reward for having helped save a world; the taking away of his loved ones. Tears of self-pity ran down his cheeks. Joe was not, normally, an emotional man but he just could not help himself. Fenner comforted him as best he could. 'Joe, we still want some more information from you, and need you for at least another week. After that why don't you take some leave, and relax a bit.'

***

Ten days later Joe took a train to the city of York in Yorkshire - even place names had changed. He had been pestered continually by phone by a girl claiming to be his fiancé - the girl in the photograph by his bed. He did not have the heart to see her. Joe had sought out Fenner, and asked him what he should do. He had suggested that he would call the girl and explain that Joe was incapacitated for a time and would contact her as soon as possible. This would give Joe time to get himself together. Fenner knew the pilgrimage that Joe would have to take for the sake of his reason; the visit to Yorkshire for news of his beloved Ann.

The scientist was certain that there was little probability of Joe's family existing, but did not try and dissuade him - he had to get it out of his system somehow.

Joe, in military uniform, walked down the pretty lane to his house. From a distance it appeared exactly the same - it seemed so long ago now. He half expected to see the children playing on the well-kept lawn. He went up to the door with the roses around it. Yes there were mild differences but nothing really outstanding. He knocked. Joe's heart was pounding with anticipation. The door opened. There was Ann, unchanged it seemed. Joe longed to take her in his arms, but something stopped him. It was the way she looked at him. 'Yes, what may I do for you?' 'Don't you know me?' he blurted out. 'Where are the kids?' Ann looked at him as if he was mad, and backed away trying to close the door on him.

'Please listen to me Ann, 'he implored. 'We have so much to talk about.' He knew he was clutching at straws. 'If you don't go away, I will call the police. Joe decided to try another tack, somehow he had to try and explain to this Ann; the predicament he found himself in.

He had, after all, always been able to talk her round after disagreements in the past.

In a pleading tone. 'Please listen to me, I promise I will not harm you, I have somebody who will vouch for me, here is his number.' Joe produced a card with Fenner's number on it.

'I will stop here outside whilst you check. It is a Ministry of Defense number.' Perhaps that fact would carry weight with her. Joe felt in his pocket, 'If it is any help here is my I.D.'

Minutes later Ann appeared again. She smiled at him, and his heart leapt. This was his Ann, with the nice dimpled smile and the flashing eyes.

'Please come in Colonel Vincent. Mr. Fenner has assured me that I have nothing to fear from you, and asked me to listen to you very carefully.' Joe went into the house; the lack of change was remarkable. He sat down; Ann made tea with scones and strawberry jam, just how he used to like it. 'Well Colonel would you like to begin?' 'Please call me Joe.'

'Very well Joe, would you like to tell me all about it?' Joe stumbled through the whole story, including his relationship with Ann, and their family. She was silent throughout the revelation. It transpired that Ann was unmarried and had recently buried both parents, whom she had looked after for the last five years. She more than half believed Joe's story, maybe it was his charm and good looks, perhaps she wanted to believe him. She had had little love in her life. Her parents, particularly towards the end, had been very difficult. When Joe asked her out for dinner she readily accepted.

One month later they were married. In six years they had three children Delia, Ali and Adam. Each child was the splitting image of those on the tatty photograph that Joe had kept with him throughout the whole of his exploits...

Chapter Eleven

Future

'Heaven from all creatures hides the book of fate'
Alexander Pope

Williams was not with him that was the plain simple fact that kept hammering into his brain as he lay on the ground. Grant pinched himself, very hard, to ensure that he was not dreaming; he wasn't. What was real was the long rapier like sword that was being held at his throat.

'Well! Well! What have we here said the swordsman to a companion. He did not seem at all concerned that Grant had suddenly appeared from empty space. The two were hairless, and initially Grant could not tell their gender, eventually he settled for male. They were dressed in a seamless red plastic material; very loose fitting. Both appeared to be normal Homo-sapiens. The second man drew a handgun. 'We had better take him back with us, I have never seen anything like him, although there have been stories of others appearing from nowhere before.'

'Yes, Commander Cord will certainly want to see him; he will know what to do.' Then as an afterthought 'Doesn't he look peculiar, and phew... he smells a bit.' Both men spoke in a lilting English tongue. Grant tried to identify the sound. Yes, that was it! An Irish accent.

They were referring to Grant's hair, and very scruffy appearance. Under normal circumstance he would have taken great exception to these comments, even to the extent of some physical violence. Grant stood up - he had no choice. He was led away to a small transporter and bundled into the back, being handcuffed to a ring in the floor. The vehicle hovered six inches above the ground. At first Grant thought that it rested upon a cushion of air but noticed that no dust was disturbed by jets of air. Then he realized that it must be an anti-gravity device; indicating a very advanced civilization. The propulsion, however, appeared to be based on a conventional reaction principle, and speeds of well over a hundred miles per hour were reached. Altogether a very smooth ride!

During the trip Grant had time to view his surroundings. The landscape was typical of American prairie; perhaps it was. They were, presumably, on the planet earth, but in what year, wondered Grant. There were no clues to be seen, the prairie stretching away in all directions as far as the eye could see. He decided not to ask any questions just yet. That would come when he met the "Commander".

The sun was high in the sky and it must have been around noon. The sky was blue and cloudless. It was very hot, and despite the air conditioning in the transporter Grant was starting to itch. He hadn't bathed in some time, and he knew that he was starting to smell, even without the rather unkind comments from his captors. He shifted uncomfortably, and was prodded in the ribs with the gun for his pains. Gazing out of the viewing window he saw a large herd of buffalo in the distance. He wondered about this. In his time period buffalo were all but extinct, and efforts were being made to preserve the dying breed. Grant thought that maybe they were bred for food. After two hours travel a large dome hove into view - at first it looked like a dome of substance; it turned out to be pure energy.

They went through a security system, and eventually were shown into an office which was very well furnished, with an oak desk and a large leather covered chair. In the chair sat another baldy, his dress was similar to the others, although there was an insignia of rank on his breast, two crossed swords with a crown inscribed above them. By now the heat and the itch was almost unbearable. The Commander saw Grant's discomfort. 'Take him away and get him cleaned up, 'he ordered, with a large smile on his face.

Grant was whisked away, stripped and searched, bathed and dressed in some of the loose fitting clothes he had already seen. Sometime later he was back facing the man in the leather chair again. The man rose to greet him, he was short and lean, but radiated tremendous authority - this was obviously the man in charge. The worry lines on his forehead indicated his responsibility; his small beady eyes suggested that it would be difficult to put anything over on him. Grant wanted to laugh, but decided against it, he must have looked just as amusing to these people, as they did to him. In any case he wanted to keep them sweet. They hadn't threatened him as yet, and he wanted to keep it that way. It appeared as if he was in the future, maybe many hundreds of years by the look of it.

After the initial shock of his unscheduled visit to the future Grant was beginning to enjoy himself. What a unique opportunity for him to study the earth of his future.

At the back of his mind he still had a nagging thought about whether he would ever see home again; perhaps Williams was home now, and worrying about him. Before the man could speak Grant said 'Forgive me, Sir, but you have the advantage of me. My name is Doctor John Grant and I would dearly love to know where I am, and in what year.'

'As I thought from my men's account of your sudden appearance, you are a time jumper' exclaimed the man. 'My name is Cord, Commander of this City. The year is 3031 AD, and you are in the continent of the Americas.

Grant let this sink in; he had been catapulted far into the future, in fact far beyond his expectations. He was way beyond his own time. '3031' he repeated, incredulously, as if not really believing what he was hearing. 'I am from the year 2030, and lately from 33.' Cord let this information pass without comment. 'You have, I think come across time travelers before,' continued Grant. 'I thought that time travel into one's future was impossible, according to our researchers anyway, can you explain, please?'

'You can only visit your own future if you have visited the past first' clarified Cord. 'Under certain conditions a sling shot condition is possible, which catapults you beyond your time - as has happened to you. Now I wonder what you were up to in 33?' Grant felt rather like a naughty child as the other's keen little eyes studied him without blinking.

'That is rather a long story, but if you wish I can...'

'No, no! That is not necessary at this time, you will be questioned later by "Big Q", and your answers analyzed very carefully' Cord added ominously.

Grant wondered who or what the hell "Big Q" was, but thought that he would find out soon enough, and decided to change the course of the conversation.

'Commander, forgive me, but I am just dying for a drink, and I haven't had a square meal for days, and if it wouldn't be inconvenient, I would like a rundown on the last thousand years.'

'Your first request we can do something about immediately.' Cord went over to a recessed contrivance which, to order, dispensed a very passable meal - what looked like veal with potatoes and a green vegetable - with a large glass of beer and a hunk of bread.

Grant tucked in, with relish, watched by Cord. When he had finished, the eating utensils were placed in the device and spirited away.

'You obviously enjoyed that,' commented Cord. 'Now for your other request, please follow me and all will be revealed.'

Grant walked just behind the little man, wondering where he was being led. After five minutes brisk walk, down long corridors, they entered a small medical laboratory. Grant was laid on a bed, a small metal cap, with electrodes, was attached to his head by a technician. In minutes he was asleep.

What seemed like days passed - in fact only forty minutes elapsed; during this time he got a complete update on earth's history, post twentieth century. The potted history lesson was absolutely fascinating and incredible. In 2083 North Korea dropped an "A" bomb on South Korea. Horrified nations of the world became really united for the first time in history. A "World Government" was set up, with teeth: all conventional armies were disbanded, and replaced with a World military force, taking men and women from each of the disbanded armies. All atomic weapons were dismantled except for a few held by the World Authority.

Satellite mounted laser cannons were requisitioned for use by the military force, if required, against any dissenters. In fact any countries Executives not falling into line were punished severely. All members of the North Korean military Government were executed.

Instead of countries competing against each other, both military and scientifically, all resources were pooled, and by 2191 biochemists had cooperated with electronics engineers and physicists to produce the first intelligent computer. The monster computer had been constructed to help in the day to day running of the world - a concept that had been thoroughly discussed by scientists and politicians, probably since the first microchip was produced.

Despite gloomy predictions that the computer would take over from its human creators, and eventually run the world as a dictator, things seemed to work out well. The quantum computer - which even with micro-engineering covered an area the size of a small city - brought man into a wonderful era of prosperity. The Computer was known as "Big Q". This culmination of man's technological development had been built deep under the Sahara desert. Completely self-contained it was serviced by robots, and powered by solar panels, which covered ten square miles in grid formation. The selected site made certain of vast quantities of energy and the huge maze of specially developed batteries in the complex ensured power during the night. A hydrogen fusion cell powered system was used as a backup. Man had been designed out of the computer complex completely and utterly. "Big Q" was self-repairing, self-perpetuating, and what was more, self-developing.

Even before the appearance of "Big Q" time travel had been prohibited. Grant searched, mentally, for a reference to the "Jesus Project" and finally found it; however it appeared that, soon after its inception, it was wound up. Grant wondered if it was due to his non-appearance. With the pitfalls inherent in time travel, all governments in the year 2035 had put a bar on it. This was fairly simple due to the vast resources required. Only Governments or huge Corporations could afford to sponsor such projects.

Man continued to evolve over the centuries; one of the more bizarre effects was the hairless nature of the present inhabitants of earth. Their E.S.P. facilities had been developed to the extent that some gifted people could now actually read minds and indeed influence those of inferior intelligence. Intellectual capacity had increased tremendously, due to some very advanced nano and quantum physics. Conventional learning techniques were largely obsolete except for human tutoring. The full potential of a child's brain was realized instead of being largely wasted. I.Q. values of 150 were normal in this age. In Grant's time 100 was the "norm" the 150 value being a one in a thousand phenomenon.

Man had conquered the solar system, but had still not developed an efficient star drive. In any case all space travel had been banned from 2455. This was the year that a space virus had been brought back, which had contaminated the wombs of ninety five percent of all females. To maintain a stable population it had been calculated that two point four children must be born to each couple; hence an end to civilization and life on this planet was a distinct possibility.

A sociological disaster was only prevented by "Big Q". It took over the running of earth completely. The few women left who could bear children were treated like Gods. Using techniques developed by the giant computer, these women produced many babies a year.

That is to say scores of eggs were fertilized in their bodies, and then taken away to be nurtured by artificial means. The problem was that approximately ninety five percent of the girls born were also contaminated.

Cloning had been tried by "Big Q' in earth's laboratories, but without success. This puzzled Grant, as even in his era some success had been achieved using small animals. The problem here, apparently, had been deterioration in brain cells, and after five years the products of the experiments had to be destroyed. It seemed insoluble, and even with the advanced facilities that they had, cloning as a method of repopulating earth was dropped.

This failure was a huge blow, and possibly the only chance that earth had, excepting an outright cure for the virus. So, despite all these efforts earth's population was still desperately low. The remaining people on each continent lived in self-contained cities.

Grant had ended up in one of these cities in the Americas; geographically the old West of North America. The cities were protected by energy screens, ostensibly against adverse weather conditions. In fact psychological protection was desired. With space travel banned, and the population decimated, the inhabitants of earth had begun to suffer from severe melancholia, that if allowed to continue would turn in on itself, and destroy Homo-sapiens.

"Big Q" had no wish to administer a depopulated planet, and reacted quickly to the situation. His people needed cheering up, needed stimulation and excitement. In an incredibly short space of time, hundreds of ideas were conceived by the computer, and then rejected by It. Eventually THE idea. "Big Q" set up planet wide competitions. Annual entry was compulsory, and for the masses a system of grading and handicapping was established.

At this level all kinds of intellectual games were played; as well as the more athletic. In each city local and area championships were established, in both handicap and scratch categories.

The ten area scratch champions in each city vied for the title of city champion. It was at this stage that the competitions began to get deadly serious. "Big Q" thought, rightly, that men and women (there was an equivalent championship for females) at this level of competition would not settle for a safe, lack luster type of competition. At this advanced stage the whole cities population watched; either at the huge games hall in each city, or on the 3d Holo-Screen systems. At least two out of ten were dead by the end of the five day competition, such was the intensity of the contest.

From this point a Continental champion was found by pitting the twenty city champions against each other. After this the champion of the world from the six Continental victors.

The death toll from these championships always hovered around fifteen to twenty percent.

At the end of the history lesson the scientists in charge of the procedure subjected Grant to a wide range of tests; both physical and intellectual, after which he was allowed to rest for two days.

"Big Q" was pleased. There was no doubt about that. It was rather like a dog with two tails, or a kid with a lollypop. His circuits hummed away, analyzing the data from Grant and the missing Williams, who had eventually turned up, albeit forty-eight hours after his friend.

In the months to come the two men were to look on "Big Q" as a friend. They never considered his gender, but if asked would have probably plumped for male.

The giant computer had never been as happy; as the nitrogen cooled systems kept his circuits at workable temperatures, and prevented the nutrients feeding the biological parts from boiling. That night his army of service robots was kept busy as he worked at full capacity, predicting events on earth for the next hundred years due to the sudden appearance of the two men from the past.

"Big Q", whose powers were so fantastic that even the scientists of this age had failed to comprehend them, knew that these men, Grant and Williams, would indeed have a phenomenal effect on events to come.

The computer had not as yet worked out how the two time-travelers would be used in its grand scheme, and was still working on it. The electronic subsystems of the huge brain would be working flat out for hours yet on the accumulation of data, whilst the higher biological regions rested, for the time when data was presented to them for analysis, conclusions and decision.

***

John Grant was in the hands of the Dark Brotherhood. He knew, now, that Williams was dead, that Christ hadn't been crucified, but quietly murdered in an alleyway. The Dark Brotherhood's plan had succeeded and their efforts had all been for nothing. Joe's people were doomed. What was worse the worshippers of the "Dark Prince" had now set their sights on the alternate world. Grant's world...

Chapter Twelve

A Confrontation

'The argument of the stronger party is always the best'
La Fontaine

Grant woke in a cold sweat; his dream had ended badly. The devil had just begun to flay him alive, the flesh stripping from his bones. He awoke suddenly, as often happens during a nightmare, opened his eyes and saw his nurse. Even without hair she was lovely, although he doubted whether he would ever get used to women without their crowning glory. Her name was Sara and she had bright blue eyes and a lovely full body under her coverall. Grant realized just how long it had been since he had made love. In fact his whole being suddenly just ached for her. He realized that he was staring, and averted his gaze - he didn't want to embarrass the girl,

'You have been out a long time' she said, in a low husky voice. Then without pausing 'Would you like me?'

Grant was rather taken back by this forward young madam, then realized that this behavior could be normal in this future world. He stuttered a bit as he affirmed his needs. He was gently taken by the hand and led into an adjoining room in which there was, what looked like, a large water bed. It turned out to be an air filled mattress under high pressure, which was found to be very comfortable indeed.

He felt his manhood rising under his loose fitting clothes. Sara looked down and laughed, reaching down and unzipping him she took hold of his organ, giving it a squeeze. Grant nearly ejaculated on the spot. Sara quickly undressed both Grant and herself, revealing her glorious delights; plump firm breasts and buttocks, beautiful long legs. Her skin was like satin as Grant, fumbling like a school-boy in his eagerness, caressed her.

Sara laid him on his back and straddled him, like sitting astride a horse, working herself on him. He climaxed very quickly - after only six movements. She seemed disappointed as the subject of her pleasure shrank, but shrieked with delight as it almost immediately swelled up again.

Now it was Grant's turn, and he rolled Sara over onto her back and entered her. For what seemed an eternity they made violent love, gradually softening into something more civilized as their passions were quenched, and eventually satisfied.

As if nothing had happened Sara got up off the bed, which had taken such a pounding, slipped on her clothes and walked out. She was followed, shortly afterwards, by a somewhat fatigued Grant, who had a very large smile upon his face.

***

Grant lay on his bed looking up at the white ceiling whistling untunefully but with great energy. The sort of sound which Williams had once opined could easily drive a man mad. After a short refreshing nap he now felt really good. During his sleep Sara had brought in two of her friends, to view her latest conquest, and they stood in a corner giggling and making pointed remarks about him. They were quickly shooed out as Grant stirred in his sleep and seemed about to wake up. Sara promising to introduce him to them at a more convenient time.

Later on Commander Cord paid a surprise visit. He found Grant studying some technical data on a computer screen.

'Morning, Grant, hope you are fully recovered. By the way we picked up a friend of yours while you were in dreamland' Grant leapt to his feet 'Thank God; I had given Williams up for lost.' He was momentarily overwhelmed with relief.

'So that's his name. We picked him up by grav-copter just west of here. He was wondering around in circles, dressed like you were. He is in our hospital suffering from dehydration and exhaustion.'

'Can I see him?' asked Grant.

'Later,' answered Cord 'When he is rested.'

'Okay' replied Grant. 'Can I have a look around the city?'

'That you may, I am very busy at the moment, but my second in command will give you the "grand tour".'

Colonel Foster was a jolly roly-poly character. He was introduced by Cord as "Colonel Foster, Guardian of the City." When pressed by Grant it was explained that this was the title given to all City Champions. The title was enhanced by a neat one piece royal blue uniform.

Everywhere the two went they got odd glances. This was due to Grant's hairy appearance. Williams and he had grown beards during the last week or so; in this world there was no head or body hair at all. Perhaps this was the reason why Sara had found him so desirable. He had hoped that it went somewhat deeper than that - male pride perhaps?

Many of the cities' population wore side arms and swords. He asked Foster the reason for this. 'Protection,' was the reply.

'But protection from what?' queried Grant.

'From each other, from life, from everything!'

The Colonel threw up his arms in seeming frustration. Then he tried to explain it to Grant.

'You may recall the days of the American West when guns were worn. In fact the whole American nation became fanatical about their right to bear arms for centuries afterwards.'

'There were periods in English history when many wore swords. In the early days it would have been for protection; because of the lack of law and order. In this present period it is psychological; you know our position, the planet wide depression after our population was so brutally reduced. People feel more secure with an energy screen around the city, and a sword or gun at their side. Sometimes the weapons are used for purposes other than psychological, or for mere decoration. Under certain circumstances a challenge may be issued and a duel fought to the death'. The Colonel spoke matter-of-factly, as if this might have been a regular occurrence.

'I see,' said Grant. 'At least I think I do.' He was naturally intrigued by the information - that duels were actually fought in this futuristic world. He decided to drop the matter at this stage; undoubtedly it would be raised at some future and convenient time when he could get more information. At the moment he wanted to concentrate on the conducted tour.

The tour was done partly by grav-copter, and partly by the vast network of moving walkways. There were five walkways, each moving at different speeds, from around five miles per hour up to twenty-five miles per hour. No ground cars were allowed within the city. The grav-copters were anti-gravity ships, carrying up to six people, which obtained forward and lateral movement by using powerful air jets. Vertical movement was controlled by varying the degree of resistance to gravity. This meant that the vessel was highly maneuverable.

To Grant the layout of the city was not much different to cities from his own time, except for the walkways, and the refreshing lack of traffic. There were supermarkets, hospitals, houses and flats; parks, sports halls, universities and schools. The huge nurseries were the real contrast between the present and the far distant past. In the large white buildings the eggs were nurtured and brought to fruition. The babies so produced stayed until they were three months old, before going to special small unit homes.

Grant wondered what the long term effects of the lack of natural mothering was. He thought of the abortive attempts by the Nazi's to create a super race, by mating selected men and women of the "master race", and then removing the result of the union to one of their nurseries as soon as it was born.

On leaving the nurseries they were passed by a large matronly looking lady, dressed entirely in purple; including an ornate head dress. She was surrounded by well-armed men, who seemed to watch her every movement. An armored grav-copter hovered to complete the guard on her. Foster answered the obvious question on Grant's lips. 'The future destiny of our planet depends upon her, and the few like her,' he said with a sort of whispered reverence. 'She must not be allowed to come to any harm. Because of the demands made upon her body even the smallest scratch, at this stage, may be crucial to the litter she will produce.' Grant shook his head in disbelief, what sort of a world had he come into? He made no comment, and asked no questions; Grant had no wish to embarrass his guide.

Grant wondered why no matter transmitter had been developed for ease of transport. He remembered the device that had taken Sir Felix, Williams, and himself from the formers home to the "Jesus Project" plant; just prior to taking off. Was this alien technology he wondered? Surely, if there was such a device then, it ought by now to have been developed to a high degree. He asked Foster about this.

'Five hundred years ago the device was invented, but it had one small problem, on average every fifty pay loads - human or material - one was lost in the intervening space. Even more serious was the damaging effects of the ultra-high frequency radiation given off by the irreclaimable mass. Some lives were forfeited before the horrific consequences of the research were discovered. This research was immediately terminated, and never restarted.'

Grant suddenly started to sweat. Either the system he had experienced was alien, with all the bugs ironed out, or they had been in considerable risk with a device not yet proved.

There were several amazing technological developments that interested Grant immensely. One concerned the electrical battery. He had wondered about this when he had got the "update" on this period. "Big Q", he remembered, had as its main source of energy, solar powered batteries.

In Grant's time period, in the twenty first century, storage of electrical energy was still limited by the batteries of that era. Even so, in the early part of this century, great strides had been made with LiPo cells - Lithium Polymer batteries and the nano battery using nanopores - giving much improved performance. He asked Foster the reason why "Big Q" should use, what to him, was a totally inefficient energy storage and power supply system.

Foster told him that the basic reason was, the complete rethink in the materials used: the electrolytes, and the plates. By some miracle of chemistry - which even Grant could only guess at - the negative plate took electrons from an electrolyte with ten times more available electrons than with conventional electrolytes. The positive and negative elements were incredible alloys, which allowed for this massive increase in potential capacity. Hence a battery was built in 2183 with one hundred times the capacity of conventional batteries.

Furthermore they were almost indestructible; small wonder that "Big Q" used this rechargeable unit as his power, source energized from the sun's rays, not having to rely too much on his backup - the fusion capability.

Grant was also interested in the advance of the laser weapon, in particular the life of the power pack used in this era. He was informed that the average hand weapon could be held on full power for ten minutes; the size of power pack was that of a pack of playing cards, built into the weapon handle.

Having expressed his disbelief, Grant was told by Foster, in a somewhat patronizing tone, that the lasers used were somewhat more efficient than in Grant's time - ninety-nine point nine percent. The man from the past remembered that the first lasers were a mere 25% efficient, and even the later, military, development only reached 48%

Another major factor was that a tiny fissionable element in the unit provided the energy for the laser. In John Grant's time the principle of the rechargeable power pack depended upon energizing a complex sandwich of capacitors. This gave a very limited pulsed output from the laser, with a maximum life of ten seconds at full power. Its development, however, could be fired in bursts, or continuously at maximum power for considerably longer.

***

After three hours Foster took Grant into a small restaurant, where they ate an excellent meal. Apparently meat was now completely artificially produced. Animals were no longer the source of man's staple diet. Grant was glad that the buffalo he had seen would not end up on somebody's table. The "steak" he was eating tasted just like the real thing, he could not tell the difference.

Grant had always considered that killing animals for the food they gave was morally wrong. Most people, like him, did it out of necessity, and because they had been brought up in this way. This was certainly a plus for the future. One other piece of very good news was the fact that the animal population hadn't been affected by the virus; otherwise the complete ecological balance of the planet would have been upset.

Then an incident occurred which was to seriously affect both Grant and Williams and their involvement in future events, which would unfold on earth in this era. There was a rather loud mouthed individual seated at an adjacent table. He was dressed in royal blue; Grant should have noted the fact. The man, called Haigh, abused the waiters and kept making loud remarks about Grant's appearance. His friends tried to keep him quiet; to no avail. Foster apologized to Grant, he shrugged his shoulders and said, 'Forget it! I know how hot headed and arrogant the young can be!'

Apparently this particular young man had very keen hearing. He got up, pushed his chair back and strode over to

Grant's table. Foster got up to try and stop a scene.

'Keep out of this old man' said Haigh. 'This is no business of yours. In any case I cannot challenge a former City Champion.'

The people in the restaurant suddenly stopped talking, all eyes were focused on the little drama that was being enacted before them, and Grant had time to study Haigh as he advanced on them. He was around five feet ten, and appeared extremely well muscled, with broad shoulders, and a slim waist. It was the face that took Grant's attention; it was cruel and hard with pale blue eyes set very close together.

'This man is a guest of the City, and must be treated as such,' retorted Foster.

The exchange between the two stopped when John Grant stood up.

'Let him say what he came over for.'

'But you don't understand, 'pleaded Foster.

Haigh slapped Grant across the face. Grant with a reflex action slammed his aggressor in the mouth. The man was hurled back across the room. The blue suited Haigh lay across a ruined dinner table, with red wine dripping down his right leg, and his arm in a plate of stew. He wiped a dribble of blood from the corner of his mouth. Staggering up, his friends supporting him, he glared at Grant, and in measured tones said, 'You are a dead man, whoever you are, and from wherever you come from. I challenge you to personal combat tomorrow at dawn, in the dueling hall.' Without another word he turned and tottered out, Grant's blow had been a hard one.

Foster buried his head in his hands. 'Do you know what you have done?' he cried. 'You have been challenged by the current "City Champion" - may God help you!'

'Do I get choice of weapons?' asked Grant.

'Yes,' answered Foster bleakly.

'Swords I think. Will you be my Second?'

'Of course!'

The diners turned back to their eating, and the mess created by the brief disturbance was quickly cleared away. The inhabitants of this world were used to such goings on.

'Come on Colonel, lets finish our meal, we mustn't let that young fool spoil our meal' said Grant. Foster agreed, and they sat down again. 'I really don't know what Cord will say about this,' observed the little man.

Afterwards they continued the tour, and by late afternoon both of them had had enough. By mutual agreement they headed back to base. In the administration block. Cord made no comment on the events of the day. Grant wondered why; but didn't press the point. All he wanted to do was to see that his friend was alive and kicking. Colonel Foster walked him over to the hospital block.

Williams and Grant were eventually re-united with much back slapping and congratulations. After a great deal of discussion of the events of the past four days, they couldn't think of any reason why they should have been separated by the transfer from ancient Judea, and why they had been thrown so far into the future. Then Grant remembered that he had been hit on the head, during their fracas with the Jewish bandits and that this had, presumably precipitated the "sling shot" effect.

The two men agreed that an attempt to transfer again, before the nano-unit in Grant's skull was checked, might be just as problematic as their previous attempt. In any case they wanted to get a good look round this futuristic world first; this really was a marvelous chance for them; this glimpse into the future. Grant hadn't yet told his friend about the little duel he was going to fight, with the bad mannered City Champion. He had decided to keep it from Peter until it was over. There was no point in worrying him needlessly, particularly after his recent ordeal outside the city.

The two were housed in some very spacious accommodation, having separate suites of rooms. Foster told them that they were normally used for visiting dignitaries and could consider themselves lucky. He let Grant into his room last. 'I will give you a call early tomorrow morning,' he said. 'I still have the arrangements to make, see you then, goodnight.'

'Goodnight Colonel.'

Alone at last, thought Grant. What bliss! Like most people he appreciated privacy; at least some of the time. He hadn't been on his own for two weeks now. Grant examined his surrounding, and found to his delight that the living room had a well-stocked library, of conventional books. Most of the classical writers had endured the test of time: Shakespeare, Shaw, Wild, Poe, Twain, Dickens, Kipling... John Grant spent what was left of the evening reading David Copperfield, by Charles Dickens, one of his favorites.

***

Whilst Grant was thus engaged, Julian Haigh was busy living it up. Haigh was not used to people actually objecting to his behavior - to his face, that is. If they were brave enough to object within his hearing, he challenged and killed them; it was as simple as that. He always kept to the letter of the law in such matters - that was his excuse.

After the affair in the eating house Haigh cleaned up, and went back "on the town" again.

He had acquired a small group of so called friends; they were the usual type, the natural hangers-on of life, who hoped that some of his glory would rub off on them; or who were just scared of him, and maybe thought that his friendship would save them from the worst of his temper. Despite the thousands of years of civilization nothing had really changed in man's basic character.

The rest of the evening was spent in a drinking establishment, where they had back rooms in which the oldest profession was plied by willing girls - they were still very much better than the best sex aids available; even in this advanced culture.

Most of the girls kept clear when Haigh and his companions came in. He tended to mix his sex with an extreme streak of cruelty. But there was one with whom he regularly kept company. Her name was Gill, and a patchy sort of relationship had begun between them.

She was a buxom girl, just past her prime, and was in this business because she enjoyed it, and for no other reason. Haigh had just told her that he was to be involved in yet another duel, as he knew that the news would upset her.

'Oh Julian why must you put yourself in such danger? 'She asked.

'None of your business' was the curt reply 'I don't tell you what to do; How many have you had tonight?' he added nastily.

Gill was silent, she knew there was no reasoning with Haigh in his present mood, and did not want to bring his anger down on her; she still bore the bruises from the last time.

'Come on then slut, let's get on with it'...

Later on Haigh went to his living quarters and stretched out on his bed. Yes, it had been a good evening, even though Gill had been her usual dumb self. He thought about the possibility of getting a replacement for her sometime, but in a way he was rather fond of her. He started to think about the duel tomorrow, he had no doubt as to the result. Haigh had never felt fear in his life, and certainly this upstart from the past would prove no problem at all. After that he would have to get into shape for the next stage of the games, and then for the final - Haigh had no doubt at all that he would become world games champion this year.

Chapter Thirteen

The Duel

*'My good blade carves the casqued of men,
My tough lance trusted sure'*
Tennyson

A tap at the door interrupted Grant's early morning preparations. Foster was there.

'Come in Colonel; help yourself to coffee whilst I finish up.'

'Thanks John,' said Foster, helping himself to some of the brown liquid from the automatic dispenser, in the corner of the room.

Grant had risen early in order to give himself plenty of time to prepare himself for the coming ordeal. Having slept well he exercised; going through a simple loosening up drill. He showered - luxuriating under the hot needles of high pressure water before finishing with the control on ice cold, to close the pores.

After examining the contents of his wardrobe he selected a bright red track suit and what appeared to be training shoes; to wear to the dueling hall.

Next he breakfasted on bacon and eggs, toast and marmalade, orange juice and coffee. This repast had been dialed up on the dispenser, which seemed to have a capacity for an infinite variety of dishes and drinks.

Foster made himself comfortable in an armchair and sipped his coffee. He was dressed in a royal blue two piece track suit, open at the neck. His name was embossed on the right breast of the suit top. Although Foster was over-weight, Grant could see that great power resided in the portly body. You could tell by the way the man moved.

The Colonel waited quietly whilst Grant went through his meditation routine. When John finally came out of his trance Foster coughed to gain his attention.

'Come on then,' exclaimed Grant 'Something's up; you have been sitting there with a face as long as a fiddle ever since you came in.' Foster half smiled, 'As your official second I must advice you on protocol and tactics. As a friend I must warn you to try and pull out of this fight with Haigh.'

'Sorry Colonel, I don't think so.'

'Very well then, Haigh has an astonishingly good record with the rapier, which you as challenger have selected. Last night his second contacted me - the duel will be held at 0600 in just' - looking at his time piece - 'Thirty minutes.'

'Haigh is a slippery customer' Foster continued, 'he will be up to all sorts of tricks, and will never fight fair. The other bad news is that he is the best in the City, and has never been defeated.'

The next few minutes were spent in discussing the rules and a quick rundown on Haigh's strengths and weaknesses, although there were not many of the latter.

'By the way John, daft question I know, but have you fenced much before?'

'Just a bit,' was the rather guarded reply.

At 0545 the two men left for the dueling hall. When they got there Haigh and his second were already warming up. The current City Champion stared across at Grant, fixing him with his pale blue eyes. The men were locked in this psychological battle for a few seconds until Grant decided, much against his better judgment, to make an attempt at reconciliation with Julian Haigh. He thought he owed it to Foster; the man had seemed very concerned about the impending duel.

'Haigh would you accept my apology for the whole incident?' He asked.

'Not a chance, you are not going to wriggle out of this, you yellow bastard.' Answered Haigh with venom. 'You will pay for your insolence with your life.'

That may be true thought Grant; these duels, he had learnt, were fought until one of the participants was either dead, or so badly wounded, that in the opinion of the referee he was unable to continue. A refusal to fight was a capital offence. There were safeguards, and if somebody thought that an unfair challenge had been made, for some reason, a board of five senior officers was convened and a decision made, which was binding. This would have been Grant's only chance of getting out of the duel, other than by mutual agreement.

Julian Haigh had fought twenty duels with sword, laser handgun and unarmed combat. He had killed ten men, and counted on Grant being the eleventh.

The referee, a major, offered Grant choice of a matched pair of swords. He selected one at random, slashing it through the air, trying it for weight and balance. Finding it to his liking he said 'I'll have this one.' Haigh took the other.

The dress for the duel was simply, a light singlet and trousers with special grip soled shoes. Grant hardly heard the referee's instructions when the two men were called together, as a small voice in his brain kept telling him he was going to die.

'You will fight on, without a break, until one of you is either dead, or so badly wounded that you cannot go on,' said the major. 'Any attempt to break off the fight, without my permission, and I will kill the transgressor with this' - he pointed ominously at the laser handgun he held ready, with the safety catch off. There were no buttons on the sword tips, no protective shields for the face, or protective clothing.

Again that insistent voice hammering into Grant's head, the message was about his impending demise, and how much he would suffer before it. He started to believe it. Grant was brought out of his daze by Foster whispering into his ear.

'Watch him, John, he will try and put you off by using his mind probe facility.' Grant snapped back to reality, and fought the mental attack on him. He was now very angry indeed. That such an insidious assault should have been perpetrated on his mind was beyond his belief. Grant in his normal even tempered mood was a very formidable opponent; in his present ugly mood he was extremely dangerous.

His anger was soon under very tight control, and this conditioned his body to face any eventuality. Grant was thirty four years old, at the peak of physical condition; his muscles were tuned to perfection, his reactions razor sharp, the weeks preparing for Judea were to prove crucial. Haigh had made a terrible mistake in treating his opponent like an inferior species; but he appeared to make a habit of this sort of behavior by all accounts.

The two men circled each other. Grant projected, mentally, a message to Haigh. 'Keep out of my mind!' From then on it was man to man, good old fashioned combat. The two might have been battling it out in a fencing establishment in France or England, during the Napoleonic wars.

Haigh wanted a quick kill, and came in fast with a fierce thrusting action. Grant reacted like a tightly coiled spring, retreating across the area until his back was against a wall, parrying Haigh's flashing blade. Then the "compressed spring" released itself; with a quick thrust, and a flick of his wrist Grant's astonished opponent was disarmed, his rapier skidding along the floor to a far wall.

'Had enough?' asked Grant, hardly able to believe that this might be an end to it - he was to be disappointed.

'No' answered Haigh savagely, 'why don't you finish the job, you had a bit of luck that's all; go on kill me!'

In retrospect Grant was to wish that he had; but in the circles that John Grant moved in, you just didn't do that sort of thing. Honor, chivalry, kindness, a helping hand for the underdog; that was his code and always would be.

'Pick up your sword, 'was Grant's answer. 'Let's see if my luck continues to hold.'

'You fool,' shrieked Haigh, as he picked up the fallen weapon. 'You're stupid honor will prove your death warrant.'

Haigh was now very careful, studying his antagonist through narrowed eyes. He had seen his opponent's skill, and had decided that his best strategy was to wear him down. The city champion was, in fact, a very good swordsman, as well as being intelligent, strong and, despite his despicable character, brave and without fear; that's how he had got to be city champion. The problem for Julian Haigh was that Grant refused to give way and showed no sign of tiring. The battle continued.

Now the contestants had been at it for twenty long minutes. Grant's right shoulder had been pierced, and his sword arm hung useless by his side. Haigh had come in for the kill; he had no scruples, murdering a defenseless man did not worry him at all.

A small crowd was gathering, and becoming larger all the time as word got around that somebody was giving Haigh the fight of his life. They gasped as Grant changed his sword to the left hand - he was ambidextrous - and at this moment very grateful for the fact. Haigh visibly slumped as Grant successfully defended the attack, despite his wound. Both men were now very tired, the two week celebrations, after the City Championships, were now creasing Haigh. He had spent the time in eating, drinking and wenching; he was nearly spent. Grant thrust through his guard, slicing through the flesh of the upper sword arm.

Haigh's weapon clattered to the floor a second time and he slumped to his knees. John Grant placed the point of his rapier to the throat of his rival. The crowd suddenly went quiet. Haigh hardly knew what was happening, his eyes glazed, waiting for the quick thrust which would mean his death. Grant merely gestured to the referee.

'Major, would you please call for some medical attention for this man.' Then the victor threw down his blood stained sword, and lurched off with Foster supporting his tired frame.

A ripple of applause swept round the considerable crowd which had now gathered. Shouts of 'Well done,' could be heard across the early morning air. Quickly gaining momentum the polite clapping turned to cheers. Haigh was not a popular man in this city. But what had really impressed the spectators was the sparing of the man's life.

'Well done,' congratulated the colonel. 'It's about time he was taken down a peg or two. We should get you to the medical center to have that wound attended to, I will call up a "copter".'

Grant was slowly recovering his composure. It must be said that although he was a superb exponent of the art of fencing, he had no experience in duels to the death; but he was learning, and would be even more formidable in any similar situation which might arise.

The crowd opened up their ranks to let the "hero" and his second out of the sports hall. They were met by an irate Williams.

'What the hell have you been up to John?' he asked. 'Someone said you were fighting some sort of duel. My God you are hurt!'

A shaken Grant managed to smile through the curtain of pain, and swayed. Williams lifted him up gently and carried him into the sports medical center. They patched him up and took him to the City hospital accompanied by his friend. Reports of the result of the clash between Haigh and Grant were immediately flashed to a relieved Cord, who was in three way communication with the "World Council" and "Big Q".

All major decisions in the running of the planet were left to "Big Q"; although he first listened to all arguments and discussions of the various Council members. In this way the best possible judgment was always made; the combination of the biological quantum brain being infallible. Some very important discussions were, at this moment, going on; concerning Grant and Williams. If the intrepid adventurers had only known what was in store for them, they would have certainly attempted a return home there and then.

***

Cord staggered into his living quarters, and was greeted by his wife with a kiss, and one of his favorite tipples, a very strong lager type beer.

'God what a day it's been. Young Grant came through though, thank "Big Q",' he added with feeling 'I don't know if I can stand much more of this.'

'There there, Love, come and sit down.'

Like the dutiful husband he was, Cord enquired after his wife.

'What sort of a day have you had?'

'Quite nice, thank you Francis.' In the next few minutes they indulged in the usual small talk, common between married couples throughout the ages.

'Think I'll have a "needle shower" and turn in, Jenny' concluded Cord.

Later on, greatly invigorated, Frank Cord went to bed. Jenny had stopped up to watch some 3d Holo-pics they were showing some old romantic adventures...

Cord lay on the air bed, the soft plastic mounding to his body; he felt as good as he had been all week. Yes by God! John Grant might be the catalyst that we need to save us, he thought.

Earlier the City Commander had had a long session with "Big Q". He remembered every word, particularly "Q's" parting shot.

'Well Commander, we must now leave matters to fate; with a little help from me of course' Cord had almost detected a snigger. But how could a machine duplicate such a human trait?

Cord had been City Commander for eight years, he was fifty-six years old, and soon due for a place on the "Twenty Cities Council." He had been dealing with "Big Q" for many years now and still, in his own mind, considered it nonhuman, merely a system of nuts, bolts and Qubits. The well-modulated tones of "Q" emanating from the speakers never fooled him for a moment - such an effect was merely due to modern scientific effects. Cord never voiced his opinions on "Q" to anyone, not even his wife. He thought that if his misgivings were to be known it might jeopardise his future career. Nevertheless he accepted "Big Q's" logic and decisions without question - they had been proven so right in the past, he could hardly do otherwise.

Laying there, his mind filled with so many thoughts, he found sleep hard to come by. He started to think about himself; in all his life what had he really achieved? Everything had been so easy. Every decision of any consequence was made by the Computer. Cord had been earmarked for advancement from the nursery stage; every child in this world realized their full potential, and Frank's potential had been better than most. In fact he was in the top 0.0001 percent of the population. His ability, however, to his everlasting regret, was mental rather than physical.

The dream had been to be "World games champion." Granted, he was no slouch, physically, but had only managed good local placing's in the championships; being eliminated easily at the next stage. He sighed, that was always the way of it. Even genetic engineering couldn't make people happy with their lot in life. Cord made up for his considerable disappointment by being an avid follower of the "games", watching all the Holo-pic analysis and personalities.

Cord's other loves were Jenny, of course! And war games; another very popular pastime with earth's population; in lieu of the real thing. He could fight, albeit on Holo-pics, every major battle in earth's history, and change their course; if he was skillful enough - in this era there was "Fully Immersive

Technology" which meant some fantastic viewing experiences.

He was a military man that had never seen raw battle. If only he could return to the past and take part in those real battles, in the flesh, instead of in a game.

The Commander had once mentioned the possibility to "Big Q", and had been treated to a few seconds silence before, kindly, having his request rejected. Nobody was exempt from the time travel rule. He knew he had been foolish to ask, to show such a quirk to the Computer, who could block further advancement for him.

Jenny Cord came in, much later, and found her husband sound asleep curled up like a baby in the womb - every woman had seen pictures of this wondrous event, even though it hadn't happened for centuries.

Jenny kissed him, he stirred but did not waken; it had been a long day. She undressed and got into bed beside him and lay there, her eyes open, staring into nothing less. The sight of her husband curled up like that had awoken such longings of motherhood. The fact that no woman, in this age, could have a child by natural means created tension in women, which even "Big Q" could not do anything about; the giant computer continually worked in the hope of finding a remedy to the virus, and perhaps wanted to retain maternal feelings in earth's women.

And yet Jenny Cord was happy in her own way. The position of the Commander's wife did not, by itself, give her any real privilege in this, theoretically, classless society. But she always felt the envy of her friends, and other women because of her marriage and this did give her a lot of satisfaction. Before her marriage she had been a top grade administrator, in the security section and this is how she had met Frank. She still worked in the security complex, and because of her position she had regular contact with "Big Q".

One day, during the course of her work, she had cause to consult the computer, and had asked it about the possibility of natural childbirth - again that silence as if the computer did not want to hurt the feelings of somebody about to receive bad news. Yes, it was still working on it. No, there wasn't any progress. Well she had asked, and got the expected answers, and had thrust the facts from her mind; that is until today. She started to cry, the tears rolling down her face, she shook uncontrollably until her husband awoke, and tried to comfort her. Frank Cord knew what was wrong; in fact this sort of behavior was becoming more and more common amongst the women of earth. He sighed; even "Big Q" could not come up with a solution.

There were now, of course, these twin problems, the lack of basic motherhood, and the games behavioral pattern. It was fortunate for his piece of mind that Frank Cord still stuck to the firm belief that "Big Q" would see them through it all.

Chapter Fourteen

A Question of Honor

'Honor is simply the morality of superior men'
H.L. Mencken

Grant spent a week in hospital. His wounds had almost completely healed during this time, with the aid of the highly effective medical facilities. Yet much of the treatment had, as its basis, pre-twentieth century medicine. Acupuncturing techniques, using fine needles; hypnotic therapy - the mind over matter approach. These and other methods were combined with extremely advanced drugs, computer analysis and control, together with a variety of healing rays.

Haigh would be receiving similar treatment, and Grant wondered when he would be bumping into that gentleman again. Perhaps he should have killed him when he had the chance; he put the unworthy thought from Him; he had in any case made a very dangerous enemy.

During his enforced rest he studied recordings of all kinds played on the 3d system. The effect was fascinating, you could put your hand out, and expect to come into contact with a solid object; only when your hand grabbed thin air did you realize that it was only a holographic image. In Grant's era holography had only been developed to a pale flickering representation - an obvious illusion.

Towards the end of his stay in the medical center Grant received a visit from Foster and Williams, ostensibly enquiring after his health. He had begun to like Foster - the chubby little man was a regular visitor during his convalescence, and they seemed to have much in common.

'Commander Cord would like to see us in his office, if you could spare the time.' This, as Grant well knew, was equivalent to an order. A few minutes later saw the three men comfortably seated in Cord's office.

'Glad you could make it' observed Cord. 'Congratulations on your win, by the way.' Grant mumbled his thanks.

'Anyone like a drink?' continued the Commander. 'It's likely to be a long session.'

They all selected and dialed up some refreshment, and settled down to hear what Cord had to say.

'The Earth Council has a problem,' began Cord. The idea of the games, brilliantly conceived by "Big Q" has achieved all that it set out to do. Unfortunately we now have a system that is epitomized by young Julian Haigh. Winning is everything, losing means abject stinking failure. Whether the participants are at the bottom end, struggling for position in a local competition, or in the supreme battle for Champion of this planet, we have a win at all costs syndrome. Any underhand trick is accepted as normal. In other words we have a system without honor.

"Big Q" is aware of the problem,' continued Cord. 'And is working on it, in conjunction with the World Council. The difficulty is not in changing the rules to cover subterfuge, but in seeing that the ideal of the whole game's system is not destroyed. In this situation any interference with the games rules may be disastrous.'

'But what has this got to do with us?' asked Williams.

'You will remember that when you first came to us, both of you were monitored physically and mentally as a matter of course. The results of the tests were fed into the "master computer" together with everything else known about you at that time. With this data base "Big Q" was able to run an analysis, and as a result of this evaluation initially suggested that we introduced Grant, there, as a sort of wild card in our present system. For instance the incident in the restaurant with Haigh was a carefully worked plan.'

'Why, you rotten...'

'Sorry John,' exclaimed Foster, to whom the tirade was directed. On Haigh's past record we knew that he might try and pick a fight with you.'

'But I might have been killed dam 'it.' It was Williams who finally managed to calm Grant down and make him see reason - he had been briefed before the meeting. Cord continued,

'Your showing against the City Champion was exemplary, and was normal around ten years ago when Colonel Foster was champion.' Foster nodded agreement. 'If we allow Grant to represent this City; following the old codes of conduct and if he wins, it may encourage a greater sense of ethics amongst the population.'

'I thought that Haigh was your champion; how can I, a total stranger, just bludgeon my way into the games?'

'You did that when you beat Haigh,' interjected Foster.

'Having won the games in this City he knew that nobody could then challenge him. However, he could, and did; the only problem for him was that having lost he forfeits the right to represent us. That right passes to the victor.'

'But a man could get himself killed,' stated Grant with some feeling.

'I know it is asking a lot John, but you may be our chance to get back to some sort of morality' said Cord.

'I must have time to think it over,' answered Grant.

'Could we have a decision tomorrow? Asked Foster. Our champion must start training soon, as the Continental Championships are in three weeks.'

'Agreed,' affirmed Grant. 'I would like to talk to your computer if I may, would that be possible?'

'Yes, that could be arranged for this afternoon.'

After lunch Grant and Williams went to the computer facility for the City which housed an appendage of "Big Q". Williams had come along to give Grant support. Grant had often found his friend very helpful when he was up against it, or had to make an important decision. Grant read the code he had been given by Cord into the computer mike. He expected, in response, a tinny mechanical tone. Instead, a deep resonant voice, with perfect modulation, emanated from the speakers. It was, thought Grant, as if God were speaking. Perhaps here on earth "Big Q" was God.

'Ah! Peter Williams and John Grant I believe. Welcome my friends. I trust that you are well. Thank you, for making the commitment to help us.' Grant looked at Williams questioningly. Although, in their minds, they had decided to help in any way they could, neither of them had given voice to such a decision. They let it pass for the minute. Grant didn't know whether to address the computer as Sir, or what! He settled for "Q". It made no comment.

'We would like to help you, but could we ask a few questions first please... "Q"?'

'Of course, fire away' - it really was like talking to an old friend, thought Grant. Probably the reason why the computer was such a force in the world. Before they could pose their first question the computer continued 'The answer to your question is that you have a probability of 61.3016 percent of making it back to your own time, providing the nano-circuit you have lodged in your skull is checked, in fact I will arrange it for tomorrow.' The answer verified a thought that was already half forming in their minds; the computer could read minds, as, the question that Williams was framing had been answered without him uttering a word.

"Big Q" was having a bit of fun with them. From then on he kept the conversation strictly conventional; that is based on verbal questions and answers.

'You must know by now of our adventures in the past, could you tell us if Joe reached his era safely?' questioned Williams.

'The probability of success is 92.3413 percent,' was the answer, 'I do not think that you need fear for your friend.'

'Is there any possibility that you will ever allow space travel again?' asked Grant. There was a five second pause before they got an answer. They thought that perhaps the wonder computer had somehow blown a fuse.

'You must allow me to reserve judgment on that one. The ban on space travel was not imposed lightly, you know. My circuits are still sifting through the possibilities, and have been since the virus struck this planet. From information I have at present there is a 39.1671 percent chance of allowing space travel in the next hundred years. There may be all sorts of other lethal bugs out there that we know nothing about,' the computer added by way of explanation.

'Is there a God?'

'Oh! You mean a supreme being. I think you are in a much better position to answer that than me. In fact I know that you have already accepted the existence of such a being, from firsthand knowledge. Such information is already in my data banks, and has increased the probability of there being a God by 25.0612 percent; to a figure of 74.1363 percent.'

So the questioning went on for six solid hours. "Big Q" never seemed to tire; the only part of him which could possibly get weary would have been the higher biological areas. The final question 'what is the chance of me succeeding in the Continental, and Inter-Continental Competitions?' asked Grant.

'According to comparisons made on all City, Continental, and inter-Continental Champions, over the past hundred years, with you, there is a 51.4012 percent chance on the first count, and a 16.6251 percent chance on the second. On the third possibility, that of you winning and its effect on this planet, there are so many combination that even I can only hazard a rough guess of 9 percent of your winning and being successful in changing the moral climate.' Williams seemed visibly pleased that the customary four decimal place accuracy had been omitted on this occasion.

'Not good odds,' observed Grant.

'No, they are not, but considering the importance of this experiment, I intend to shave those odds a little. You are not of this time, and have no experience of the games. Hence this means that you are at a disadvantage. I intend to rectify this without, you appreciate, actually cheating. You will get some special coaching from me; at various times. I see that you have run out of questions. You are welcome to visit me any time you like.'

'Thanks "Q" and goodbye,' said Grant and Williams together. They walked out of the complex in an absolute daze. The sheer range and depth of questions they had plied the computer with, and its answers had delighted them. There had, however, been one or two areas when "Big Q" had not been forthcoming; for instance on the subject of Extra-terrestrial visitations, and life on other planets, he would not even give the, now, expected probability. This had concerned Grant somewhat, as he might have expected very much more; way back in the late Twentieth Century scientists and statisticians had grappled with these probabilities and concluded that the chances were extremely high "Big Q" had hundreds of years more sightings and experiences to work with since then. Grant shrugged his shoulders in resignation as "Big Q" would not be drawn further. All the computer would say was: that there were some subjects that he would not discuss with anyone, not even members of the Council, and that this was for the good of all.

Grant thought about this afterwards. "Q" had acted like a parent telling a child that it was for their own good. In a way "Big Q" was the parent, of the whole world. But why the refusal to discuss that particular topic? The trouble was that like a child, John Grant could not get out of his head something that he was denied knowledge of.

'Did you get that?' asked Williams as they walked back to their living quarters. 'That has just got to be the most amazing God damned few hours that I have ever spent.'

Grant nodded agreement 'Yes, no doubt about that! "Big Q" really intrigues me; it has developed to an extent where it is millions of years ahead of ordinary mortals. I wonder if they would let us look over the computer complex in the Sahara.'

***

That evening the "time travelers" had to attend a party in their honor. It was by special invitation, and included: Senior Officers and officials of the City and their wives; together with others with special interests such as scientists and researchers of all disciplines.

The men were checked in at the gate - security was very obvious - and then a walk up a long drive to the edifice which was a most unusual hexagonal shaped construction, with a low roof. The entrance was supported by white marble columns. The surrounding area was cultivated with trees, shrubs and flower gardens. A beautiful show piece of a place. The inside was equally lovely, with superb decor and a magnificent dance floor. They were greeted by attentive waiters with glasses of champagne and by members of the city council, including Commander Cord who was dressed in a handsome uniform. The ladies at the reception wore beautiful garments made of a brocade type of material, in a selection of very vivid contrasting colors.

During the course of the evening Grant broached the subject of "Q"'s" domain. He was greeted with an absolute negative. Nobody, but nobody was allowed physical access to "Big Q's" installation, on penalty of instant death. Cord patiently pointed out that no human being could, in any case, get within five-hundred miles of the area, due to the security arrangements surrounding "Big Q". The giant computer did not trust mankind. It had thousands of years of history of man's despicable behavior as an excuse for the mistrust. You could thus hardly blame it. There would however be an opportunity for Grant, at another time, for an audience with "Q", at home, under entirely different circumstances...

***

Grant was fascinated with the chain of command of the security forces of the city and the general political structure. Cord as Commander was at the top of the heap. His second in command was the Senior Colonel - Foster. The city was divided into four areas each with a colonel in charge, all but one of them, who were on duty, were present. Under them were the usual majors, captains, and noncommissioned officers and men. Nothing really changed, thought Grant, there were the leaders and the led; the system, at least as far as military rank was concerned, had endured throughout the centuries, on the other hand there did not appear to be the same class barriers. Advancement and rank were based purely upon merit; there were no other criteria, "Big Q" saw to that.

Williams and Grant found themselves in great demand and were continually surrounded by large groups of people, hanging on to their every word. Grant, due to his exploits in the dueling arena, was particularly popular. Some of the ladies eyed him with more than a passing interest, giving him obvious body signals; several times he excused himself to prevent things getting out of hand.

A little later, when the excitement of meeting the two men had died down, Grant struck up a conversation with a captain. His special interest was theology. It appeared that many of the religions had stood the test of time; in fact "Big Q" actually encouraged them. Grant was pleased to see that Jesus Christ was still the focal point of many of them.

The captain was enthralled at Grant's story of the time in Judea, and their adventures. In fact he recorded the conversation for future use in his studies.

Eventually - after a couple of hours - John Grant found himself alone in a corner of the large hall, he felt quite drowsy and sat down. The hubbub of the room, the clinking of glasses, the background music and the general chatter persisted unabated. He wanted to slip away from it all. He sighted a figure coming towards him, he groaned inwardly. Then he realized that it was Sara.

'Hello John.'

'Good evening Sara, what a lovely surprise, I didn't realized I would find you here.'

Sara was wearing a long golden gown, well-shaped around her body being matched by a turban of the same material. She wore no jewelry but the effect was simply stunning.

'You are beautiful,' exclaimed Grant, brightening up considerably.

Sara looked visibly pleased at the compliment, she smiled, and Grant felt his pulse quicken. He remembered the last time he had been with her, and he wished he could repeat the experience.

'I wanted to come earlier, but unfortunately I was detained at the hospital, it was an emergency. Have you enjoyed the party so far?'

'It has been an interesting evening but, come, let's get you a drink.' Grant took her arm and guided her to the bar and then he tried to find a more secluded spot, with less noise, where they could talk. It was Sara who suggested the garden; out in the evening air Grant soon felt better and refreshed. They walked hand in hand talking about many things, but mostly about Sara and her life and how she got to become a nurse.

It was dark now, but the air was still warm and everywhere was a sweet pervading smell he could not identify. He took Sara in his arms and kissed her passionately, her lips were soft and inviting and he felt her responding to his touch, his hands wandering down her long but rounded figure, and soon they were making love on the soft grass, oblivious of everything else around them.

The party ended towards the early hours of the morning; people were getting ready to leave. Sara and John were saying their Goodbyes to one another. Sara thought that she had been physically attracted towards him, mainly because he was so very different from any other man she had ever met before, but now, looking at him, she felt there was something else about him, something she couldn't explain. She only knew she wanted to see more of him, much more...

'Goodnight, darling, I will get in touch as soon as I can. 'Grant's words didn't carry much conviction. He had some very serious commitments coming up in the near future that would claim all of his time and energy. On impulse, he blew her a kiss. It was a light-hearted gesture, but his eyes remained serious and unsmiling.

They were travelling in opposite directions. Sara to her little studio apartment on the fifth floor of a tall but handsome building, on the outskirts of the city. She had made it very comfortable and the large picture windows on the East side looked out on a most beautiful, if ragged, stretch of land. Yes, perhaps next time she would ask John over to her flat for a more intimate and relaxed evening.

***

Haigh was extremely upset; anyone with half an eye could see that.
Just prior to leaving the hospital he had seen fit to challenge one of the medical staff, simply because he had insisted on

Haigh stopping on another day, to facilitate a complete recovery.

The doctor concerned had decided not to accept the invitation to an early death, and had convened a board who ruled, unanimously, that the challenge was unfair. In fact Haigh had been very seriously warned as to his future conduct - even the fairly flexible rules concerning challenges, and dueling, had limits, and Julian Haigh had reached those limits.

The ex-city champion had "blown it", and he knew it. He would have to battle through the whole thing again next year, before he could take his place in the continental games. Julian uttered a loud curse, as he strode down the walkway outside the hospital; he had even had his title stripped from him, and with it the right to wear the coveted blue uniform.

Several people stared at him, and then quickly looked away when they realized who it was. Haigh's black mood continued as he plotted his revenge - he would take on Grant, his idiot friend Williams, Foster, Cord, the whole dam lot if need be; yes, even "Big Q", he was behind this in all probability.

After a night spent drinking, and then a brutal session with Gill, he felt better, a whole lot better. Gill's girlfriends found her next morning, badly beaten up. They pleaded with her to report Haigh to security, but she refused point blank; perhaps even now she could save him from himself. She loved him, despite his terrible treatment of her.

Chapter Fifteen

A little coaching from "Big Q" and Friends

'What we have to learn to do we learn by doing'
Aristotle

The next few weeks were spent in getting Grant into shape for the Continental Championships. Many of the events were standard stuff like running, jumping, throwing, fencing, and unarmed combat. There was however some rather unusual competitions, which together with the complex format of scoring, needed to be studied in detail.

Williams took on the role of Trainer; regular workouts with him would keep Grant in excellent condition for the more physical contests.

Colonel Foster volunteered to take care of the other events, requiring rather more specialist knowledge. He also became Grant's Mentor for the whole project. "Big Q", in planning the games, had taken some considerable time to come up with the exact mix of events, which could ensure only the most outstanding competitor becoming champion. For example, there seemed little point in shooting at a fixed or even a gyrating target. The real test was to blast away at a human target, who incidentally was trying to eliminate you at the same time.

The games were also more than just a test of brawn, reflex action and physical power, but were designed to assess mental agility and intellect as well. To this end a complex form of chess known as three dimensional chess was included, together with a card game called Pule. Foster was worried about his protégé's chances in these two competitions, mainly because Grant had had no experience of them. He voiced his misgivings. Grant put his arm around the Colonel's shoulders, and indicated his willingness to give them both his very best shot.

Foster patiently took Grant through the basics of Pule. After thirty seconds the pupil started to smirk behind his hand. He let the Colonel finish his tutoring, and then suggested they play a hand or two, just to get the feel of it. To Foster's amazement John Grant trounced him, winning game after game, until he held all of the little plastic colored discs which they were playing for.

'You lucky bastard, must be beginners luck; complained the good Colonel. Grant had to gently inform him that Pule was a very old game, and that there was a short period in his life, when at College, that he had made rather a lot of money out of his skill at this particular pastime, which was then called Poker. The real problem was the 3d chess. Whilst Grant had represented Cambridge at the conventional game, he was not familiar with the three dimensional development. A lot of concentrated work was going to be necessary.

During the next few days Grant visited "Big Q" regularly with Foster, and was rigorously coached in the finer points of the futuristic game of chess. Using the same mental processes as he had already been subjected to on coming into this alien world, he was taught every major game played by Grand

Masters in the last hundred years. It was of course one thing to memorise the moves, it was a totally different proposition to have to actually use some of them against a skilled opponent. Foster was a "Grand Master," and past champion of the Americas Continent. Grant faced Foster across the 3d chess tower, and after ten consecutive defeats - most of them in less than twelve moves - began to hate him, with an intensity which hurt.

Foster, who had begun to feel real affection for Grant, could see how defeat was affecting him. Very cleverly he started to build up his confidence, and soon John was taking the odd game or two; some more private sessions with "Big Q", and the electronic educator, and Grant had reached his full potential. He would never be a Grand Master, but could now more than hold his own against sixty-five percent of the men he would meet in competition.

Colonel Foster now turned his attention from chess, to strategy in the competition as a whole. Grant could not help smiling, as the little roly-poly man got into his stride - just like his old headmaster at prep school, now long since dead. He listened intently, as he knew that much depended on him absorbing information quickly.

'John, pay attention,' lectured the Colonel. 'The games are in two separate parts. Part one constitutes: Chess, Pule, Standing Jump, Discus and the Mile race. Part two: Fencing, Unarmed Combat, and the Shoot Out. The top six in part one, go through to the final stage. The Jump and the Run are straight forward. We have analyzed your current form, and compared it with the competition this year. You should finish sixth or better in the Jump with a probability of 90.384 percent, sixth or better in the Run with an 87.864 percent probability and sixth or better in the Throwing event at 89.126 percent probability. I cannot see you being bested at pule, but you never know. Chess; there are some very good exponents of the art, the computer gives you only a 58.123 percent chance of finishing in the top six. Taking everything into account, the computer gives you a 91.374 percent chance of making the final six. Any question so far?'

'No, Sir. I don't think so, but I must say it all sounds very simple, there must be a catch somewhere.'

'Clever lad,' continued Foster. 'There is a major problem, or should we say nineteen problems; each of your fellow competitors will be using all sorts of underhand tricks to give them an edge. You will soon have another session with "Big Q", to help you guard against such eventualities. To give you a couple of examples of methods that you may encounter: the mind probe can be used very effectively, particularly with a strong will, against a weaker mind. Putting a little something in the food or drink is also popular. Remember, on no account must you retaliate in kind, otherwise the experiment is doomed from the start.' Grant nodded agreement.

'Once you reach the last six your troubles really start,' went on Foster quickly, hardly pausing for breath. 'It is well to take into account that all your points, from part one go forward to the second phase. Each event counts equally. The "Shoot-out" consists of a round robin between the six finalists. At this stage nobody gets hurt despite the "Wild West" nature of the event. The weapons are low powered laser handguns. The contestants wear special suits which relay "hits" to the computer. When a man is "dead", that is according to the computer, or so badly "wounded" as to be unable to carry on, the shoot-out ends. Points are awarded according to individual performance and hits.

Unarmed combat is the penultimate event; again a round-robin. This is where the really dirty stuff starts, and although each fight is well monitored, and stopped immediately there is a submission, it is of course quite possible to end a challenge, particularly if your opponent happens to be ahead of you in the overall competition, permanently... It is not unknown for a really good unarmed combat man to end the whole contest at this stage, particularly if he happens to be trailing in the competition. You may say that this is unfair, but I believe that although "Big Q" theoretically made all events equal, in fact the really exciting combat bouts can play a much bigger part in deciding the winner; this by design of the "Ultimate Computer"' - Foster added theatrically. 'The top two only go forward to the fencing, and in this event are completely unprotected; exactly like in your duel with Haigh.'

'I assume at this stage,' interjected Grant at last, 'that the only event which counts is the fencing.'

'That, young man is quite correct' affirmed Foster, fixing Grant with a knowing expression. 'But it is your best event you know,' he added with a smile.

The two men talked on for a while before Grant went off for another session with "Big Q". His computer friend was most forthcoming, and gave him a complete profile on all competitors in the continental games; their strengths and weaknesses in each contest. Most importantly "Q" talked about each man's morality; or lack of it: this man had a very strong mind and used it whenever he thought it would give him an advantage; that man would try and disable his opponent, permanently, whenever an opportunity presented itself; another was an expert in poisoning techniques, whether via food and drink, or simply by touch, through the skin.

Only good manners prevented Grant from interrupting this flow of information, but finally "Big Q" had finished, and commented 'I believe you have been dying to ask a question.'

'Yes "Q" I have, how on earth have your people managed

to get themselves into such a state of mind? - No, don't answer that! I already know from previous discussion with yourself and Foster. The real question is how the hell they cure themselves?'

'Social inertia is a massive thing,' answered "Q". 'When people are set in their ways, it takes something very special to change them. Consider the German people, under Hitler, in the thirties and early forties of the twentieth century. He changed them into a fighting machine with one aim in mind, the conquest of the world. Once set on this course only total defeat could halt them. Take the beginning of the Twentieth Century when Britain was threatened, because of successive Governments naïve attitude to so many things; it took an ice cold shock, from a determined reconstituted British Government to move their people into a much more realistic climate. In our case I believe much depends upon you,' the computer concluded.

There really was nothing more to be said, and Grant left soon afterwards with the weight of a planet on his shoulders.

'What am I going to do?' he asked his friend Williams later. 'Do they really expect me to succeed in changing the attitudes of the Billion or so people left on earth?'

'Don't take it so seriously John, you are, probably, one of several options that "Q" has. You can only do your best, remember what our mother used to say: "Do your best and shame the devil", and I think that this is very good advice under the circumstances.' So saying he clapped Grant a blow across the shoulders which made his friend wince.

'Come on lad, let's go and grab a drink before they close' the various bars in the City were serviced by humans, rather than robots. You still couldn't pour out troubles to a robot like you could to a barman or barmaid. They selected a bar at random and were soon surrounded by people, all wanting to speak to them, and ask them questions; attention they could well do without. However, they thought that it would be a good thing to please the natives, and chatted to them good naturedly.

This was the first totally classless society that Grant and Williams had ever seen; although very practically so. In theory every person in the city had exactly the same rights and privileges as the Commander. In practice the only over-riding consideration was the comfort and wellbeing of all. In other words Cord and his security forces could take what steps they considered necessary for the safety and security of the city; the rights of citizens under these circumstances were secondary. But - and this was the important factor - every decision by the security forces was monitored by "Q". Power was not allowed to corrupt in this era.

The system reminded Grant of China in the twentieth century. Here, when at work, all the citizens wore the same type of one piece clothing: the men in yellow, the women in green,' exceptions were the "mothers" in purple and the security forces who sported a very distinctive red. Those who were off duty could wear almost anything that they desired, and this led to a tremendous gaiety of colors and styles; indeed some of the women went around topless. To all this variety was added the blue of the "City Guardians" and just occasionally the white of a visiting continental champion, or the gold of a world champion - the city had not achieved that sort of success for a great number of years.

Like communist China the uniformity of working clothes, in this era, was instrumental in overcoming class barriers, making for greater efficiency. There was a general lack of the simple minded unskilled and semi-skilled worker, and no disabled; due to the genetic engineering programme, this meant that everyone in the City had to carry out a few hours community work a week like: tending the bars, waiting on table, and supervising the army of robots which carried out functions like cleaning, manufacturing and food processing.

Even highly qualified people like doctors, teachers, and engineers served their time on the more menial tasks. Williams and Grant managed to shoulder their way to the bar 'Two of your very best please my good fellow' said Peter.

'That is not the way that you address the citizens, even if they are serving you drinks,' said a voice that both instantly recognized. Cord stood behind the bar - doing his weekly community service.

'Sorry Commander' said the two in unison, somewhat sheepishly.

'I think that I had better put you two on the list for the robot sewage cleaning operations next week' mused Cord. 'Anyway, what is your pleasure, gentlemen?'

'Some of your excellent beer I think' said Grant.

'Coming up'

'Thank you very much... Commander!'

They took their drinks over to a corner table where they got embroiled in a discussion with a wizened old man in royal blue, on the state of the games now, and what it used to be like ninety years ago when he had been champion. The man admitted to being a hundred and twenty years old. 'I like the way you handle yourself,' he said to Grant. Grant's training programme had been well covered by the Holo-pic people, and he had been interviewed numerous times.

'What are my chances do you think old timer?' he asked.

'Not so much of the old, if you please: was the spirited reply. 'I could still see you off if I were twenty years younger.'

'Sorry... Sir, no offence meant, but I would be glad of your opinion,' Grant asked kindly.

'None taken young man. I believe that your chances are very good, certainly there is, at this time, only one other person on earth capable of beating you with the sword, a lad named Henderson from Europe, and you won't meet him until the world championships; providing you get that far. You have certain weaknesses in your other events. You should be more aggressive in the unarmed combat section, and you really need to work harder at your chess, some of the mistakes you make are childish.'

Grant thanked the ancient city champion, and assured him that he would certainly try and do something about these criticisms. It was refreshing to hear an educated opinion expressed by someone who was not close to him.

Almost everyone he met was a games addict; offering encouragement and advice. This population lived for the games, and Grant was sure that without them Homo-sapiens would have long disappeared from earth.

After his session with John Grant, Colonel Foster took a ground car out of the city. He kept clear of the twenty lane vehicle way grid system which connected the cities in the Americas continent. His city had been built on prairie land, and was clear for hundreds of miles around. Colin Foster drove around for a while, as he often did for relaxation He went on at a steady eighty miles per hour until he was beyond the horizon of the city, and it was getting dark. He stopped the transporter; called in to let them know he was all right, and then got out to stretch his legs.

Foster was one of those rarities - the truly happy contented man. He knew that he had achieved his maximum possible goals; both in rank and in mental and physical attainment. "Big Q" called the shots and knew exactly a man's capabilities. He would never make the council - and all that worry! He had become city champion, and had reached number eight in the continental games - it seemed like yesterday, and had been a marvelous experience.

In the "Master Index" Foster's rating was 95.1467 percent. Only a thousand other people on earth, at this time, bettered this figure; one was President of the World Council, yet another was John Grant. The index, devised by "Big Q" was the result of a detailed study on every conceivable characteristic and aspect of a person's abilities.

The index considered such features as basic intelligence - I.Q. testing used to cover this area; but on its own was considered useless. The ability to jump through hoops; to solve paper exercises is no good, without, common sense. "Big Q" had a sub-index for this previously indefinable quality. Other sub-index values were given for contentment, fulfillment, physical powers, leadership, organizational ability and E.S.P. facility. There was even an emotional quotient!

Foster looked up at the stars, they were very bright against the blackness, covering the heavens in their unique pattern.

'Will man ever make it up there again?' He said aloud, and then caught himself, and laughed; they do say that's the first sign of madness, he thought.

Yes, it's been a good life he reflected, nothing missing, nothing left out. There was always something of interest to get your teeth into. Take the time jumpers for example; they seemed to get fewer and fewer over the years, and then had come Grant and Williams - now there were real men! What fun the next few months would be. Foster licked his lips with anticipation. He was delighted to be a part of this crucial period - he liked talking to "Big Q"; sometimes they would philosophize for hours about a tremendous range of subjects. Because of the colonel's high index rating "Big Q" regularly took him into his confidence and asked his advice. That is how

Foster knew how critical the coming months would be; and Grant's involvement in it all.

Colin Foster was a very popular man; well thought of by almost everyone. He had never married; being unable to tie himself to one woman; instead, at the age of forty-four he had contented himself with a range of mistresses. The ladies liked this little chubby man immensely, and went with him not just because of his rank, but also because of his wonderfully exuberant nature. The Colonel got back into his vehicle, pointed it towards the glow of the horizon that was the city, and went home.

Chapter Sixteen

Williams has a Fight, and Wins a Lady's Gratitude

'Faint heart never won a fair lady'
Euripides

The days passed very quickly, and Grant was steadily reaching his peak. This had been calculated to occur exactly at the beginning of the championships. Every phase of training had been planned precisely by "Big Q", and on the basis of all work and no play makes "Jack a dull boy" it had ordered that John be given two complete days off, just before the contest. So it was that Grant, Williams and Sara - "Q" had given its blessing for her to be a part of the break from routine - found them at the city Arts Hall. The occasion was a concert of Beethoven's Symphonies.

The finale was his Ninth - "The Choral". Both men had been emotionally affected, and Grant had shed tears as the major work reached its conclusion. The fact that composers such as Beethoven, Mozart and Tchaikovsky had endured for so long did not surprise either John or Peter. In both their opinions nothing really decent had been written after the late nineteenth century; this opinion had since been vindicated by their experiences in this time period - the fact that the music of such composers had endured through the ages.

'I believe' observed Williams, 'that when the achievements of this planet are toted up by God, that music will come top of the list.' Grant indicated his agreement. 'I think that I would prefer our own computer generated music' commented Sara. 'Some of our "Principal Composers" have been likened to the great musicians of the past.'

'Yes, they aren't too bad' commented Grant. 'But surely the combination of man and computer gives music that lacks that certain something.'

The old masters gave their music soul. They had the ability to lift man spiritually, to bring him nearer his maker. Music, partially generated by a mere machine - even "Big Q" - will never achieve such heights.' Sara pouted, and then made a face. 'I will never understand you John Grant - you have such funny ideas.' Grant kissed her tenderly. 'I still love you even if you are a music Philistine.'

'Don't mind me,' quipped Williams. 'But don't blame me if you get arrested for indecency in a public place.'

'Let's go and eat,' suggested Grant. 'I feel rather humble and very hungry after that experience.'

The two men had been working hard; the championships were just a few days away, and they really deserved this little break. The City was in a state of excitement, and the two time travelers were now well known. Everywhere they went they were greeted like friends, and wished the best of luck. The City had not had a Continental Champion for over a hundred years, and its representative had always failed at the final contest for champion of Earth, except for one rare occasion over three hundred years ago.

Walking into the best eating establishment in the City, they were well received by the head waiter - his normal job was Chief Engineer - who said, 'It is a great pleasure to have you here, if there is anything I can do for you, you have only to ask.'

The restaurant compared well with the best that Grant had experienced: the Ritz, Savoy, and Claridges. There were rich furnishings, and expensive looking paintings on the walls, and a five piece orchestra was playing. The lights were soft and unobtrusive, altogether a wonderful setting.

They ordered after an aperitif, and found the food and wine absolutely first class. It transpired that the cooking in this establishment was done by human chefs, and for that reason, had that touch of class unattained by the computerized systems of food preparation which was normal. You can't design Homo-sapiens out of the system completely, thought Grant. The best Music, food, literature and architecture is still created by us.

The three were just on their second cup of coffee, when a group of men came in, they were laughing and joking; a lot of alcohol had been consumed, and they appeared dangerously drunk. Grant wondered why, even in this age, they hadn't taken the kick out of alcohol. He quickly came to the conclusion that most of the fun in drinking was derived from the effect of intoxication that alcohol produced.

Two women were quietly eating at a corner table when two of the drunks started to pester them. They wanted to join them, and became very belligerent when they were refused. A waiter tried to remonstrate with the two men, but was knocked to the floor. It was then that Grant recognized Haigh, and his second from their previous encounter.

Williams and Grant got up despite Sara's plea to be careful. 'Security will take care of them,' she cried.

'Stop that, now!' ordered Grant. Haigh and his friend spun round. At the sight of his old adversary, Julian Haigh quickly sobered up. Williams got to the table first, one of the girls was weeping, and the other was trying to console her. Williams was so overcome with rage that he struck Haigh. With a sly smile on his face Haigh turned to Grant.

'I cannot challenge you again because of the rules, but the next best thing is to challenge and kill your friend. As soon as he hit me, he effectively challenged me, which means that I may choose the form of combat. It will be unarmed combat to the death, tomorrow, at noon. 'I look forward to that,' growled Williams. 'In fact we could have it out here and now if you wish.'

'You had better tell your stupid friend about our code of conduct, Grant.' So saying, Haigh and his sidekick made a rapid departure from the establishment. Grant and Williams turned to the two women to see how they were. They were very concerned about the escalation of the situation. One of them, red eyed from her ordeal, kissed a blushing Williams. 'Thank you for saving us' she murmured 'would you like to join us?' Williams readily agreed, and Grant, with Sara thought that it would be impolite to refuse.

Introductions were made. It transpired that Tara and Clare were sisters, and worked for the City Civil Authority. Tara, who had been the one to reward Williams, seemed much taken with him, and he reciprocated her obvious affection. For two hours they all put the confrontation to the back of their minds, whilst they had an extremely enjoyable time. The girls seemed to get on famously, and all had now gained their composure.

Later that evening, having dropped the girls off, they went to their quarters. In the lounge, over a nightcap, they discussed the impending fight. Williams did not seem too concerned; after all Haigh had selected Peter's "piece de resistance". Nevertheless Grant felt that "Big Q" ought to be consulted, and asked for any help that he could give. Grant had had a computer terminal installed in his room, giving him direct access to his electronic friend.

On contacting "Big Q" they were mildly rebuked for having got into trouble in the first place.

'What is done is done' commented the computer rather unnecessarily.

'The point is, can you help Peter? Please "Q" implored Grant. 'Ah! Well! Let me see now, Haigh will try his mental attack, which will do him no good at all due to Peter's low E.S.P. reception. Now what else? Oh! Yes, unarmed combat is Haigh's specialty too, he has killed four men to date, and was continental champion last year in the event.'

'When are you going to tell us the bad news? 'Asked Grant. "Big Q" continued as if it hadn't heard 'Haigh has been regularly subjected to physical and mental scans by me as a matter of course. He is in superb condition and has been in training for some time now.'

'OK! OK!' interjected Williams impatiently, 'you have my scans and profile, what is your prognosis?'

'Patience, Peter, patience,' boomed the computer, 'Haigh fights in a style called Sorta; I suppose a mixture of Karate and Judo.' His technique is superior to yours.'

'Thanks!'

'But your sheer staying power and toughness should see you through.'

'Thanks again!'

'Probability of success,' intoned "Big Q", '32.121 percent in the first ten minutes increasing to a value of 61.321 percent thereafter. Your tactics are obvious!'

***

The first part of the fight went to plan. Williams kept his opponent at bay with a series of defensive ploys; backpedalling and refusing to join in major physical contact." Sorta seemed to involve a lot of shouting and chanting, but Williams stuck to his task. After some time spent moving his opponent about the area, with minimal contact, Williams became more aggressive, and executed a minor throw which seemed to annoy Haigh. Immediately he hurled himself at Williams, who was overjoyed at this indiscretion and proceeded to kick his opponent high over his head. Haigh landed in an untidy heap.

At this stage, of course, Williams should have gone in to finish the job. Grant, in fact, was calling to him to do just that. Williams was oblivious to it all, he dashed across to Haigh to see how he was, and to administer to him if necessary. Thoughts of fighting to the death evaporated.

His opponent was moaning; in fact he was only winded. Once Williams was close enough Haigh aimed a Karate style punch to the heart. Fortunately for Peter, Haigh's heavy fall had weakened the force of the blow. Nevertheless it hurt Williams a lot; in fact it may have killed him, if he hadn't managed to ride it a little. He sank to his knees under the treacherous attack. This gave Haigh more valuable time to recover. He got to his feet, and aimed a deadly blow at the injured Williams throat; Peter rolled away and shook his head, trying to clear the scarlet curtain that threatened to engulf him. This experience had probably cured Williams of being "soft" for the rest of his life; providing he survived the next few minutes, that is. Survive is what Williams did; after another ten minutes Haigh had taken another couple of falls and was sweating and panting for breath. One thing that must be said for him was his courage; a pity he did not have the moral responsibility to go with it.

Williams held Haigh in a Judo neck hold, squeezing the life out of him, there was now no mercy in Peter's soul, Haigh had to be killed so that he was no longer a blight on the lives of others. A quick twist and his neck was broken. Williams threw the lifeless body from him; his shoulders slumped with hurt and fatigue. Grant helped him away. A bully had got his just desert; but this thought gave the friends no comfort at all.

The crowd of a few hundred who had watched the confrontation, and the unfortunate result, were silent, opening up to let the two men through. They were met by Cord and Foster, who quickly assessed the situation, and hurried them away without comment.

Tara and Clare had been unable to bring themselves to watch the combat that they had precipitated; and had waited in a hallway, close to the area where Williams was suffering his "trial by combat" Their relief was obvious as Peter came through the door, and Tara ran to greet him; embracing and kissing him. This show of affection cheered him up, and it was in a little better frame of mind that he and Grant discussed the fight, and its implications, later, with the city Commander, although Peter was still very upset.

'No one blames you in any way for what happened' said Cord. 'No more than a handful of people will weep over Haigh's death tonight.'

'Will this affect the plan?' asked Williams.

'I doubt it,' answered Cord. 'Haigh was disliked by almost everyone that he came into contact with, and there have been several attempts on his life. "Q" says not to worry about it...'

'Come on Peter if "Q" says not to worry about it, we won't'

commented Grant. 'In any case I need you to see me through the competition. If you are going to mope around feeling sorry for yourself, you will be no help to me at all.' Grant knew that he had to shake Peter out of his depression, before it got the better of him.

'Sorry John didn't know I was being that much of a pain' was the reply. 'You can rely on me, but I would like to be left alone for just a little while.' Grant and Cord appreciated the situation, and left Williams to his thoughts.

***

Gill Prean greeted the news of Haigh's death with silence. She knew that he richly deserved it, but when you loved someone, you accepted all their faults; no matter what they were.

In her own mind she blamed the system. The two visitors from the past had just been unfortunate to be involved in that system. What was to be done now? Curiously enough she enjoyed her work. The city looked after her, and she was supplying a useful service, and satisfying a demand undiminished since time began.

Gill shrugged her shoulders in resignation, perhaps she might meet someone, someday, and who would be kind to her; would cherish and love her. Then the reaction set in, and she cried her heart out. Hours later, after a good sleep, she was ready for her evening trade and perhaps that "Mr. Right..."

***

The local Holo news programs were full of the fight. It had been recorded by an enterprising young cameraman, and the action replays were shown over and over again in front of an enthralled audience. Haigh's previous record was trotted out and illustrated, using 3d holograms of his previous triumphs. Deaths due to the games, and the duels were fairly commonplace, and next day the Haigh story had been forgotten to be replaced by coverage of the buildup to the annual Continental Championships.

Julian Haigh's body was consigned to the atomic disintegrator on the outskirts of the city, after a short service performed by a Roman Catholic priest. Only three people turned up. Gill, Grant and Williams. The citizens were very coy as far as the aftermath of death was concerned. They enjoyed the spectacle of dying, but steered clear of its reality.

Chapter Seventeen

Grant Shows his Mettle

'Fortune favors the brave'
Terence

The Americas championship was to be held in the "First City". When examining records and plans of the capital city, Grant discovered that it had been established on the site of New York, although all evidence had now long since disappeared.

The "First City" was a carbon copy of the "Eleventh City" where Grant and Williams had spent such an eventful few weeks. The only real difference was that the "Twenty Cities Council" was held at regular intervals in the capital, and this required some fairly extensive administrative arrangements. Further research had unearthed the fact that all the cities on the planet were built to exactly the same specification.

Grant had realized, some time ago, just what a boring period this really was: the sameness, the lack of adventure and excitement unless artificially produced. Both he and Williams could see what a tremendous task confronted the giant computer. If you take away man's hopes and dreams, his expectations for the future; if you stifle his development, for whatever reason, what has he got left?

It was decided that Foster would accompany Grant and Williams to the championships. Cord said he had to stop behind to mind the shop. At Grant's request the journey was to be made via a twenty lane vehicle way, using a ground car. He had already examined satellite data of the Americas continent, and wanted to see something of it at ground level.

There was nothing left of twenty first century America, "Big Q" had seen to that. All physical ties with the past had been destroyed. The computer had decided that the less experience earth's population had of the past, the better. The decision was based on the principle of what you haven't seen you won't miss. For this reason there had been a huge clear up operation mounted when the city system had been established, hundreds of years ago. Now earths people only had books and videos as a record of their antiquity - not nearly so damaging to them, psychologically, as real artifacts and structures from the past.

Many cars used the vehicle way travelling at speed up to 250 mph. Although each car had a computer control facility, many people still liked the thrill of driving by themselves without aid. For this reason there was a regular patrol of traffic security men along the vehicle way. Just like the old days, with traffic cops, thought Grant. "The more things change the more they remain the same".

Foster decided to trust the automatic driving facility, and the group settled back in the very comfortable seats ready to enjoy the journey. They were shadowed throughout the trip by a security vehicle - just in case!!

Looking out of the viewing windows Grant was fascinated to see the wide open plains, eventually giving way to huge fields of wheat, vegetables, and other plants from which the meat tasting compounds were produced. Great forests purified the planet's air. Wild deer could be clearly seen in herds moving through the trees.

They were three quarters of the way to their destination, when Foster received a message that there had been a major accident up ahead.

'Damn teenagers,' muttered the Colonel.

It transpired that two teenage-gangs had decided to play "chicken" on the outer fast lane, in their exceptional powerful vehicles. Unfortunately for them, and several other ground cars, they touched whilst one was trying to overtake the other, went out of control and swerved over onto the slower lanes, hitting two cars, which in turn side-swiped more cars. The result? Absolute chaos, seven of the ten lanes being closed for up to two hours whilst ambulances and the vehicle way clearing equipment were sent for. They were waved through and past the carnage. Ten people were dead and another fifteen badly injured. The men from the past had seen it all before on the motor-ways of twenty-first century England.

Foster commented that these, virtual, suicide runs were increasing all the time - just another ramification of the current problems confronting the authorities.

They finally arrived at the "First City" without further incident.

The first day of the Games and the twenty participants were divided into four groups of five for the initial competition; pule. The contestants were selected in order of past performances with seeds placed in each group. "Big Q" had seeded Grant at four. He easily won his group despite several attempts at mental pressure. The final groups and Grant had a terrible run of bad luck with the squares of plastic. The squares were automatically fed from a machine monitored by "Big Q", and although he knew that there was no possibility of the forty-eight squares being rigged; it certainly seemed like it as he lost pot after pot of the small colored discs which were being gambled for. He bluffed and went through the full range of his considerable skills, to no avail; he finished last of the group of four playing for positions one to four.

Williams consoled him, and told him that it wasn't a bad start. One of the group members Tibor Orlowsky, who finished second - a favorite for the title - shook Grant's hand. At the time Grant barely noticed the faint prick. It was only a few minutes afterwards that he started to feel faint, and guessed that he had committed the cardinal sin of allowing physical unmonitored contact. He had been poisoned. Such poison was usually lethal.

Grant, accompanied by a distraught Williams, was rushed to the nearest medical facility. His blood was replaced, and his stomach emptied. The medical team was highly skilled and experienced with this sort of thing - it seemed that they got plenty of practice. Apparently there was only a one in five chance of pulling through this sort of ordeal; but a quick thinking medical assistant had injected what he thought was a suitable antidote to the poison almost immediately after Grant had become distressed. Luckily he had selected the right one, and the worst effects of the poison had been neutralized.

Several hours later Grant was pronounced fit a statement that he stridently disagreed with. In fact he felt far from fit and wished that he had died. Imagine the effects of a long bout of sea-sickness. He felt as if he had been turned inside out.

'How on earth am I going to compete tomorrow, feeling like this?' He complained to Williams.

'The doctor said that there is no reason why you shouldn't.'

'Well, all I can say is that he has never gone through the process of being tortured like this' was the bitter comment.

***

The next day's event was to be the Standing Jump. Grant's best effort in practice had been fifteen feet two inches. Under the circumstances he was fortunate to make thirteen feet eleven and a half inches. This gave him ninth place, when he should have expected much more. Things were not going well at all.

'We cannot afford any more slip ups,' commented Williams. 'Even if you make the final six, by no means certain, the carry forward score will not be all that good. There are some very good lads in the leading six who still have their best events to come.'

As it happened one of the six lost all interest in the competition; he was found with his neck broken early next morning.

The next competition was 3d chess, a favorite with many of the population, who eagerly watched each match on their Holo-pic systems. Chess was undoubtedly Grant's poorest event; but what was worse was that he now had very little leeway in the competition as a whole, due to his poor showing in the last event. Then came a bit of luck which was to prove crucial. In the groups, which were again seeded, he had the good fortune to be in the dead man's set, which effectively promoted him to third seed in the group instead of fourth.

In the round robin, which ensued, Grant did in fact finish third. This meant that in the reconstituted groupings for the final places he made group three, battling it out for placing's numbers nine to twelve. Playing at his very best he managed tenth position - an extremely good result for him considering that sixteenth place was the most he could have expected.

The third day and the throwing event; the discus. This required absolute skill and precision. Technique was crucially important, with strength a close second. This event was very old even in Grant's "normal" time period, and it was amazing that it had lasted as a major event down through the ages. The competitors had six throws from an eight feet two and a half inch circle.

From the early nineteen-sixties onwards there had been tremendous controversy on measurement units, the metric versus imperial battle had raged into the twenty-first century. The Americans, in the early nineteen-sixties, had specified a totally metric space programme, to encourage the movement to Systeme' Internationale. The American public, however, still maintained their beloved feet, inches, yards, pounds and tons. Ultimately the whole argument fizzled out. With computers and microelectronics it was just as simple to use one as the other. As far as Grant could see in this age the imperial system was used for the classic athletic measurement, whilst the metric held sway in the technological disciplines; although individuals could choose for themselves.

An athletics coach would have described Grant's technique as text book. The only problem was his lack of bulk. Again "Big Q" had chosen well; competitors, who would do poorly in the standing jump, would probably do a lot better in the throwing event. Grant's first throw was perfect, he rotated smoothly in the circle, building up speed, getting the transfer of weight just right, before releasing the four pound six and a half ounce projectile a distance of around three hundred feet. This massive throw gave him third placing in the event; very satisfactory, especially as some of the leading contenders hadn't fared so well.

Next, the run. To just make the last six Grant had to win the foot race, which was to be held over one mile. There were conditions under which he could finish third and still make it; but this pre-supposed bad placing's from other leading members of the championship.

The mile had always been the Blue Riband event at athletics meetings in the distant past, and it appeared that it had remained so. The sports stadium was packed to capacity, with at least two hundred thousand cheering people, eagerly awaiting the main event of the day.

They had many other diversions to keep them amused, as the ladies and junior championships were being held simultaneously with the men's. But there was no doubt what the huge crowd had really come for, and as the appointed time approached there was a mood of expectancy, building to something like ecstasy as the competitors were announced in turn.

It was then that Grant realized, with horror that all nineteen competitors were to run at once; he saw now why the crowd were working themselves up to such frenzy. It was like a Roman Circus. This had certainly been a serious omission in his preparation; but he had to make the best of it. Grant decided, then, that he would run from the front; the whole four laps.

The starting hooter went, and Grant left the starting line like a greyhound, just missing an outstretched foot, trying to trip him. He had been a forty-five second quarter miler in his

Varsity days - within Olympic qualifying time - and quickly opened up a thirty yard gap.

Already the track behind him was littered with sprawling bodies; in fact by the end of the second lap he was rapidly catching up on some of the stragglers who had been so disposed.

He needn't have worried about interference with his progress as they were all attempting to improve their positions, and in any case he was tiring fast. He was no longer a twenty-one year old Cambridge Blue, but, now a rather jaded thirty-four year old. John Grant gave the last two laps his all, and won with two yards to spare, amidst tremendous enthusiasm; the crowd had never seen anything like it; and cheered him to the echo. This result gave Grant fifth position overall. The next two days were rest days, and he certainly needed it. During this period the eliminated thirteen fought it out for the minor placing's which to them and their supporters were extremely important.

***

And so to the fourth day. The "Shootout took place in a specially constructed arena, consisting of narrow ways, open spaces, and cover. Each contestant had a laser handgun capable of six shots only. Grant rather enjoyed this part of the Championships; it was like the old westerns that he had seen as a boy. It was particularly pleasant, as nobody could be killed, or indeed hurt - just like childhood games.

The "round robin" took all morning to complete, and by the end Grant was slightly ahead with one match to play. The seedings had operated so that he was paired with Orlowsky in the final round - as it happened the computer was absolutely correct; Orlowsky was in second place. Whoever won this match would take the event. Orlowsky almost immediately scored a hit - catching Grant off guard - which the giant score board above their heads registered as a level three wound, level one was the least serious, level five; you were dead.

The action took place under a glass, sound proofed, cover so that the huge crowd could witness the whole thing. They, of course, were in the privileged position of seeing the action unwinding; the two men, crouching behind the plastic walls, scurrying along the passageways moving quickly across the open areas.

Grant had loosed off four shots without even singeing his opponent. Orlowsky had fired five times, but had caught Grant again as he was running from cover to cover; this time a level two hit in the leg. Because of Grant's relatively mediocre showing in some of the previous events, he really had to win this one. His only hope was a "kill". Grant could now afford to take chances - if the worst came to the worst he would finish second anyway. He decided to draw Orlowsky to him, by showing himself. His opponent would have to be careful with only one shot remaining. It worked! Tibor Orlowsky hesitated for a split second, when both had a sight of each other, and Grant's two last shots took him in the chest. The scoreboard flashed a "kill" and that was that.

In the penultimate event, anything could happen. Although Grant knew that he had edged into second place with his result in the shoot-out, a broken arm or worse in the "Unarmed Combat" section would of course eliminate him. A submission or an inability to defend oneself signaled an immediate end to a match. Electronic monitors made certain that anyone continuing after this point was detected, and punished by disqualification; however, a lot of damage would be inflicted during the bout itself. It was common practice to scan all competitors, to prevent any poisoning incidents of the type that had so nearly laid Grant low earlier.

There was no seeding in this event, and in round one Grant found himself up against Orlowsky, who had gained a healthy respect for this outsider. He was so cautious that he was quickly overcome, and tamely submitted under a simple arm lock; Grant thought that there must be some other reason for his lethargy.

The other pairings produced some bitterly fought results. One man was killed outright with a chop to the throat. Another lost interest in the proceedings with a broken leg; the result of a heavy fall.

Grant thought about the "Ten Little Indian Boys" he hoped the next one to go wouldn't be him. Orlowsky didn't seem to be doing as well as he lost again; then collapsed. A quick check showed that he had been drugged. Despite all the safeguards, somehow a drug had been introduced into his system. 'Poetic justice, I suppose,' was Grant's considered opinion.

John Grant needed to win just one more bout to reach the final. His next match was against a Julius Grozier; a giant of a man. He had the power to break Grant in two if he laid hands on him. Ducking and weaving Grant kept out of trouble, whilst aiming subtle blows to critical pressure points on the man's frame. He made certain that the blows merely slowed the man down, and would not incapacitate him permanently. This fact was not lost on the, largely, knowledgeable crowd. Instead of killing the man at the end of this exercise, Grant simply asked him if he would like to submit - Grozier did! This was absolutely unheard of in recent times. Under normal circumstances no mercy was shown to such a weakened opponent.

After Grant's earlier sportsmanship with Haigh, when he

had allowed him to pick up his weapon, (this was public knowledge) and now this; some older people remembered the days gone by when such honorable behavior was normal. A buzz of conversation spread round the arena, then isolated bursts of clapping; in minutes the whole crowd had joined in as they spontaneously paid tribute to Grant.

There was one other match between Grozier and a man by the name of Carl Schultz. Schultz had really come from the back in the competition as a whole. One could not help feeling that much of his success was due more to luck and under-handedness, than to actual skill. The winner would meet Grant in the final. This brawl; it could not be called anything else, was obscene. It ended with the death of Julius, killed when his back was broken; totally unnecessarily. The crowd was silent; then started to cry out with dissatisfaction; finally booing. Schultz strode off the combat area, whilst his opponent was dragged out feet first.

The final event, on the fifth day, was a complete anti-climax, Grant totally out-classing Carl Schultz with cool superior swordsmanship. The fight ended with Schultz, totally unmarked, being disarmed and submitting after sixty-three seconds. Losers at this stage were usually carted off to the surgeons; or undertakers.

***

Grant was fated as champion of the Continent; everyone wanted to shake his hand. Foster was beside himself with glee. Williams jumped up and down on the spot with sheer joy. They were presented to the leader of the Twenty Cities Council before going off to the banquet held in Grant's honor.

The "Eleventh City" representatives took their places at

the top table, and Grant found that Sara was there next to him, they embraced and kissed.

'Sara!! What a marvelous surprise,' said a very happy Champion.

'Yes darling, we have Commander Cord to thank for this. He was so positive that you would win, that we came over yesterday, to watch today's events. Well done John, you were absolutely tremendous, but that's not the only reason that I love you.'

Commander Cord brought the general chatter to a sudden halt, when he proposed a toast to the Champion of the Americas, and the fervent hope that Grant would be successful in the final conflict; in the battle for the supreme title "Champion of Earth".

Later that night Grant and Williams got away from the celebrations, and back to the sleeping quarters. They were both utterly tired, and staggered into Grant's room for a night-cap, before retiring. Opening the door John Grant got the shock of his life...

Chapter Eighteen

A Visitor from the Past

'We are Tomorrow's past'
Mary Webb

Sitting on Grant's bed, blinking in the light, was an "old friend" of the men. Cato sat there; large as life, and very very ugly. The last time they had seen him was in Judea, during the crucifixion. Again, as in their first meeting, he had them at a distinct disadvantage; a weapon in his hand. He waved them over to the far wall.
Williams spoke first. 'How did you get here? I thought that all your kind had been eliminated after the crucifixion.'
For the first time Grant had a real chance to study Cato, one of the leaders of the since defunct Dark Brotherhood, at close quarters. He was a tall man with a very spindly frame, and wore the clothes of this period. His black eyes were sunk deep into the sockets, and were mean and hard; the nose was hooked, and the lips thin, tight, and unsmiling; his head was shaven, in an attempt to merge into his surroundings.

'As you will both die in a little while, it will do no harm to tell you how I managed to escape, when all of my Brethren were eliminated, due to your meddling in our plans,' cried Cato, his face twisting with controlled fury. 'Just before the end, when I felt our existence threatened, I attempted a time jump beyond my own period, and into the parallel time continuum. It worked! I am the only representative of my kind alive, in fact a total enigma, as I have never actually existed.' Cato's voice was becoming high pitched, and out of control.

With an effort he restrained himself.

'I spent sometime in the country called North Korea and managed to precipitate a war with South Korea, in an effort to destroy your world,'

Cato continued, with some glee as he saw the looks of horror on the faces of his captives.

Williams looked at Grant and then, back at Cato. 'Why, you dirty misbegotten creature!' he exclaimed, 'North Korea dropped an "A" bomb on South Korea in 2083, which I assume you encouraged; unfortunately for you it only served to unite the countries of the world.'

'Yes,' commented Cato, 'but in my next jump I found your world in even more serious trouble than atomic war could ever have created; I refer of course to the space virus. The accursed computer has, however, stabilized the situation. I now intend to change all that by destroying the baby farms.'

Grant had been rendered speechless by this turn of events, and his mind had been churning over; but now he had cooled down and was calm again, planning a counter-move against this devil's spawn preening himself before them.

'How the hell do you intend to carry out such a plan,' he said with some passion.

'You really must keep calm,' leered Cato. 'In my travels through time I have always kept a fix on you and your friend;

being able to follow you any time I choose. You will also find that my powers have been considerably multiplied, due to some unknown factor; probably the billion to one chance which saved me.'

Grant considered this for a moment. 'You won't get away with it you know.'

'It seems you require a demonstration of my powers,' said Cato...

Both Grant and Williams were suddenly picked up, as if by invisible hands, and flung heavily against the wall. Lying there, their minds were taken over, and they were forced to kneel before Cato. He laughed at their discomfort.

'I can control many people at the same time, nothing can stop me now. You will be allowed to live long enough to see the end of human life on your world. After that, I intend to jump into the alternate world - my world. With my massive power setting up a new Dark Brotherhood will be simple; you see, in addition, I also have communication with my master the "Dark One", Lord of all men, and ruler of the universe. I am his tool.'

Grant's very soul chilled at Cato's boasting, in his heart he knew that the man was indeed capable of such acts; he was in league with the very Devil himself. It could be that Lucifer was responsible for Cato's life and present powers.

'At midnight my agents, in each city on this planet, will move in and destroy the baby farms, using very dirty nuclear devices. This will ensure that eventually, once the air within the cities has been totally contaminated, all human life on this planet will cease; and I will have achieved my revenge,' concluded Cato.

There was yet forty minutes to go to midnight, and Grant racked his brains for some way out. Even these private thoughts were denied him, as Cato was monitoring his mind...

'You have no chance of changing events, Grant' gloated Cato 'You would do better to prepare to meet your God; that God who has failed you so abysmally. At midnight I shall make the time jump across to the alternate world, the year 2043, on our calendar, looks particularly promising.'

Just then a message flashed into Grant's brain; initially he thought that it was Cato playing with him as a cat plays with a mouse, but it was somebody or something else...

'Do not show that you are in communication with me,' the mental signals indicated. 'This is "Q" and everything is under control.'

Grant, with an effort, did not register his amazement at this turn of events to Cato, who was too busy gloating over the two men.

'We have been aware of Cato ever since he came into this time period; and of his links with you,' continued "Big Q". 'His agents have been rounded up and are being treated to counter the hypnotic state he has induced in them; in order that they carry out his orders. Some, unfortunately, are permanently damaged. Your thoughts are now shielded from Cato, and you may therefore communicate with me freely.'

'Thank God,' thought Grant. 'I might have guessed you would pull the chestnuts out of the fire.'

'I do not comprehend, that information is not in my data banks,' commented the computer.

'Never mind' thought Grant. 'How do we go about overcoming Cato?'

'You will do it with my help. My power is now yours; channeled through your mind.'

'How may I use this power?'

'Relax; in a few seconds I will remove the shield, and you will join the mental battle with Cato.'

The shield came down, and Grant was again subjected to severe mental pressure. Rather like a baby learning to walk, he falteringly tried out his new powers. There was a look of amazement on Cato's face as his mental grip on Grant began to waver...

Once Grant got the hang of it he rather enjoyed it. Cato started to sweat and panic as the mental probe went in, and started to pulverize his brain cells. Williams was released, but Grant waved him back as Peter adopted a fighting pose.

Cato's mouth was wide open, as he was forced to his knees, the roles were now reversed. The sort of power that "Q" was bringing to bear on that scoundrel, through Grant, would have burnt out the mind of a lesser man. Cato's eyes closed, and he suddenly disappeared.

'What on earth is happening?' asked Williams.

Seemingly from thin air "Big Q" said, 'I was afraid that would happen; he will not attempt another sortie into this world in a hurry, my memory circuits certainly have no record of him during my life-time. If he did visit us he did no major harm. If he tries his luck again, I shall be ready for him and will surely destroy him. Almost certainly he has now gone back to his own world. I would, by the way, be glad, if you did not mention these additional powers of mine to anyone. Nobody knows that I can control minds, or communicate without normal electronic aids. You are the only two humans in whom I have confided this knowledge. I know that I can trust you.'

'Your secrets are safe with us' Promised Grant. 'I presume that none of your people are aware, or will ever be aware of tonight's events.'

'That is correct my good friend, it would not help their state of mind to know of this threat to us.'

'By the way John' Continued "Q", 'You will find that you have been left with a gift, with my compliments. Due to the effect on your neural circuits, in acting as the transmitter of my power, your mental abilities have been considerably increased, to the extent of mind persuasion powers, and greatly improved telekinesis ability. Try it some time, and develop it; you have tremendous potential.' It was to be sometime before Grant found himself in a position to develop this gift; but he was to be, eventually, eternally grateful for his new found abilities.

"Big Q" never mentioned what had occurred that night again. Shortly afterwards its "presence" diminished, and then left them altogether.

Grant, without a word, went to a cupboard and took out a bottle of a special brew, which he had had synthesized. It tasted exactly like the best "scotch whisky".

The next two hours were spent in some quiet drinking by the two men before finally making their drunken way to bed.

"Big Q" wondered how many more time jumpers he would have to deal with. Cato was rather different from the normal "jumper", and with his abilities, fueled by hate, had proved a very dangerous opponent. The computer had channeled his power through Grant's mind, using the man as a dual amplifying and focusing agent. The fact was that "Q's" raw energy would not have been enough to defeat Cato. It needed the concentrating lens effect of a suitable mind.

The other "jumpers" had been a strange bunch, and due to the instability of their devices, and weak mental ability, had very quickly disappeared back to their own time period. All, excepting Grant and Williams, were working illegitimately, on limited funds and resources.

The computer contemplated the situation. Things were going to plan. On the other hand it was all very well relying on predictive mathematics, but occasionally the unexpected did happen - Cato for instance!

More and more "Big Q" felt that it was being pulled into a confrontation between good and evil. Whilst having complete control of Earth it knew that there were Universal powers over which it had no authority at all. Luckily there always seemed to be a balance between the dark and light side, but if that condition ever changed, and evil gained the ascendency, Mankind would be in real trouble, and "Q" knew that even it would be unable to help.

I am Man made, thought the computer, and yet on Earth I am God. Yes! God! Man-made - an interesting concept indeed. Perhaps a chicken and egg situation - that expression at least was in its data banks. Who did come first? God or Man - where did the Devil come from? Questions, questions! No real answers, it mused reflectively.

If there was life after death - another possible phase in man's existence - would it be a part of it, or, merely, like the destruction of an old machine system, just recycled; its molecular particles simply being reconstituted, without any awareness on its part. Have I got a soul? "Q's" circuits had been investigating that indefinable characteristic of man for hundreds of years now. Many people think of me as human. I wonder if God does, thought "Q".

For many hours the Computer ruminated about life, death, good and evil; the meaning of its own existence. Eventually it rested, without having come to any real conclusion at all.

Chapter Nineteen

Grant has Thoughts about Luck

'Diligence is the mother of good luck'
Benjamin Franklin

Grant watched the early morning newscast whilst breakfasting. There was a rather interesting item tucked away towards the end of the programme. Apparently three men had been apprehended trying to get into the cities' baby-farm. They were drunk, so the report went on, and resisted arrest. What started as a joke turned to tragedy as the men were killed by the security guards, acting in self-defense. Grant knew, with utmost certainty, that this little charade had been enacted in every city on the planet. All the people involved in Cato's plot were eliminated, one way or another.

The big news of the day was, of course, Grant's triumph. Right now Grant didn't feel particularly triumphant, probably because of the heavy drinking that Williams and he had indulged in, plus the reaction to a situation which at one time looked like proving critical. He looked at himself in the mirror, his eyes were puffy, and he really did look like death warmed up; he would have to give the booze a rest.

A knock at the door, and his friend came in; he looked equally under the weather. 'Good morning John. Boy, did we hit the bottle last night!' Grant got off his bed and staggered, partly from the previous night's alcohol, and partly from the physical effects of competition.

'I feel like sleeping for a year,' moaned Grant. 'I just don't know if I will be able to go through the whole thing again.'

'You'll be right as rain, after a few days. We have three weeks before the finals. You ought to get down to some serious work; after a bit of a rest of course.'

'It is alright for you to talk Peter, I seem to be doing all the work, and taking all the risks'

'Well John, you know what they say, behind every successful man is somebody like me.'

'I don't think you have got that quite right, but I see what you mean. Anyway we have come this far; and will see it through. I would like a chat with "Big Q", sometime, to get his views on the situation to date.'

They spoke to the computer later that day. It congratulated Grant on his performance, the previous night's episode remaining a closed book.

'Your behavior in the games is already a talking point in the city, and certainly it will not be long before the world knows of you. There is a worldwide Holo-pic profile of you tomorrow, with an interview by Cher Starr!' Grant cheered up a little, and smirked to himself, Cher was something of a favorite with him. Williams noted the sudden change in his friend.

'I thought that might do the trick,' he confided to "Big Q". It laughed as if sharing a dirty joke with drinking friends.

That was the thing about the Computer. It always judged the right remark or action at any given time. Its grasp of human psychology and reaction to given situations and attitudes was so perfect. Small wonder; it had the experiences of thousands of experts in the field of the human mind over the years; which began with Sigmund Freud, the Father of it all.

One minute you would be as mad as hell at the Computer, the next it would have you eating out of its quantum hand. What a weapon to have on your side, thought Grant, you could master the Universe with the right sort of psychology.

'There has already been a move to have you disqualified from the games on the grounds that you are not of this time period.' "Q" informed the two. 'This was roundly defeated by the World Council, who think that, in you, they have the best chance of a change of attitude in the Games. The seeds of chivalry and honor have been sown by you. We must now see if they have been sown on stony or fertile ground. Wherever possible they must be nurtured.'

'What of the competition in the world finals?' queried Williams, rather abruptly, and with an edge to his voice, always practical, he subscribed very heavily to a code of honor, but wished people wouldn't keep on about it; after all you shouldn't have to teach it to people, should you?

'Ah, yes,' answered "Big Q" 'as you know the continental championships are held simultaneously, and your five opponents are now known. I am collating all information concerning them, and will report to you both later, so that you may know what Grant is up against; and his chances. Tomorrow you go back to the Eleventh City. I suggest a few days rest and relaxation, and then preparation for the finals, which will, by the way, be held in England, in the capital city of the European Continent.'

Back at their base city Grant and Williams were greeted like heroes by the huge crowd, which had gathered at the vehicle-way terminal to greet them. They were however quickly whisked away by Foster and Cord rather prematurely - just as they were beginning to enjoy the adulation.

Once inside the Commander's Office, the four men sat down, Cord looked serious, and Grant wondered why; he soon found out.

'We must all be on our guard from possible assassins; Cord grated through clenched teeth. 'There has been even more butchery this year in the other continental championships; eleven men dead, fifteen badly wounded. In the sixth city, of Africa, there was a riot, and over a hundred people were killed; all due to an electronic error in the master score board. Whole areas of the arena had to be sealed off, and the people in them tranquilized.

'Steps have been taken to monitor all visitors to the City; particularly intercontinental visitors' continued Cord. 'You will both have a twenty-four hour guard put on you.'

'Do you really think that's necessary?' Queried Williams.

'I think that's a bit extreme, too,' agreed Grant.

'You, gentlemen, do not realize what we are up against, and will do exactly as you are told,' stated Cord. There was really no valid argument to that, and the friends became suddenly silent - they knew when they had met their master.

'Don't feel so bad about it,' said Foster, taking their silence as resentment, 'sadly, the games is all we have left; and games competitors and their supporters will kill to achieve success, we must do everything in our power to protect you.'

The three days' rest and relaxation granted by the Computer were spent in various ways. Grant and Williams wanted to see much more of the City and to study the scientific and technological development - since their time - and thus opted for a conducted tour of the city, and the scientific facilities, to see for themselves the "state of the art." The evenings were spent in a less formal way with Sara and

Tara.

The tour was very revealing. Here everything was recycled; materials could be broken down to their component elements very easily, which made their re-use extremely simple. There was no pollution, everywhere was scrupulously clean, a far cry from the huge rubbish damps, and polluted atmosphere of earlier times. The reasons for this lack of contamination was; the cutting back of the human population (man, the only living thing who could alter his surroundings); the fact that gases, oils, and coal no longer had to be burnt to produce energy in quantity.

During the walkabout the two men noticed three rather large policemen, shadowing them; they were very heavily armed. In the open they were surveyed by a couple of the grav-copters. Security cameras tracked them inside the various buildings.

All design and manufacture was done by computerized automatic systems. Grant could not help thinking that the designs so produced lacked flair, and ingenuity, particularly the clothes and shoes. At least the best food and drink was prepared by human experts.

Everyone had the same potential standard of living, and access to the same sources of pleasure, food and entertainment. People worked, or not, just as they pleased, (apart from the compulsory community service). A waiter could be waiting table one night, and dining on the same table the next. Most people had a job, simply to relieve the boredom. Many spent hours a day practicing for the games.

Only people, who broke the few laws laid down, were denied access to the pleasure areas, by the simple process of taking away their status for a period of time. This meant that only the most basic food dispensers, and living quarters were available to them. What was worse was their total exclusion from the Games.

Big brother 1984 version might have got a big kick out of this age; all the ingredients were there; every person, at birth, had a monitoring implant placed in his body - impossible to remove, without a fatal result. This meant that wherever you were "Big Q" could monitor you - he knew exactly what you were up to at all times. Hence normal crime was almost unknown, for example theft, fraud, violent crimes such as rape, child abuse and the like.

On the other hand it could be argued that much of the violence which did occur, within the rules of dueling and the games, would have definitely been outside of the law in other, earlier, time periods.

Biologically there were no physically crippled people born in this world, genetic engineering had seen to that. What "Big Q" had not done was to filter out potential murderers, and psychopaths, on the premise that they produced the excitement that people craved for. It also failed to warn its security forces of potential assassinations and killings by such psychopaths - it trusted security to do its job and worked on the principle of giving the murderers a sporting chance.'

Such trust was put to the test on the third day when Williams, Grant, and their guard were strolling down a walkway; there was a loud yell from one of the policemen. Both Grant and Williams were thrown to the ground and in the same movement their Protectors drew handguns and fired simultaneously into a doorway. There was the sound of two heavy bodies hitting the floor, each with their own weapons half out of the holster.

This was to be the first of two murder attempts. The second saw one of their bodyguards killed with a burst from a grav-copter hovering close by; which was blasted into oblivion by a security aircraft split seconds later. Both attempts were by visitors from two of the other Continents.

Grant and Williams took a much closer look at the Baby Farms; and were enormously impressed by the attempt to re-populate the world, after the virus attack on the female population.

After the break, it was back to hard preparation for the finals. Grant's opponents had been scanned and analyzed, the conclusions of the computer were listed as follows:

Probable Results:
Pule 1. Grant 2. Smitt 3. Henderson 4. Critchley 5. Patel 6 Ling. Grant 2nd or better - probability of 87%.
Jump 1. Patel 2. Henderson 3. Ling 4. Grant 5. Smitt 6. Critchley. Grant 2nd or better - probability of 23%.
Chess l. Henderson 2. Ling 3. Smitt 4. Critchley 5. Patel 6. Grant. Grant 2nd or better - probability of 11%.
Discus 1. Smitt 2. Ling 3. Grant 4. Henderson 5. Patel 6. Critchley. Grant 2nd or better - probability of 63%.
Run 1. Henderson 2. Grant 3. Smitt 4. Critchley 5. Ling 6. Patel. Grant 2nd or better - probability of 82%.
Shootout 1. Critchley 2. Smitt 3. Grant 4. Henderson 5. Patel 6. Ling. Grant 2nd or better - probability of 71%.
Unarmed Combat 1. Patel 2. Henderson 3. Ling 4. Critchley 5. Smitt 6. Grant. Grant 2nd or better - probability of 17%.
Other Information;
Probability of 10% of being unable to continue due to injury.
Only two through to the fencing - the final event.
Probable finalists; Henderson and Smitt.
Grant - chance of fencing final 38%.
Percentage value to two significant figures.

There was a lot of information, including Holo-pics of every competitor in all events, Williams and Grant studied these in the evenings, after hard days spent in workout. Foster helped with coaching whenever he could. They all knew that, on the day, computer analysis meant next to nothing. Luck played its part of course; a turned ankle, a slip, a fall, these could all influence competition results.

Grant had told himself many times, that there was no such thing as bad luck, you made your own luck in life; then the academic took over, the accomplished physicist, and mathematician, and he had to admit that, just as there was a small chance of throwing say six consecutive sixes with a dice - in fact one chance in six to the power six, or one chance in forty six thousand, six hundred, and fifty six - there was also a slight chance of him missing his footing in a fencing match, due to a fault in the matting, and losing because of it.

It was unfortunate that, human nature being what it is, man has always tended to blame bad luck - that very small chance of an adverse event occurring - for performing badly; instead of their lack of ability or talent. In the current situation there was of course other bias to consider - the breaking of the rules by the competitors to gain an advantage for instance. To be honest, Grant thought that the Computer was helping him rather a lot. But on the other hand almost all the information available to him was also on tap to anyone who cared to ask for it. The other competitors were undoubtedly studying Grant's performance statistics just as avidly as he was studying theirs.

Chapter Twenty

'The Death of Close Relatives'

'The death of a loved relative is something most of us experience, but never quite get over'
T.P. Edwards

'I managed to get a "Times" after all, the last one left,' exclaimed Vera Grant with great satisfaction, to her husband, who had his nose deep in a novel. She sat down beside him, having received a mumbled response. There were only a few minutes left before their New York flight was called and Vera decided to keep her precious "Times" for the flight, she was unlikely to see another edition until they returned in a month's time.

Vera wished that he hadn't begun another book until they got settled on the plane. She enjoyed the pre-flight rituals; visiting the duty free area, studying their fellow travelers, criticizing the facilities, and watching the aircraft through the large viewing windows. Half turning in her seat Vera scrutinized her spouse without disturbing him. She loved Victor very dearly, but wondered sometimes what he saw in her. He was a handsome man with smooth even features; the blue light weight suit was an exact fit on his slim but powerful body. A marvelous tan compensated for his complete lack of hair, and accentuated a perfect set of teeth. She was short, plump, with a Roman nose and bad skin. Her hair was raven and unruly.

If Victor Grant had been asked why he adored his wife so, he would have smiled, and shrugged his shoulders. She had an indefinable something that he could not put his finger on. He could have had his pick of any number of women over the years, but he had always remained faithful to Vera. She was fun to be with, a willing partner in love making, and a wonderful mother to their only child, John.

'Victor!'

'Yes darling!'

'Do you think that we should have left little John with the Williams' for so long? He has never been without us for more than a few days at a time.'

Victor kissed her tenderly. 'You really will have to stop worrying; this is supposed to be a complete break from routine - including our son. Just think, four weeks in the States, and it won't cost us a cent.'

Victor Grant was a highly sought after computer engineer, who had been offered a post in America with "Computer World", a giant Corporation. He was beginning to think that it was an offer he couldn't refuse. The trip had been a further inducement. He was to visit the Corporation headquarters in New York for a formal interview, lasting a few days. The rest of the time was to be spent on holiday, at the expense of the company.

Their flight was called, and off they went down the interminable moving walk-ways, until eventually they reached their departure point, some half a mile from the lounge.

They boarded the huge Pan American Boeing 747-300, and made their way to the first class accommodation. The stewardesses were very charming and attentive with their "fixed" well-rehearsed smiles. The Grants were shown to their seats and settled down, preparing themselves for the six hour flight.

The 747-300 was one of a series of "jumbo jets". Its maximum capacity was three hundred passengers. Vera had been staggered by its sheer size. It had been the first time they had seen it at close quarters. Victor seemed to take it all in his stride, being totally unimpressed by this feat of modern technology. There were no delays, and very quickly the craft took its place in the take-off queue, before moving off up the number two run-way and into the air. In a short while they were cruising at five hundred miles per hour, seven miles above the earth.

Champagne was served with a light snack; the airhostess serving the Grants was blonde, with bright blue eyes, and pert breasts. If Victor had been at all interested he would have noticed a considerable quantity of female body language being directed at him, but he wasn't, and settled down with his book, much to her chagrin. Vera smiled to herself; she was used to this sort of thing.

Vera listened to the captain's speech - probably recorded - about how pleased he was to be at their service. Then the oration of the magnificence of the aircraft that they had the good fortune to be travelling in. Their load was about 350 tons, equivalent to the total weight of nine Lancaster Bombers, each loaded with a 22,000 lb. "grand slam" bomb; its fuel capacity of 42,466 imperial gallons was sufficient to run sixty family saloon cars each for 20,000 miles, or forty cars around the world. Further; the four engines developed 47,000 lb. of thrust which was ten times the power of the jet engines fitted to the first jet fighter aircraft entering service with the

Royal Air Force, and the United States Air Force twenty-five years ago.

The meal and waffle over, Victor tilted his seat back and had a nap. Vera thought that she would stretch her legs and then take in the film they were showing, it was to be South Pacific, and although she had seen it five times before, it was one she loved - in any case it would help to pass the time.

Vera soaked several paper hankies during the film. She loved every minute of the classic musical, and knew every scene and melody off by heart. She would drive Victor crazy over the next few days with her rendering of the popular tunes.

During the interval Vera had got talking to an American couple, who were on their way home after a holiday in the United Kingdom. Their names were Hank and Doris. Vera was immediately impressed by the couple, both in their late fifties. They were modestly dressed, and a far cry from the brash, loud Americans portrayed as typical, nightly, on the television. They confided in Vera that they had had the holiday of a lifetime in the "good old Motherland".

Doris suggested that Vera and Victor join them for a drink after the show, just before dinner. Victor wasn't too keen when Vera came to get him; he had just woken up from an extended nap and really wanted to get back to his book. He decided not to argue, a dutiful husband, he usually gave into Vera's little whims and fancies.

The bar area was crowded, but Hank managed to shoulder his way through to order whiskies for Victor and himself, and Campari and soda for the ladies.

As it happened Victor got on extremely well with Hank. The big American was a construction Engineer, and talked Victor's language. They swapped small talk for a time, the men chatted about sport, and their respective work; the ladies about their families and home making. Addresses and phone numbers were exchanged, with an open invitation to visit on both sides. In fact Doris insisted that once the business end of the Grants' trip was completed that they come over and see her and Hank in Los Angeles; an invite readily accepted by both Vera and Victor.

Unfortunately the Americans were booked into tourist class and the couples were thus segregated for dinner. Vera was getting very hungry; the combination of the film, meeting Hank and Doris, and the aperitif had given her an appetite. She was looking forward to "first Class" fare. Although the Grants were reasonably well off, caviar and champagne was not part of their day to day diet.

It was nice, thought Vera, to be treated like rich people for once in their lives. Although she was not a pretentious woman, Vera rather hoped that the offer of a job in the States might mean a "quantum leap" in their status and living standards.

Marrying Victor was undoubtedly the best thing that Vera had done in her whole life. The daughter of a builder's laborer she had originated from a Bradford slum, but had passed the eleven plus and gained entrance to the local grammar school. From there, hard work had ensured a place at one of the "red brick" universities, where she had read history, gaining a second class honors degree.

Vera had always fancied teaching as a career, and had stopped on at the university for another year to gain teaching qualifications. Her first job had been in Leeds in one of the major comprehensive schools in that city. It was here that she had met Victor. She had been happy in her work, and got on well with the children in her care, but her social life lacked any sort of real sparkle. One night Victor had turned up at a party attended by Vera and her date, who had left early with her best friend - that sort of thing was always happening to Vera. She was beginning to look forward to a life on the shelf, at the ripe old age of twenty-five.

Vera had wiped the tears from her eyes, and consoled herself with a pineapple juice. She could not bring herself to look at anyone in the hall; staring down at the floor with shame - she knew everyone would be talking about her.

'Would you like to dance?'

Vera looked up and saw a bald-headed young man standing there. He had very kind hazel eyes; there was a sort of aura about him that was impossible to resist. For a second her heart stood still, and then started to pound. She felt herself blush - the pulse racing.

'Yes please, I would love to' She managed to stammer. Victor seemed to take her shyness in his stride and took her by the hand, leading her into a slow foxtrot. Vera felt as if she was dancing on air. At the end of the dance she fully expected to be left, but Victor complimented her on her style, and asked her if she would like a drink. . From that moment on he didn't leave her side, they had every single dance together. She noticed the envious looks of the other girls in the hall as Victor held her close to him during the last waltz.

Afterwards he took her home to the small flat she rented in the city Centre. Kissing her gently he arranged to meet her next day for lunch. From then on they saw each other every day.

Despite her happiness one thing concerned Vera. Victor had made no passionate overtures, only polite kisses on greeting and leaving her. She was worried that he didn't love her in a physical sense. She kept thinking of ways to encourage him - without appearing too wanton. At twenty-five years old she was still a virgin, and desperately wanted to lose her purity to Victor.

They made love for the first time after three weeks, and Vera breathed a sigh of relief. Victor was very gentle with her, seeming to know - without being told - that it was her very first time. He affirmed his love for her and her for him. Six months later they were married. A year after that John was born.

Vera had often realized just how little she knew of Victor's past. She had never met his parents, and knew nothing of his origins. It was not that he was secretive in any way just that his recorded life seemed to have started when he was twenty. He had no memory before this time. They had once, together tried to establish his past, without any success at all; there was no evidence or record of a life before the age of twenty.

Eventually they had decided to forget it. There seemed no point in spoiling their life together because of something they could do nothing about. Vera loved so many things about her husband. They were as compatible as any two people had any right to be. They talked for hours about anything that came into their heads, they never argued like most married couples; instead any differences were rationalized by discussion. Their relationship was always loving. Their son was brought up in an atmosphere of love and affection.

Some years before meeting Victor, Vera had acquired a beautiful tri-colored Cavalier King Charles spaniel that she adored. His name was Woozy - a silly name really, but one which seemed very apt when she had chosen him from the litter. Fitting nicely into the palm of her hand, and blinking in the light away from his mother, he had seemed dazed and confused.

When introduced to Victor it was love at first sight - on both sides. The dog jumped up onto his lap - spreading hairs all over the place - and proceeded to lick his entire face. Vera often caught Woozy looking up at Victor, with those liquid brown eyes possessed by the breed. Those eyes which Vera swore you could drown in. It was as if there was some sort of telepathic link between them.

There were several strange aspects about Victor. He seemed to have a certain power over people. For example he always managed to persuade everyone to see his point of view. Bank managers and salesmen were putty in his hands. He always got the best deals, and any sort of loan that he required. Another thing was his ability to anticipate situations. It was uncanny - almost as if he possessed clairvoyance. As far as his technical ability was concerned, Victor had been described as a genius, several times, by people who should know.

'Well that was nice of them, I think that we must make an effort to try and get to see them, don't you Victor?'

'Yes darling, I agree, let's have some dinner, shall we?'

The three course meal was excellent. Smoked salmon, steak, strawberries with thick rich cholesterol forming cream, all washed down with a very agreeable champagne. Vera was feeling a little tiddly after a third glass.

***

She blinked her eyes two or three times. A man in a torn sports suit was standing five paces from her. He seemed to appear from empty space. She must have had more drink than she thought. There was the champagne on boarding, and then the large Campari and soda pressed on her by Hank and Doris, then more drinks with the meal. The man was still there staring at her; nobody else seemed to have seen him. Vera was about to dig Victor in the ribs, and point out the apparition in front of them, when a violent explosion rocked the plane, she caught the man's eyes briefly before he suddenly vanished, they looked vaguely familiar.

Next the panic as the stricken craft banked and spiraled downwards, faster and faster. There was no time for anything but a quick prayer. Victor held onto her hand, gripping it tightly.

'I love you Vera'

'I love you Victor'

Then there was terrible pain, next merciful unconsciousness, followed by oblivion...

Chapter Twenty-One

To Final Glory

'The paths of glory lead but to the grave'
Thomas Gray

The journey to the capital city of Europe was made in a ship which could only be described as a flying saucer. Grant made a mental note to check on the drive of the craft, and its antigravity principle which he had met with on the small ground cars and grav-copters used in this era; that is when he had less pressing matters to consider.

The outer shell of the saucer rotated, cutting through the air, giving it very efficient aero-dynamic properties. Grant guessed that the gyroscopic effect thus produced could be an important feature of the anti-gravity principle.

Part of the center of the ship's floor was transparent; Grant and Williams spent the time - only twenty minutes for the total journey from the Americas continent to Europe - in viewing the various land masses, and the sea. The geography hadn't changed much; excepting the fact that now there were huge areas lacking any population; only being broken up by the occasional energy dome, indicating a city, and the food growing areas and forests.

The saucer landed just outside the "First City" of the European Continent. The city was situated in the country that used to be the two men's home - England, and on the very site of London although, as in the case of New York, there was absolutely nothing left of the older city.

At an official reception Grant met the competition. Although very much on his guard, he was particularly impressed by the general demeanor of one Lewis Henderson; the favourite for the title, who was to represent Europe. Grant studied each contestant intently as he was introduced to them. Over the years there had been some tremendous intermixing of the races, but the basic colors and characteristics of race could still be seen; albeit on a reduced scale. Common names of ethnic groups had also been intermixed. Grant expected Smitt, for example, to be pure blooded German, instead he was coffee colored, and turned out to be champion of Africa. Ling was representing Asia, but was coal black.

Language presented no problem at all as everyone spoke English. Many hundreds of years ago "Big Q" had decided on a standard tongue; the biblical tower of Babel, and its effects, had at last been laid to rest.

The full list of competitors in the championship was:

Smitt for Africa
Grant for the Americas
Henderson for Europe
Ling for Asia
Critchley for Arabia and
Patel for India.

Security during the period of the championships was extreme and competitors were guarded everywhere they went.

***

The games got off to the best possible start for Grant as he won the Pule contest with consummate ease, endorsing "Big Q's" faith in him. The game went on for around four hours, with first one competitor dropping out - usually with a curse - then another. All six formed this particular card school, and final placing's were simply made up by the reverse order of elimination.

For some reason or other the Jacks were missing from the suits of plastic squares. Thus there were only forty-eight instead of the normal fifty-two. Smitt and Grant were the two players left, exactly as predicted by "Big Q". Skill in this kind of game was just as important as the sort of skills required in running, jumping, chess or most other games - intellectual or physical. Grant was extremely glad of his, partially, misspent youth, although he never thought that he would be using it in such a way.

Smitt's full house, queens high, fell to Grant's aces high; first blood to Grant. The amazing thing was the congratulations that he received from each competitor. They appreciated his skills.

In the Standing Jump, a super fit Grant excelled himself with a massive sixteen feet five and three quarter inches to give him second place, behind Patel's sixteen feet six inches. Grant at this stage was the man to beat, and a good section of the huge crowd combined, with over five thousand fans from the America's, to support him. The vast majority of the two hundred thousand assembled fans got behind their own champion, Henderson, who had started well, gaining third place in each of the opening contests, with his best events to come.

So, the first day ended with Grant comfortably in front. Although tired he managed to smile into the Holo cameras for the worldwide interviews which all competitors were expected to participate in. Although the interviewer tried to make him come out with some controversial statements, he kept his cool, and was suitably nice about all his opponents.

The interviews and general chit chat went on for what seemed like hours, until well after the huge crowd had left. Later on the giant stadium was silent and deserted; the only people active were the security men who seemed to be waiting for something to happen. Grant, more than once, noticed small groups of them conferring in whispers. At various times a squad of grav-copters circled the arena noiselessly and unobtrusively - like great bats searching for their prey.

'Come on John, you had better go and get a massage and a hot shower, otherwise you will stiffen up' ordered an ever attentive Williams. It was at this point that Grant suddenly felt queasy, a chill ran down his back, and he was aware of his body reacting to some sort of attack on it. He wondered if perhaps he had caught a chill or virus of some kind. He swayed involuntarily, and Williams had to support him. Immediately they were surrounded by security men, officials of the games, and reporters hot after a story. Grant began to feel claustrophobic. Anxious faces studied him as he reasoned with himself. Security eventually cleared the crowd away, and he stumbled off to his room, helped by Williams, where he was sedated by one of the medical team. The physician said that he was tired and suffering from mental and physical strain and merely advised a good night's sleep. A very worried

Williams was hustled away, protesting that he wished to remain with his friend.

***

Despite being drugged Grant retained his mental facilities, and laid on the bed, eyes closed. He still felt very cold, and icy fingers seemed to be exploring his entire body. What appeared like several hours passed, when the mind that was Grant's was disembodied? He felt as if he was flying and it was as if he still had a physical form. He was able to look down onto his own body lying on the bed. Was this to be yet another meeting with the disciples of darkness? Or, more probably, a dream.

Grant's spirit or psyche moved off into the night. He was not in full charge of his flight as he soared up into the air. Eventually he could see the world thousands of miles beneath him. It was as if he was being directed somewhere. Outwards from earth he moved at mind boggling speeds. It was an exhilarating experience, as Grant passed first the moon and then onwards to the outer planets. At the extremities of the solar system he sighted a small reflected light, which gradually got larger, until he found himself looking at a massive space station; not the standard rotating wheel design, but something resembling a very large multi-storey building. This meant an artificial gravity system not relying on centripetal forces.

Through the outer and inner skins of the structure went Grant's psyche. Long corridors within the station were thronged with people going about their various tasks. They appeared humanoid, and Grant heard them speaking English.

He was eventually directed into a large room, which appeared to be part of a command center. Ten uniformed men and women sat around a huge square table. A bearded man with gold leaves on his shoulders was speaking.

'It is now hundreds of earth years since we introduced the space virus into their females. Since then we have maintained this station to monitor the planet, and to give us an indication when we may take over the planet for ourselves. Generations of our people have been involved in this project, which is still no nearer a successful completion.

The wretched computer guards its people well and, as you know direct invasion is forbidden. Another factor has also been recently added, the man Grant, from another time period. This, coupled with the probability of the computer coming up with an antidote for the space virus in the near future, means that things do not appear to be going favorably for us.' Throughout his oration the man's eyes were constantly on the move studying his audience, observing their reaction to his dialogue.

'Shortly, I will be reporting to the "High Lord" and recommending the abortion of this project. We have already wasted far too long on it; Dak only knows how many Trillions of credits have been spent on this enterprise. I personally want to see an end to it.'

Many of the group agreed with their commander, as they nodded their heads in acquiescence. The Commander continued 'If it wasn't for the Amalgamation's rules concerning direct intervention in a planet's affairs, I would now recommend earth's invasion.

It was hoped that the subtle introduction of the virus would soon have run the population down to a point where annexation would have been within the laws of the Amalgamation, but that now seems highly improbable. Any comments, please?'

'Yes Sir,' answered a fair headed handsome man on the Commander's right hand - probably the second in command.

'I know the strategic value of earth to the "High Lord". There will soon come a time when our system will break away from the Amalgamation of Star Systems, he will then order all-out war against the other systems in the Amalgamation in order to establish an Empire. With him as outright ruler, instead of that lily livered Council which we have at present. Why doesn't our illustrious leader make the break immediately? Then we may invade earth now, simply eliminating the entire population so we may take over unopposed.' This line of action also seemed to have its supporters.

Grant began to study this very callous group of people who could hold the fate of his world in their hands; perhaps eventually the whole galaxy. They looked ordinary enough but he detected beneath that outward air of normality, an insidious, evil intent. To even think of killing a whole planets people defied belief. He wanted to get back now, and report these events to "Big Q", but still he was held there watching, waiting and wondering.

Refreshments were brought in and the meeting carried on with what amounted to trivia - the general running of the station. Suddenly Grant was aware of another presence within the room besides himself and the senior officers of the station.

'Do not be alarmed, it is only "Q"' was the communication. 'For many thousands of years I have been trying to determine the cause of the virus, and if there were any external influences involved. A few days ago it was established just where the perpetrators of our horror were. I thought that I would experiment with you as the medium through which I could act. You seemed to have more potential for this sort of thing than anyone else. It has worked beyond my wildest dreams. Now, using you as my agent I may eliminate earth's enemies.

Using his colossal powers, through Grant, first one of the group sitting around the table slumped forward stone cold dead, then another. Each one with a look of complete amazement on their faces; until all were exterminated.

'John, please do not waste sympathy on these vermin, they deserve all they got.' "Q" had detected some stirring of conscience in Grant.

There were loud noises from outside, and alarm bells were being set off, as "Big Q" started to affect the mental balance of the station crew. Fighting broke out and explosions were next heard, the station being shaken violently, as it was forced from its original stable orbit in the solar system. Grant was well on his way home when a massive explosion destroyed the stricken structure, and everyone in it.

'I do not think that we will have any more trouble with the "High Lord" and his gang' commented "Q".

Minutes later Grant joined his sleeping body.

"Q", he thought, 'just how the hell did you do that?'

'I really don't think that you would understand if I told you,' was the reply.

'Perhaps you are right.'

'How do you feel John? I hope that the experience was not too uncomfortable for you.'

'Alright, I guess, considering that I have just been instrumental in saving Earth.'

'Get some sleep now John Grant, for tomorrow you will attempt to save Earth again.'

***

At 0830 next morning Grant was woken up by Williams who had been allowed to take him breakfast. The second phase of the competition was due to start at 1030 and Peter was getting worried that his friend wouldn't make it.

Within seconds Grant was under a shower and drinking orange juice and coffee, singing at the top of his voice, Williams quietly left.

Later that day, Grant finished sixth in the 3d chess, with Henderson improving his position; winning the event. Although Grant expected the worst, he was beaten so thoroughly that it was almost humiliating. He consoled himself with the fact that his opponents were certainly in the super-star class, as far as 3d chess was concerned.

At this point in the proceedings Grant lay in third position behind Henderson and Smitt. The next day was a rest day; and the competitors went off to a relaxation center. Here they could spend the time physically and mentally recuperating before the next phase.

The whole complex, for security reasons, was set aside for the exclusive use of the competitors, and their handlers. Williams and Grant had a great time, swimming in the warm aerated waters, treated chemically in a way that the two men had never experienced. It gave the body a wonderfully invigorating feeling. They sampled the dream machines which induced any sort of dream you wished - Grant had the exquisite feeling that he was back home again, and walking through the sun kissed fields of his youth.

Williams's choice was rather more down to earth, and involved numerous females, pandering to his every whim.

Afterwards Williams suggested a drink, and they drifted off to the cafeteria area where they found the rest of the competitors, and handlers drinking and chatting. By the end of the afternoon they had made at least two more friends,

Lewis Henderson and Patel, champion of India and Pat to his friends. Grant sensed a genuine comradeship amongst these men. He wondered if this would extend to the more physical man to man competitions later on.

In the evening their ladies were allowed to join them for dinner. Henderson brought along a magnificent Amazonian specimen, coal black with large sensual lips and a body to match. The tight fitting dress left absolutely nothing to the imagination. Lewis was going through his sowing of wild oats stage. Patel's choice was of Oriental stock, petite and very sweet.

The girls got on famously with one another, and soon Tara and Sara were swopping intimate details with the other two. The talk amongst the men was of a more serious nature, with the competition uppermost in every one's mind. Later on the conversation got around to "Big Q" and the virus situation. Grant ached to tell them about the space station and the possibility of an antidote to the evil plague. Unfortunately he had been sworn, again, to secrecy on the computers activities.

The next event of the games was the discus, one of the oldest of the field events in the history of man. When Grant hurled the disc of brass and wood away from him, watching it spin away, he was reminded of the "saucer" that he had travelled in just recently.

The bulkier men - the throwers - had all been eliminated in earlier competitions. This meant that the superior technique of the stocky Grant would count very heavily in his favor. In fact, he took some time to get going, and after the fourth round was only fifth. His next throw was a life time's best, three hundred and five feet six and a half inches. He was duly adjudged victor after the last round; Henderson was second and Smitt third.

Henderson showed his class in the mile run, and was easing steadily into the, computer predicted, final. Smitt and Grant were opening up a considerable gap on the rest of the field in their battle for second spot.

The spectators were going mad and it was obvious that Grant was their second favorite for the final although even now Smitt might disappoint them.

Security was still fanatically tight and now becoming something of a bore. The crowds were pretty well behaved, except for a few fighting drunk supporters, who were soon put into the cell block for a period.

In the shootout a long protracted struggle saw Patel first and Ling second. Henderson finished third, with Smitt and Grant fourth and fifth respectively.

The games now reached a fascinating if critical stage. The penultimate event even now might see Henderson with a broken limb, or worse, and therefore unable to continue. Even the men lower down the scoreboard could see a chance, however slim, of reaching the final stage, and the chance of the ultimate prize. Grant knew that the combat section would again require skill and technique, in the absence of brute strength.

Smitt and Grant were level, and this was Grant's second worst event. The giant scoreboard, at this stage, read:-

	Pule	Jump	Chess	Discus	Run	Shoot	Total
Henderson	4	4	6	5	6	4	29
Grant	6	5	1	6	4	2	24
Smitt	5	2	5	4	5	3	24
Patel	1	6	2	1	1	6	17
Ling	2	1	3	3	2	5	16
Critchley	3	3	4	2	3	1	16

The only chance for three of the contestants was to cripple the men above them; things could get dirty and Grant fervently wished that Williams could replace him in this particular event. As far as the computer was concerned Grant was bottom of the heap in unarmed combat.

Patel was a brilliant exponent of the martial arts, and fully confirmed his number one ranking. The incredible thing was that he did not take full advantage of his superiority. Grant guessed that he could have probably killed both Smitt and himself without breaking into a sweat. As it was Patel merely went through the field obtaining submissions in rapid order.

Even Henderson was no match for him, and succumbed meekly in thirty-one seconds - perhaps he was saving himself for the final! The crowd warmed to the twenty-six year old Indian, who was entertaining them in such spectacular fashion. Williams enthused that Patel was the finest exponent of unarmed combat he had ever seen - better, even, than some of the Japanese masters he had encountered.

The whole planet watched as this act was played to its climax. There were no major injuries suffered during the whole event. Ling and Critchley seemed to settle for their lower placing's, both defeating Smitt and Grant; but with magnanimity.

The final pairing was for the right to meet Henderson in the final. Neither Smitt nor Grant had yet opened their account in this section; but this really didn't matter, as everything depended upon the result of this one match.

The match started quietly enough; both men looking for openings. Although totally outclassed by Patel and Henderson, Grant and Smitt were both black belt class, around third Dan standard in various kinds of martial arts. Smitt tried a series of kicks: probing Grant's defenses. None of them came off, as Grant formulated the various defensive techniques. Grant attempted a hip-throw, which was neatly countered by Smitt. More circling and sparring then suddenly Grant was caught with a reverse punch to the chest, countering an attacking move by him; knocking him backwards. Smitt came in to take advantage, but his opponent regained his balance, moving in for another attack.

The fight went on, rather like a chess match, and both men were battered and bruised by the blows which breached their defensive screens. After ten minutes, they stood back, weighing each other up; then back to the, now, bloody battle. Grant began to think that he would never get that crucial opening. Smitt's nose was broken, and Grant's lips were badly swollen with loosened front teeth from a severe contact with Smitt's fist.

After an hour it was little more than a bar-room brawl, with both men covered in each other's blood. All thought of finesse gone, the men swapped punches, leaning upon each other for frequent support. The place was in an uproar, nothing had been seen like this since the games had been instigated hundreds of years ago.

There was a hub-bub of conversation from various quarters, and the main topic of conversation was comparing this match with the best of previous matches over the years.

Most agreed that this was positively the best. The two men were so evenly matched that; really, a draw would have been the fairest result. But somebody had to end the victor in this one.

Eventually the men collapsed; pandemonium reigned and the vast crowd was on its feet, imploring one of them to get up, and thus win the fight. It was Grant, through a veil of pain, who finally staggered to his feet, and was adjudged the winner.

The crowd erupted; Smitt finally gained consciousness and shook Grant by the hand, and wished him luck.

'Well done John' he said. 'You just had that edge, and at least with your record with the sword you must stand a real chance against Henderson. 'I would have been beaten before I started.' Through the swelling Grant managed to lisp 'I will try and live up to your expectations of me.'

There were now two rest days before the final event. Grant spent them under various healing rays, getting rid of his aches and pains. Thanks to the first class medical facilities of this age he was soon in fine physical shape once again, despite the beating he had received.

Lewis Henderson sat in his room, cross legged, meditating; using techniques from long dead civilizations. He often relaxed in this way before and after games events. The day had gone well; he thought.

He had never liked the tag of "games favourite" - favourites had a nasty habit of disappearing without trace; either due to external intervention, or simply because they were not good enough.

Henderson had an impeccable pedigree, a master index of ninety-seven percent and a past record of achievement in the games - he fully deserved the top ranking. What would the future hold; he wondered. He had studied Grant's fencing techniques, in detail, over the weeks up to the planet finals. Henderson knew that if Grant could, by some chance, make the final event that there was an evens chance he could win. Grant was possibly the only person with any real chance of success against him in this last and most important of events.

Somehow the man from the past had made it; against all the odds, and Lewis had a very strange feeling that maybe the favourite wouldn't become games champion after all.

Henderson was the ultimate result of hundreds of years of genetic engineering. He was as near perfect in mental and physical ability as it was possible to be; given the present stage of man's evolution. Yet it appeared as if he might well fail to a man born hundreds of years ago.

Chapter Twenty-two

Finale

'The sabre is your pen; write with it finely and with grace'
Italo Santelli

Grant knew how the Gladiators must have felt before going into the arena in ancient Rome. Loudspeakers blared out "Entry of the Gladiators" and Henderson and he were given the full hero's treatment, as they were escorted into the dueling area, between security guards in dress uniform. The crowd rose to greet them, amidst the cheering and thunderous applause which lasted ten minutes before, eventually, silence was restored.

The two men were introduced by the President of the games. Then the rules for the final confrontation were announced. These rules were already etched in the contestants' brains. Everyone watching knew them off by heart from the age of five, but protocol dictated that they be repeated before each duel: light sabres, no protective elements at all; participants clothed in shorts, singlet, and shoes only. The match to continue until one of the combatants is dead, or in the opinion of the referee so badly wounded as to be unable to defend himself.

The light sabre was developed by the Italians in the late nineteenth century. It was not to be confused with the heavier military sabre. Whilst the rapier type of sword, such as the Epee wounded with the point only, the sabre was a cut and thrust weapon and ideal for duels fought in this era - for those who liked lots of blood, that is.

The preliminaries being over the contestants faced each other; taking up the on-guard position. Both men were now deadly serious, any friendship between them put to the back of their minds. Fencing at the top level is a very graceful exercise, and these two boys were the very best in this age; and probably any other. In the next ten minutes they thrilled the onlookers as they went through just about every move in the fencing book; attack, defense, counter attack, parry, thrust, counter-thrust, feint, parry, riposte; and so it went on.

The crowd, used to high standards in the games, thrilled to the skilled exhibition of swordplay. The two men took a breather; circling each other, still probing; still looking for that vital opening. Henderson made the first move, a complicated compound attack, but in doing this he momentarily exposed his sword arm, Grant, grabbing his chance, executed a fine stop hit, with the point of his sabre; drawing blood.

Grant now changed his strategy to press home his advantage. He changed his sword arm. For a time this disconcerted his opponent; but gradually Henderson established a good defensive base from which he suddenly mounted an aggressive attack. Grant, who had enjoyed a small advantage up until now, was taken by surprise. He tried to back up and tripped over his own feet and fell. Lewis Henderson took the chance and Grant found himself with the sabre at his throat. Under normal circumstances that would have been that; a quick thrust and Grant would have been gurgling his life onto the mat flooring.

To Grant's immense surprise the sword was removed, Henderson gestured to the dropped sabre, and retreated. The crowd was utterly silent. Grant wondered just how much this had cost the young man. The World Champion was set up for life, and had everyone's admiration and respect.

'The young fool,' was how one on-looker described Henderson, but many did not agree with him, being caught up in the spirit of the moment, cheering his gallantry; meanwhile the battle continued as before.

After an hour both men were covered in blood due to numerous sabre cuts on their arms, and upper body. Grant's right upper arm had been pierced in the fleshy part, and was useless. Now it was Henderson turn to fall, more from exhaustion than anything else. The crowd had long been silent; if truth be known they had ceased to care who won; they just wanted an end. Grant gave it to them; he dropped his sword, and offered his hand to Henderson; and helped him up. The two men walked off with their arms round each other's shoulders.

A low chant emanated from the arena surrounds, building up to a crescendo of pulsating noise. Henderson's and Grant's names were being chanted over and over again. Earth seemed to have recovered its honor; and how!

Effectively the result was a draw, but Grant wanted to leave this age with Henderson as champion, and at the victory presentation he withdrew, to leave Lewis as undisputed Games Champion. The Games would never be the same again; still competitive but with honor and sportsmanship.

***

'Well, my friend,' said Peter Williams sometime afterwards. 'You have certainly made your mark here; I don't suppose you actually want to stay, do you?'

'Not really, Peter,' answered Grant. 'But maybe you would,' he looked at his friend questioningly.

'Yes John, I would, I have found happiness here, and I want to settle down with Tara. I went through a form of marriage with her last night; whilst you were resting. How are things between you and Sara?'

'We said our goodbyes last night, it wouldn't have worked out, and we are both free spirits and neither of us wants to settle down just yet. Sara is the sort of girl that I would like to meet, in say six or seven years. But I have so much more to do before I contemplate a wife and family and carpet slippers in front of the fire, but - turning to his friend - 'I really do wish you all the very best luck in the world.'

Just then Foster put his head round the door. 'You two were required with "Big Q" five minutes ago' he joked!

Grant clapped his hand to his head, 'Damn! I had forgotten.'

When they got to the computer room there was Cord, Henderson, Foster, Tara and Sara, and several other people that Williams and Grant had come to like and regard as friends.

'John Grant,' boomed "Q" through powerful speakers 'your arrival here has completely changed my people's outlook on life. You also seem to have brought us something else; luck!'

An embarrassed Grant didn't really know what to say, eventually he muttered, 'Very good of you to say so.'

'Not at all, not at all! By the way I have some good news for the peoples of the world' the computer paused, in a way that was irritating to many - just another of its human traits.

'Tomorrow, in a planet wide announcement I will give the news that in a year we will be able to lift the sanctions on space travel. Our laboratories have been able to isolate the space virus and have generated an antidote against it. What is even more wonderful' - you could almost feel the emotion from the computer - 'is that a complete cure has been found for all our barren women. Williams and Tara will be able to have children.'

There was a stunned silence, and then everyone seemed to be talking at once, clapping each-other on the shoulders, laughing, kissing, shaking hands and whooping. Even the normally staid Cord was caught up in the excitement, grinning widely.

After some time, when "Q" deemed it proper, it coughed, the sort of clearing the throat operation embarked on when you are trying to gain somebody's attention. It was so natural that nobody gave it any thought, except to be quiet as required by the computer.

'I would like you all to leave now, except for you John, I would like a word with you on your own.'

They quickly left, wondering what on earth "Big Q" had to say that was so secret. Grant himself was very puzzled indeed.

'What I am about to tell you may be upsetting to you,' began the computer. 'You may have wondered, indeed I know that you have wondered how you are able to perform so well both intellectually and physically against the best we have to offer; why it is that I could use you, first against Cato, and then against the enemy space station; why in the twenty-first century you were counted one in ten million because of your paranormal attributes.' The computer paused as if for breath, but Grant knew better, it was simply a human ploy to let information sink in.

'Yes, that is true, I thought it was merely a question of good fortune.'

'The reason,' continued "Q", 'for your special powers is very simple, it came to me just two days ago after considerable efforts by my problem solving circuitry. They have been on this particular project ever since you came to us.'

'For God's sake get to the point' exclaimed Grant. The computer was again showing human characteristics in keeping the subject waiting for the punch line.

'The sperm that created you comes from one million years from the future.'

Grant, who until now had been standing, sat down, rather heavily.

'How do you come to that conclusion?'

'I admit it took some time. We analysed all the factors: your physical and mental powers; the blood and skin samples taken when you first came here were subtly different; your memories of childhood - the recollections of your parents; your para-normal faculties. Eventually we came to the inescapable conclusion that your father was a refugee from one million years in the future, with a probability of ninety-nine point nine nine percent.'

'Well, I'll be damned: was all Grant could stutter.

'There is good news, too, friend Grant, your life expectancy may well be, naturally, in excess of two hundred and fifty years.'

Grant by now had pulled himself together. 'It's alright "Q", I suppose in a way I always guessed I was different. What intrigues me is why my father came back in time, and how he met my mother, and I wonder if he told her. Then meeting his death in such a way...'

'Yes, the unanswered questions are very interesting, unfortunately we shall never know. I have done all I can.'

'Thank you "Q", for letting me know, it makes it easier to come to terms with myself.'

Later on Grant had what was to be his last conversation with Williams, for some considerable time.

'Man's future seems to be assured' he said.

'Yes,' answered a very sober Williams, 'Again they have hope and real adventure to look forward to. Women can have their own children. "Big Q" has also indicated that his circuits have nearly come up with a space time warping theory which will open up travel to the stars. The Games will carry on for a time, but in brotherly love, and sportsmanship. Never again will there be a death unnecessarily! More importantly Earth will be re-populated.'

Grant had never heard his friend talk like this before. He had always thought of him as a down to earth, good natured man not given to such philosophical utterances.

'Just think John, we have been put in two God given situations, one which has stabilized history, and the other has ensured a future for mankind.'

'Yes, Peter, that is true, I certainly wouldn't argue with you.'

'Do you believe in fate, in destiny?' asked Williams, for once monopolizing the conversation. 'I do, I believe that we are all here for a purpose'

'Yes you may be right'

Then, changing the subject 'I hope you are sure about stopping here with Tara. What happens when I return, the micro unit returns with me, and may create problems for you; making your physical being unstable, and creating a condition for a return home.'

'Put your mind at rest John, "Q" has seen to all that, I shan't suddenly follow you back through time. Hell! I really am going to miss you. Still I suppose it had to happen sometime; we were bound to meet a girl with whom we wished to settle down, eventually; I have just beaten you to it. I would be obliged if you could take these letters back to mum and dad for Me.'

'Of course, old man.'

They spent the time left talking; well into the night... Tomorrow Grant would be off.

***

Whilst Grant and Williams were thus occupied, Henderson was having a session with "Big Q".

Lewis knew that his title of "Games Champion" had depended upon Grant's magnanimous withdrawal. On the other hand Henderson also realized that earlier on in the match he had had Grant at his mercy. He didn't know why he had given him a chance after slipping so badly, but he had, and he was now very glad of it.

'Well done, Lewis,' said the computer. 'Things have worked out very well. Grant is off tomorrow; but we have not seen the last of him.'

'How on earth do you know that?'

'That for the moment must remain a secret. But depend on this, you will see him again, and you will both be very much involved in events that will take place in the foreseeable future.'

"Big Q" quickly changed the subject, and Henderson could see that he was not to be drawn further in that area of discussion.

'The third city in Africa needs a security chief; you are

hence promoted to Commander, and will take up your duties immediately.'

Henderson, at this stage in his career, was a mere captain, but took his very rapid promotion in his stride. He did not suffer from false modesty, but realized he was a protégé of the computer, and would have to act accordingly. Perhaps he might end up as the World Council President - Lewis thought this over - on the other hand perhaps not. "Big Q" played certain hands very close to his chest.

Lewis Henderson was not really an ambitious man, and was more likely to be taken along by events. If he had one fault it was probably his lack of driving ambition. "Big Q" did not have the job of president in mind for his protégé, but something far more important...

Chapter Twenty-three

A Little Spot of Trouble

'Man is born into trouble as the sparks fly upwards'
Job Chapter 5 Verse 3

All was ready, goodbyes had been said, and Grant was ready to go home. Some time ago the all-important brain implant had been checked over and repaired. "Big Q" said that this time there should be no problems; Grant hoped that he was right.

Next the blankness of the transition after which Grant looked up, hopefully, from where he lay; half expecting that he would be strapped into the couch in the time chamber. He was disappointed. The landscape was unfamiliar, but was lush green and reminded Grant of his native Surrey. It could be somewhere in England; but what year was it? He felt despondent, and with a sinking heart realized that getting home was not to be that simple.

Grant studied his surroundings, turning through three-hundred and sixty degrees. He was in the middle of a large clearing, set in the center of a dense wood. There was no sign of human habitation or life in any form. It was impossible to tell what age it was.

Taking stock of his predicament Grant knew he was totally unprepared for a lengthy stay in this sort of environment. They had been so sure of a successful trip that he had virtually only what he stood up in, a smart twenty-first century sports suit, with a laser side weapon, provided by his erstwhile friends. He rubbed his beard reflectively - an adornment that he was becoming quite attached to since Judea.

With one hand on the laser - for moral support - Grant tried to think. A little voice in his head told him not to panic, he thought about it, and eventually decided that it was pretty good advice. He shivered and noticed the sun low in the east; it was early morning.

Everything was absolutely silent, not even the sound of a bird. Was this a parallel word where life just hadn't begun? Had he travelled into a far flung future where life was extinct? Questions! Questions! But as yet no answers.

What to do? Explore; and hope that by traversing the hill to the south perhaps he might see some sign of life. Grant walked into the undergrowth, there was no natural path and he soon ruined his suit. At least he had on a pair of reasonably stout shoes, and gave silent thanks for that small mercy.

After twenty minutes the trees and brambles became less thick and he eventually emerged into the open, and started up a gradual incline which would take him to the crest of the elevation he had seen from the clearing. The climb took him an hour. On reaching the top he had a good view of the surrounding countryside. Grant would have bet his life that this was England, probably late spring. But what year was it, damn it!

At just about this time Grant had planned on sipping champagne with Sir Felix and friends at the reunion. Instead he was hot, tired and very thirsty, scrambling about in, as yet, an unknown land. The cold of early morning had now given way to a humid hot day. He would have given a considerable amount, at that minute, for a pint of ice cold lager.

He strained his eyes for telegraph wires, the national grid, and pylons, anything that would indicate civilization. He used small but extremely powerful binoculars; given to him as a present by Colonel Foster as he left. Eventually he saw, to the west, a small group of huts and in the far distance what looked like a castle. Grant made a decision, that in retrospect he was to regret. He shrugged off his terrible thirst and growing hunger and strode off towards the settlement; after all he could afford some time to spy out the land before attempting another return home.

On arrival at the settlement Grant was greeted by a score or so of peasants dressed in rags; the children looked very sickly, and the adults had sores and rotting teeth. The headman, at least Grant assumed that was who he was, spoke in Olde English.

'What is your pleasure master?'

Grant could smell his bad breath from three meters away. The man looked about fifty, but was probably nearer twenty-five.

'What year is this?' asked Grant. The headman looked puzzled.

'I do not know what you mean Sire, perhaps you had better see our Lord Du Barry at the great castle.'

Grant did some quick thinking, and realized that he was in an England of the Norman Conquest. He wondered what he should do, he was certainly intrigued enough to want to look around some more; maybe he could gain information about this period. The decision was however taken out of his hands as something hit him hard on his neck and shoulders, and darkness enveloped him; the peasants had decided that their Lord might be interested in this strangely dressed, slightly tatty man.

Grant awoke, and wished he hadn't, his neck and shoulders ached from the recent blow - probably from a hefty stave. He tried to stretch to relieve the pain, but found that he was trussed up like a chicken - lying on a hard stone floor. He had a mind to chance his luck and try for home there and then, but his eyes gradually focused, and what he saw put all thoughts of home aside, for the time being. He was in a small, well equipped high tech facility. Much of the equipment was recognizable. There was a computer and printer, several large screens, and what looked like a transmitter. Various instrument panels were recording parameters, as yet unknown to Grant.

Seated before one of the screens with his back to Grant, was a blond man with shoulder length hair. He was talking into a small microphone. The man, hearing the noise of Grant awakening, turned and said 'Sorry, you have been so roughly treated by my people, but they are under orders to report anything that is strange or out of the ordinary.'

He came over to Grant and untied him - helping him to his feet. A sudden cramp seized the freed man creasing him for a minute.

'Please accept my apologies, if you look in the cupboard over there you will find some pills which will take the hurt away.'

'Thanks' said Grant, taking him up on the offer.

'What is your name? I am called Stephen, Lord Du Barry to my serfs.

'Well Stephen, you will never believe me' Grant started to say, as he disappeared from view...

Grant materialized in front of a shop window which had blazoned across it "HAPPY NEW YEAR 2313" It was very cold and he shivered in his light clothing. Some people hurried by, warmly wrapped up in furs. They gave him some very curious looks. A young girl stopped and handed him a coin, before hurrying on with an older woman, he heard them talking about him, saying, 'Poor man he will freeze to death.'

Should he try again? Home! What a lovely ring that had. Just then Grant would have given his soul to the devil to get back to his own time, intact. He concentrated desperately on March 28th, 2030, 2031 hours the exact time, give or take a few seconds, when Williams and he had left home.

This time Grant found himself in Napoleonic Europe, but now he understood exactly what was happening. He carried out an analysis on his movements through time, using his small, but very effective pocket computer. He appeared to be oscillating; following what he thought was a third order polynomial equation. The Good News? It was a damped oscillation, and another three attempts should see him back to base. The bad news was his current physical and mental state after his experiences in Norman England. He hoped that this would not influence his efforts; maybe the blow he had received had affected the all-important relay switch.

The next jump and he found himself standing in the middle of an aisle on board a large passenger aircraft. He noticed that the people around him were eating and drinking champagne - he had landed into the first class area of a scheduled flight, which by the look of it took place at around the turn of the new millennia Grant recognized the interior of the Boeing 747-300 Jumbo Jet.

At the end of the aisle, facing him, were two people. The man was deeply engrossed in his meal with a book resting on the tip down table in front of him. He was completely bald, but much bronzed, and extremely good looking. The woman sat studying Grant intently. She was the only person to have noticed the time-jumper. Grant felt memories stirring within him. The two people were vaguely familiar. He struggled to remember...

He was about to speak when the 747 shuddered from what seemed to be an explosion. In a second there was pandemonium as people panicked. There was shouting and screaming. Through one of the windows Grant saw the port wing break off, the craft lurched. Realizing that the passengers were doomed, he quickly made another jump. Just before the transition he caught the eyes of the bald headed man who had now leapt to his feet. The realization came to Grant with absolute certainty. The man was his father, the woman his mother.

Grant's next hop through time changed from the damped mode into something very different. Consider a swing whose pendulum motion is dying down, when suddenly it is given a good shove as it reaches its maximum height. The oscillation increases in magnitude, and at each maximum position of the swing another hard push is delivered. Something like this was happening to poor John Grant as he began some violent oscillations through time. In fact he was achieving a resonance situation, due to some external force pushing him at the same frequency as he had been oscillating.

There was no vacancy of mind for Grant this time; instead a roaring in his ears, scenes whisked by his eyes - rather like a video being run at high speed. He was conscious throughout the whole thing. He visited the world at the height of the

Greek Empire, then into the future; what looked like a Golden age for mankind with huge sprawling cities and space ports. Into the past again, and the Egyptian magnificence in the days of Moses. He visited huge swamps, vast deserts, and large icy wastes. At times the sun was full; blazing down with intensity he had never met with. In another instant the sun was small and weak giving off little heat.

Grant was swinging millions of years into the past, followed by an excursion of millions of years into the future. If the process went on he would see the birth of his planet, and its death, in successive beats. That is if he wasn't dead by then. The experience was rapidly weakening him, and he did not know how long he could stand the strain. His breath was becoming labored, his chest was hurting...

***

'Hasn't the little man had enough?' asked Desolina to her companion.

'Nuts answered Deneb, as he adjusted the controls of the device which was causing Grant's present problems. He giggled effeminately as he studied Grant's features, during his ordeal, on the screen before him.

'Doesn't he look funny,' continued the man. 'I hadn't had so much fun since we cross polarized that sun over in Alpha Centauri. Proxima Centaur wasn't it? Those stupid people on Gruna thought the end of the world had come.'

Deneb settled back in his seat, his plump face with full sensual red lips, a picture of delight. 'What a piece of luck, monitoring somebody making a time jump, the odds against must be astronomic. Did you see how quick I was to catch him in mid swing with the ships computer and the ultra-ray system?'

'You know what Thord said, in fact he was most adamant about it,' protested the girl. 'No interference with other planets in any way,' she emphasized the points being made with a stamp of her small foot, and tiny clenched fist.

'Oh! Put a sock in it,' retorted Deneb, 'you are always spoiling things for me. Last time you had an attack of conscience I was banned from space travel for thirty standard days.'

Desolina pouted very prettily, but kept quiet. She knew that they were playing with fire and that if her father, Thord of Lund, leader of the planetary council, found out about their escapades, there would be considerable trouble, she was not too old to be whipped, and Deneb could be sent to a penal planet.

The two were in a small "flyer" of the "elite" class. These crafts, using hyper-space, could travel from one side of the galaxy to the other instantaneously. They also had a fair turn of speed in their own right; around a quarter light speed.

Hiding behind its cloak of invisibility, keeping it from prying eyes on earth, the ship hovered just above the planet's atmosphere.

Deneb and Desolina had been cruising in the solar system, exploring the area until they had come upon the only inhabited planet. On their instruments they had espied the time jumper, and Deneb was having his little game; giving Grant subtle energy inputs, which were causing his wild oscillations through time.

To the people of earth, in the early twenty-first century, the planet hoppers would have been considered as super-beings. To "Big Q" they, and their kind, were mischievous, and malevolent: and a threat to earth.

Deneb had sadly misjudged the level of technology on earth; probably due to the small wide spread population. His invisibility screens were useless against "Big Q's" probing rays. "Q" was about to take action against the small ship in order to save Grant. In just thirty seconds the craft would be blasted into oblivion.

'Please do stop, you will kill him,' pleaded Desolina.

'Oh, all right, I would like to get back soon in any case, Joss is having a party later, and you know how good they are. We will come back here again, soon, and have some more fun.' Deneb declared wolfishly.

He touched a sensitive finger pad, cutting off contact with Grant; punched some information into the ships computer, once the flyer was well out of the solar system; away from the nagging effects of gravity, Deneb would order the computer to take them home, the ship moving smoothly into hyper-space, winking out of existence in the solar system, before re-emerging one thousand light years away across the galaxy.

This, unfortunately for the precious pair, failed to happen as "Q" decided to teach Deneb and his partner a severe lesson. The pair was almost certainly responsible for the 747's destruction as well as Grant's discomfort. He destroyed the ships warp capability and communication facility, Deneb wasn't going anywhere fast and he was unable to call for help, so he was marooned in this backwater of space for ever; an adequate punishment thought "Q" What a waste! The giant computer's weapons stood down, and "Q" heaved an electronic sigh of relief.

Just as quickly as the forced oscillations had begun, so they ended, and Grant entered the damped mode once more...

Chapter Twenty-four

Home

'And the hunter home from the hill'
R.L. Stevenson

Grant found himself back in the time chamber, well strapped in. The chamber was still rotating at maximum speed; he could hardly believe his luck; here he was, home at last.

He had been away for something like a year in "his time"

In fact only a fraction of a second had elapsed for Sir Felix, watching anxiously through the viewing windows as the spinning container slowed down. Grant disentangled himself from the strapping, opened the heavy chamber door and stepped gingerly out into the laboratory.

'What's happening? Queried the old man,

'Why haven't you gone yet?' Is there something wrong with one of the systems?'

Then, suddenly, he noticed Grant's remarkable change, exclaiming incredulously, 'What has happened to you? Where the devil is Williams?' as he discerned the absentee.

The fact that Grant was now bearded, smelt a bit and had completely different clothes on from when Mortimer had seen him seconds ago, knocked that titled gentleman for six. He looked absolutely thunderstruck. Grant himself was speechless from the terrible ordeal that he had so recently been through.

Sir Felix eventually pulled himself together, and began to realize that the untidy figure before him had actually experienced a considerably longer time interval than the few seconds that had passed for him. It was now that Mortimer also became aware of another event - the cessation of the noise of battle. He cocked his head. 'The attack seems to have stopped.' He observed.

At last Grant regained his voice and said rather huskily 'I think you will find that is because the black strike force is no longer in existence. We are free of them and their masters, as are our friends in the parallel world. Oh! Of course you know nothing, you have no idea... I have so much to tell you.' This much Grant managed to get out before his voice went again which was just as well; he was becoming tongue tied with his efforts to convey information.

Felix's sharp brain started to go into overdrive, piecing together the fragments of information from Grant. He smiled, for the first time in many months. His whole face lit up, the flesh creasing like an old leather glove. He hugged an astonished Grant to him, tears of joy rolling down his cheeks.

'Thank God, it's over at last,' he finally managed to blurt out, overcome with emotion.

Sir Felix let go of Grant, having gained his composure, taking out his cell phone he briskly dialed up a series of pre-programmed numbers speaking briefly and issuing orders to his staff, then turning to Grant, 'Come on my boy, we have people to see and things to do, but first you must have a physical, and then some rest.'

Grant spent the next few hours undergoing a complete medical. He was X-rayed, subjected to ultra-sonic scans, urine tests, cardio graphic tests, brain scans, psychological tests and many many more... At the end of it he felt as if he could sleep for a thousand years. But they hadn't finished yet. The unit locked in his head had to be removed first, and this entailed some extremely delicate surgery, whilst he was awake...

Then they let him sleep for forty-eight hours. Felix had to fight the urge to hold the final debriefing earlier; he was impatient to pump Grant for information, because although he had guessed some of it, he knew that there was much more of crucial importance.

The debriefing was finally organized around Grant's bed. The whole thing was done behind closed doors, after a complete security scan had been carried out. Every word was recorded, and before any sort of information was communicated to the outside world, it would be stringently vetted.

Those present, at the debrief included Steven Bennett, Alan Donaldson, Helen Wood and the Bishop of Guildford - the nominated representative of the Church, who had been involved from the start of the "Jesus Project" in a consultative capacity.

They all warmly greeted Grant, shaking his hand, and congratulating him with enthusiasm. Felix had told them something of what had happened - just enough to wet their appetites. What came next was completely unexpected. Mortimer began the proceedings with a lengthy statement. It appeared that there were facts about the events of the past few months that even Grant did not know about. It transpired that Mortimer knew about the Dark Brotherhood, and the parallel world from which they had come. As well as the Dark Brotherhood others from their world, Joe's people, had also made the trip, and had made contact with Sir Felix.

The matter transmitter had been their invention; it had enabled Grant and Williams to get to the lab on time for their trip to Judea, before the Dark Brotherhood could break through to destroy the time chamber. Grant remembered the conversation he had had with Foster, concerning the transmitter's reliability, and again breathed a sigh of relief. He implored Felix never, on any account, to use the device again.

Everyone was fascinated by Grant's revelations of his temporal travels. The only disappointment was the loss of all the recording equipment; but the time travelers report was very detailed. They were all very saddened about the absence of Williams, but assumed that he was happy, even if it was in a different period of time.

Grant's progress through time had been monitored, but on a time scale of milli-seconds. If Sir Felix had been watching, really closely, he would have seen Grant disappear for a fraction of a second. During this time he had experienced all his adventures. When the monitoring equipment's memory had been played back, and allowances made for the greatly shortened time span, Grant's movements on his return, as he had calculated, simulated a damped oscillation, followed by resonance when Grant bounced about wildly in time, exceeding the instrument readout scales.

The scientific teams were looking into the reasons for this unprecedented phenomenon; perhaps the relay released a little too much energy for each transfer, causing an overshoot. Nobody could guess why the unstable variations had occurred towards the end; maybe one of the Gods having a little game with Grant?

Grant, on "Q's" instructions, omitted to tell anything about his special relationship with the computer, and his various projects for and in co-operation with the computer. The final revelation as to its origin also went unmentioned. As far as his fellow scientists were concerned, "Q" was an unthinking box of mechanical and electronic gadgetry used by man to control and run the planet in the future.

On the advice of the Computer, Grant also did not reveal the tragedies to come in Earth's future, because of the problems inherent in trying to prevent them, doing more harm than good. Perhaps the Computer feared for its own origins and development. Grant's own derivation was also a closed book.

There were certainly shortcomings in knowing your future, and Grant prayed that his own individual future would never be revealed. It was hard enough knowing a world's collective future. In any case part of life's interest was not knowing what was to come, that is unless you were a gambler wanting a sure thing.

After four hours of non-stop talking Felix decided to call a halt. John you look bushed, get some sleep now, I would appreciate a start on your written report soon. I must compile something for the board to look at in the meantime. I have called a full board meeting for next Monday at 1400 hours.'

Felix stopped behind after the others had left. 'I thought that an apology is in order for keeping you so much in the dark, having seen the expression on your face during my input, I was surprised that you kept your temper. Thanks for not making a big thing of it.'

'That's okay Chief, I must admit it was a bit of a shock, but right or wrong you must have had your reasons. Let's leave it at that, shall we.'

***

Attending the Board Meeting were several representatives of His Majesty's Government, including Mortimer, the head of UK security Sir Gerald Templer, and the Minister for Information Rex Raynor.

The board members had had several days to peruse the final report on the events of the last few months, but Grant was still bombarded with questions some of which he answered honestly, others he cleverly parried.

After considerable discussion it was decided to put an end to the whole time travel project. It was considered too dangerous to continue. Meddling with events in the past or future could prove a very big mistake. Grant had been lucky, but there was no guarantee that he, or anyone else for that matter, would be so fortunate again.

The next item on the agenda was the future of the Company. Owing to the secret nature of the original project, and the Governmental involvement, shares in the company set up had been in the hands of a few trusted parties. The next obvious step was to set up a public company, with shares on the stock exchange.

The products to be marketed would be the spin offs of the "Jesus Project". These included: cryogenic development, high density magnetic field generation, study and applications of the paranormal, vindication of much of the Gospel; the list was endless.

Once marketing experts had been briefed, fortunes could be made for all those involved.

Everyone on the payroll was given a handsome bonus, together with a packet of shares in the new company being taken on for research and development in the new projects.

These included an anti-gravity system. Grant had not

wasted his time in the future, and had taken the trouble to examine their devices thoroughly. It really was something of a paradox; would an anti-gravitational system have ever been developed for the future, if Grant hadn't gone into the future for help?

He gave the project team as much help as he could, then despite considerable protests from Mortimer, and many other colleagues, he took a two year sabbatical.

Grant needed time to relax, to rest, and to consider his future. He thrived on achievement, and excitement; he would not be idle for long.

***

The South of France was nice at this time of the year, and Grant booked into an expensive hotel in Cannes - he thought that perhaps he deserved it!

Having got settled in he came down for lunch. During his meal he noticed a girl sitting at a table across the room, she was lovely with a deep tan and wearing exquisite clothes, she was alone. Grant thought that maybe he would go across and introduce himself when suddenly she stood up and came over, their eyes met and Grant thought - I think I'm in love!

'My name is Anita, and for the last few minutes I have had the uncontrollable urge to come over and introduce myself.'

Just then John Grant remembered his experience with "Big Q" during the Cato and space station crisis. "Q" had mentioned a little present that he had left Grant with. Somehow, in using Grant as a lens for its powerful mind probe, together with his father's advanced evolution, Grant's neural circuits had been affected, giving him certain powers.

Because of the pressures he had been under he had completely forgotten about this. He had obviously "persuaded" Anita to come over. Grant was a gentleman; but this did seem too good a chance to miss, and in any case she did not seem to require too much encouragement when he suggested that she join him at the table; and later in his bedroom.

Grant spent the next month with Anita, soaking up the sun. She was an English girl, from Essex, who worked in London as a personal assistant of the managing director of a publishing company. Her mother had just died and Anita had spent some years looking after her, and had had no time to form lasting attachments. This was a holiday she had been promising herself for years. Anita was twenty-five, a natural blonde, with bright blue eyes. She and Grant got on famously.

During a very pleasant month Grant found time to experiment with his new found "gift". He could move objects such as pens, books, and hair brushes across the room, and his mind reading and persuasion techniques were becoming better all the time.

One evening Anita and Grant went to a night club, where there were gambling facilities. After dinner and the floor show, he suggested a small wager on the roulette wheel; he bought 1000 Euros worth of chips.

'When we have lost these we will go back to the hotel.'

'Oh! John, are you sure. I have never done anything like this in my life. I don't want to lose all your money.'

Grant grinned, 'Tell you what, if you lose the lot you can pay me back tonight in kind, how's that! Anything you win, you can keep.' 'John Grant you are absolutely terrible, and I shan't have anything else to do with you if you keep that up 'responded Anita.

Grant had great fun in manipulating the small roulette wheel ball. After six straight wins on black a small crowd started to form to watch the action. Anita had started playing with low denomination chips, but began to get bolder as the pile in front of her increased. Grant whispered to her, 'Put half on number seven.' Whilst it was comparatively simple for him to direct the ball into a black or a red slot, a specific number was rather more difficult. To achieve it the ball took an unprecedented hop from the number three slot just before the wheel came to rest. The audience gasped and Grant noticed that furious signals were being made from the croupier, to one of the "heavies" across the room. Grant decided not to be quite so obvious the next time, after all another 1 in 35 shot would, indeed, look very suspicious!!

'Put the lot on red.'

'We might lose,' Anita was getting caught up in the spirit of the thing, but went along with the suggestion anyway. Grant sensed that the wheel and ball were being biased in some way - probably using a magnetic field. He still managed to force the ball into a red slot. A cheer went up as the croupier reluctantly pushed a huge pile of chips to join a similar pile in front of Anita.

Grant felt a slight pressure on his arm, then almost in a whisper, 'The manager would like a word please, Monsieur, Madam. If you would come this way. I have been given instructions to close this table down.'

Not wishing to cause any sort of scene, Grant exclaimed loudly to Anita, 'I don't think we will chance our luck anymore. Let's cash up and go home.' The crowd groaned, they wanted to see more of this phenomenal run of luck.

The "heavy" accompanied them to the cashing up kiosk.

'The manager would like to pay you personally; he always does this with big winners.'

Anita and Grant followed in the wake of the six foot six bouncer clad in his neat "monkey suit". He had shoulders on him like a house.

'Are we in trouble,' cried a worried Anita.

'I don't think so, the manager just wants to thank us for our custom, and send us on our way.'

The "house" tapped on the door, with manager embossed on it, and let the two into a large office with all the comforts, ominously he came in behind them, and closed the door, standing there with his arms folded.

'Drink?' said a voice from across the room.

A small ferret like man rose from behind a large mahogany desk.

'Thanks, yes, dry Martini for the lady, and a whisky for me - straight, no ice, no water.'

'I like to see a man who knows what he wants.'

The "ferret" poured the drinks, with brandies for himself and his employee.

'Sit down, this won't take long.'

'How did you do it?'

'Sorry?' asked Grant, acting innocently.

'Let's put it another way, you tell me how you tried to take us for nearly two hundred thousand Euros, and Jean, there, pointing to the "house" will only break an arm, before we send you home without, of course, the winnings.

Should you not comply; a mild chastisement will become a little more serious for you, with something a little special for the lady.'

Grant hadn't wanted his little prank to go this far. He put his arm around Anita and said with conviction, 'Don't worry love, in half an hour we will be at the hotel, with your money, with no harm done.'

'Just listen to him,' jeered the ferret 'trying to show off to his lady friend. Teach him a lesson!' Jean lumbered forward. He was used to dealing with drunks and half fit play boys. He swung a club like fist to Grant's midriff. Grant used the man's momentum, adding a little for good luck, sending him crashing across the room, ending up sitting against the wall. Shaking his head he staggered to his feet, and reached inside his jacket for the shoulder holster Grant had noticed some time ago.

'I wouldn't do that if I was you' warned Grant.

'I am going to kill you,' menaced the very angry Frenchman.

The large "beamer" was produced and waved in front of Grant, the finger tightened on the trigger, nothing happened. Jean tried again. How was he to know that Grant had activated "safety"?

Jean threw the "beamer" at Grant's head and rushed him, seeking to take him by surprise. Grant had finished playing around, and a quick chop to the neck rendered the man incapable of any further nastiness. He turned to see a white faced "ferret" groping under the desk for the alarm button...

Grant clamped off the supply of blood to the man's heart, by applying pressure to a main artery. He released the pressure, before doing lasting harm. Ferret collapsed in his large leather covered chair, the fear etched deep in his face.

Madam would like her winnings in cash please; you should have enough in the wall safe over there. Ferret tottered to his feet, and complied with the request, he had no option.

***

Anita and Grant walked back to the hotel, hand in hand, in silence, both deep in their own thoughts, until finally she asked the questions that had been on her mind for the last few days.

'What sort of a man are you?' asked Anita. 'I know that you have strange powers; you tell me that you are independently wealthy; a playboy in fact, but I do not believe you. You have come to mean a lot to me these last few weeks. Please don't spoil it for me by having secrets.'

Grant related to her the full story from start to finish, leaving out nothing; he felt that he could trust her implicitly. She listened with amazement, a part of her mind wondering if he was having a game with her, but she knew in her heart that it was all true.

'Thank you for being so honest with me John, you know that I love you, and that I have never been so happy in my whole life.' Grant did not answer for a moment, and then he took her in his arms and kissed her. 'I love you too!' They both knew that a man like Grant could never commit himself to a permanent relationship; at least not yet.

***

They travelled back to England together, she had to start work again soon, and they wanted to spend a few days in London over the weekend.

John had been putting off a visit to his foster parents, the Williams.' He still had to give them Peter's letters, and to tell them that they would never see their son again. God, how he was dreading that moment. He had discussed the position with Anita, and she had suggested that they go together; she had wanted to meet them anyway, and she felt that her presence might serve to calm the situation. Grant agreed, and on the Sunday evening, after a marvelous couple of days in town, they found themselves outside John's old home.

'Go on John, knock.'

'I don't know if I can.'

Finally Anita knocked on the large oak door, using the brass door knocker, freshly shined that morning. The door was opened by Mrs. Williams, 'Hello John; my word who is this you have brought to see us?' His mother wore a clean white pinafore and stood straight and upright, as Grant had always remembered her. She was still a very handsome woman, adored by his father. Grant hugged her to him, and introduced Anita. They kissed and exchanged pleasantries.

'Where is dad?'

'Oh! He is resting.'

Then, 'Where is Peter? I thought that he was working with you on some sort of new project. He was very excited about it.'

June Williams noticed the look on Grant's face; she hadn't been his mother for so long without knowing when something serious was up.

'You had better get dad in, no don't worry mum, the last time I saw Peter he was in excellent health.'

Mr. Williams hobbled through the lounge door.

'Hello dad,' said Grant. 'Been chasing any girls lately?'

'No, I have not, you young bugger,' was the heated response.

They shook hands; Grant was saddened at Fred Williams's lack of grip.

The next half an hour saw Peter's letters read, a few tears shed, and John and Anita desperately trying to play it down.

'Anyway mum, dad, you still have me; and now Anita' - he smiled warmly at her. 'Peter is alive and well, and who knows we may still see him again someday.'

Mrs. Williams was a practical woman, and immediately saw that her son John was indeed right, and they would have to make the best of it. Fred Williams was probably more upset. He knew that he wouldn't have much more time to live, and in all probability would never see Peter again.

Anita, seeing the problem took over, and used her womanly wiles and charm on him, and soon got him out of his sense of loss and his sadness.

'Are you stopping with us?' asked Fred.

'We can stop overnight, but I am afraid that Anita has to get back to work tomorrow, and I have lots of things that I must do.'

Mrs. Williams was used to this and took it in her stride. 'I understand, still it's nice having you over even if it is only for a short while.'

Next day Grant and Anita parted, going their separate ways, but promising to keep in touch: Neither knew whether this promise would be kept.

Grant went back to his flat in Guildford; he had letters to write, and books to read. He wanted to catch up a little on life in the here and now.

EPILOGUE

The christening service, occasioning the baptism of Peter and Tara Williams' son, seemed untouched by the millennia. It was performed by an ordained priest of the "Methodist" faith.

After the preliminaries the priest turned to Peter, Tara, Colonel Foster, Clare, and an "eye" of "Big Q". He asked them, as the respective parents and Godparents to: confirm their beliefs in Christ, to repent of their sins and to renounce evil on behalf of the little baby cradled comfortable in his mother's arms. This was the first baptism of a naturally born child, since the virus had struck earth, and was being broadcast planet wide.

"Q" had been cajoled into being a godparent on this very special occasion and had happily accepted. It wished that it could have responded to some of the priest's questions with a degree of probability, particularly with regard to those concerned with the Christian faith. Nevertheless it bit its electronic tongue, and went along with the whole process of baptism without comment...

'Francis Williams, I baptize you in the name of the Father and the Son and of the Holy Spirit.'

Commander Cord's face lit up and his chest visibly swelled at the compliment paid to him...

Later on, at the celebration party, the toasts were proposed, the most emotive from Williams. 'Here's to John Grant, wherever he may be - God bless him.'

***

'Sir, a person wishes to see you, he says on a most urgent matter' said Heather Lampton to her boss via the intercom. She managed to inject a certain disdain and disbelief into the statement. It had been a particularly difficult day, and this was not helped by the "person" now taking his ease on one of the visitors' chairs in the corner of her office, viewing her through narrow penetrating eyes.

Heather had dealt with some weird ones before - protecting her employer with all the tenacity of a "she cat" defending her young - but this one was different. The tall angular man had somehow just walked through all the security checks without being monitored. He had made the tenth executive floor without hindrance.

Heather was proud of her job, and the status it carried. She was personal secretary to the chief executive of the largest security operation in North America. Tom Smithers was a good boss, there was no doubt about that, but his voice had an edge to it as he answered, 'I really am very busy Heather, can't you deal with it?'

'He is most insistent Mr. Smithers, and says that it is to your advantage that you see him. He mentioned something about a deal that he wanted to put together with your help... Oh, yes! And he also said that a friend of yours, a Miss Sally Dickson, might also be interested...'

There was a prolonged silence at the other end, and Heather thought that there was something wrong. Finally, curtly, 'Better send him in and see that we are not disturbed. What did you say his name was?'

'A Mr. Cato, Sir!'

Heather turned in her seat; the man had already got up in anticipation of the positive response to his request. He towered over Heather and she shrank back.

'Oh! Mr. Cato, Mr. Smithers will see you now, please go straight in.' The door closed behind the dark suited man and Heather wondered why Tom had decided to see him. He normally only saw people with an appointment and then only after very careful vetting. He had sounded a little strained on the phone. Then there was the strange thing about security. She decided to ring Tompkins to see if there was anything wrong, it wasn't like them to be this slack.

She started to dial Phil Tompkins's number - the head of security would certainly want to know of any shortcomings in his system. Suddenly, in mid-dial, she felt a compulsion to forget the whole thing. That nice Mr. Cato was, after all, an established businessman who wanted to put some business Tom's way. She remembered now, he had been passed through the security system, and everything was alright. She really ought to complete the letter she had started...

'Good morning Mr. Smithers'

'Right now! Cato, isn't it? I will give you five minutes, and then get security to kick your arse off the premises. How you managed to get this far I really don't know. All I can say is that heads are going to roll.'

Cato seemed totally unperturbed by this outburst. 'I have a very interesting proposition for you Mr. Smithers,' he started smoothly. 'One that will make you extremely rich and powerful. How does Governor of the State seem to you for starters......!!!!'

The End

Made in the USA
Charleston, SC
23 September 2016